D0852697

Changing Heaven

OTHER BOOKS BY JANE URQUHART

The Whirlpool
Storm Glass (short stories)

CHANGING HEAVEN

A NOVEL BY

Jane Urquhart

DAVID R. GODINE, PUBLISHER
Boston

First U.S. edition published in 1993 by
DAVID R. GODINE, PUBLISHER, INC.
Horticultural Hall
300 Massachusetts Avenue
Boston, Massachusetts 02115

Originally published in Canada by
McClelland & Stewart, Inc.
Copyright © 1993 by Jane Urquhart

Library of Congress Cataloging-in-Publication Data
Urquhart, Jane.
Changing Heaven : a novel / by Jane Urquhart. — 1st U.S. ed.
p. cm.
"Originally published in Canada in 1990 by McClelland & Stewart
Inc. . . . Toronto, Ontario"—T.p. verso.
ISBN 0-87923-895-X
I. Title.
PR9199.3.U7C43   1993   91-7919
813'.54—dc20   CIP

FIRST EDITION
Printed in the United States of America

*This novel is for Emily B. and Emily U.
and in memory of Ken Adachi*

How still, how happy! Those are words
That once would scarce agree together;
I loved the plashing of the surge,
The changing heaven, the breezy weather

—EMILY BRONTË

SHE WANTS TO write a book about the wind, about the weather.

She wants the words *constancy* and *capriciousness* to move in and out of the sentences the way a passing cloud changes the colour of the page you read outside on a variable day. She wants there to be thunder, then some calm, then some thunder again. She wants to predict time in relation to change and to have all her predictions prove wrong. She wants recurrence. That cloud that looks like the face of a man you might fear or love–she wants that cloud to appear on the horizon, then disappear, then appear again. She wants to be forced indoors by tempests and driven into air by heat, to be caught miles from shelter by a squall. She wants to see the Great Lake altered by the activity of the sky, to see a still moorland reservoir develop white-caps for the first time in its life, to look upon the spines of animals whose fur is being blown in the wrong direction; to see their eyes reflect rain, sleet, snow. She wants the breath of the wind in her words, to hold its invisible body in her arms. She wants the again and again of that revenant, the wind–its evasiveness, its tenacity, its everlastingness.

"We're blessed and cursed by the wind here," one of the villagers might say to her, shouting to make himself heard above the gale. And in the weeks, the months to come, she will change her mind about the wind, as often as the wind itself will change its mind about the organization of the sky or how much further it should twist the trees.

Sometimes this is a direct, purposeful wind, which, if you are to believe the villagers, inhales deeply on the Russian

Steppes and hurls itself, with remarkable speed and accuracy, across vast distances to Haworth Moor in Yorkshire, England. Not a subtle wind, but one that is icy, fierce, and constant. It brings the white invisibility and lack of detail connected to Arctic places. It brings sound – a roar rather than a whistle or a howl; a brutal statement. Because it is a pure wind, a wind of the sky rather than of the earth, it brings weather. In the manner of a swift parade, patterns of clouds are moved by it to announce their intentions over and over again on the horizon.

Sometimes the wind rarefies, becomes more amorous, less aggressive, more disturbing. Then it is a wind that has been around for a long, long time; a wind that, according to the ancient Greeks, was born about the same time as chaos; or that other semi-human, a Cyclops called Brontë – the Greek word for thunder. And what is thunder, hereabouts, but a strong voice making itself heard in a rough wind?

She wants to write a book about disturbance; about elements that change shape but never substance, about things that never disappear. About relentlessness.

About sky, weather, and wind.

PART ONE

Wind

This is my home, where whirlwinds blow,
Where snowdrifts round my path are swelling;
'Tis many a year, 'tis long ago,
Since I beheld another dwelling.

–Emily Brontë

A R I A N N A E T H E R and her entourage climbed the steep main street of the village. All except one of the small assemblage bent their heads into the fierce north wind which, though not cold in early September, was not warm either. The one who walked tall, took the wind in his teeth and the low evening sun in his eyes, was a man of perhaps thirty-five years, dark-haired, of a slim, strong build with wide shoulders and broad hands. He wore a red scarf and a waistcoat of green corduroy – the latter having the effect of turning his eyes the same colour – for he had the eyes of a changeling: eyes that are fickle and true in their colour only to that which is near to them. These eyes, surmounted by perfect black brows, were the predominant feature in a face of extraordinary beauty. He was a beautiful, beautiful man with a character to match – if we are to take as evidence his unwillingness to let the wind, the sun, the hill get the better of him. However, on closer examination, one could see undeniable lines of acute anxiety branching out from the jewels of his eyes like the spidery threads of railways on a map. This man was clearly anxious, and had been for a long, long time. Around his mouth as well (this time like small streams on the same map) were traces of continued unhappiness mixed with the very stubbornness that would not allow him to bend his head to accommodate the dogged wind.

At his side walked a woman who appeared to be the most delicate lady in England: a tall, pretty woman, exceptionally slender, with fine, fair, curly hair that would not lie flat upon her head regardless of the army of tortoiseshell combs and barrettes called into action for that purpose. Her hair, or part of it, was now lifted by the ridiculous wind as were her pale blue skirts and, it would seem, her arms as well since she held them slightly out from her sides, and walked as if she were balancing on a wire. In fact, it seemed the wind might carry her away altogether, so weightless did everything about her appear to be. Every man in the village who was watching this little parade, and most of them were, fell immediately in love with her, wanting to hold her down with his strong shepherd's arms, wanting to construct black millstone grit walls to protect her from the weather, wanting to smooth the wind-tossed tresses from her forehead. And at exactly the same moment every man in the village fell to hating her handsome companion, who was apparently oblivious of this angel at his side, staring straight ahead, offering her no help at all in her negotiation of the perilous ascent of the main street, at the top of which waited the Olde White Lion Hotel, and shelter.

All of the men knew the stories about Arianna Ether, which was, of course, not her real name at all—though they didn't know that. It was rumoured, for instance, that she had levitated in the cradle, so lighter than air had she been, from the beginning, that her mother had to use twenty blankets secured by large stones merely to confine her to her bassinette. Her father's pet name for her had been "Milkweed" since she had, as a child, and even now, resembled the interior of the pod of that plant; both in her almost white, silky hair and in her inclination to float away. Later it was said that he had special iron shoes made for her, so that she would not be in danger of drifting up into the clouds when she played with the other children. And at night . . . at night her parents dared not leave the window open even a crack, for Arianna M. (for Milkweed) Ether could easily, as a result of her incredible thinness, have sleep-floated through even the smallest opening and disappeared into the cosmos beyond.

So why, the outraged men wondered, as they searched shyly beneath her skirts for the iron shoes, and they wondered if perhaps she wore iron undergarments as well, why did her handsome companion not lay, at least, a friendly, steadying hand on her shoulder to weigh her down as she made her way up the street of this unfamiliar windy village?

And what a village it was! *What a village this is*, thought Arianna (whose real name was Polly Smith), as she trudged against the wind over damp, unhealthy-looking cobblestones. When she had caught the first glimpses of West Yorkshire's unique architecture from the train window she had been horrified, and this village, perched though it was, was merely more of the same. Rows of weavers' black cottages, interrupted occasionally by a graveyard full of greenish-black stones or the square solidity of a black pub. She had at first blamed the dark village on the factories; still, there were no industrial chimneys in this elevated section of Haworth since the owners and builders had made use of the water power in the valleys below. "Millstone grit," Jeremy had told her on the train, not bothering to explain. Those were the only words he had spoken to her all day.

Arianna lifted her head now and the ferocious wind brought sudden, emotionless tears into her pale blue eyes. She could see they were almost at the inn. Was there a church? she wondered, gazing around. Then she remembered, ah yes, the church and the clergyman's weird daughters who had, fifty years before, written books and died young; the latter fact not surprising in a place like this. Arianna had not read these books because, as she perceived it, the only function of a book would be to weigh you down if you happened, for whatever reason, to be feeling lighter than air.

At this moment the crowd, spellbound though it was by Arianna and her menacing companion, turned its attention towards two burly men who were leading a horse and cart up the street. Or, to be more exact, towards the contents of the cart: a display of disorderly and colourful rumpled fabric. Necks craned, eyes narrowed, silent conclusions were drawn until, at last, one of the taller members of the gathering and one whose eyesight had remained miraculously undamaged by childhood diseases, announced with certainty:

"Aye . . . that be balloon."

While the crowd gathered round the wagon to examine this deflated world wonder, Arianna lingered for a few moments at the door of the inn with her back turned to the public. Then, as always, displaying her most dazzling smile, she turned around and said:

"I'm happy to be here and I'm looking forward to tomorrow's performance."

This short speech was answered by cheers as Arianna, after waving one pale hand, followed her companion, who had let the door slam in her face, into the inn.

The men were wrong about this handsome man. He weighed her down all right. He weighed her down very well.

The interior of the inn was dim and decrepit, but warmed and cheered on this most special of occasions by a wood fire – a thing unheard of in this coal-consuming district in any season, let alone September. The landlord was a rotund, red-faced man whose visage mirrored, almost exactly, those on the decorative china tankards that lined his walls. Upon seeing Arianna enter he left off speaking with her dark companion and rushed forward to greet her, enthusiastically uttering his welcome in a language which was as foreign to Arianna as if it were Polish or Greek.

"Tha'll be agait aboon in t' sky with birds," he expostulated, "tha'll be and only tomorra, God bless, and t'owd wind wutherin' around tha'. And aw'll be there watchin', aye that aw'll. Darnut goe aboon wi'out tha iron shoon, tha'rt that light – a slip tha'rt! T' rahnd balloon, it were lakly skift t' Lancashire, it were."

"Thank you," replied Arianna, baffled.

"Naw, a'wl fetch t' vittels," he announced as he scurried into an inner room, from which came sounds of iron pots and cutlery. "Sit tha' doun."

Arianna pulled out a chair beside her handsome manager. He had already ordered a pint, which he was now moodily consuming.

"Ah, Jeremy," she said, "I feel as heavy as lead." And she did, she felt as weighted down as she had in a long time. They had been travelling, travelling, landscapes skimming by the sooty windows of railway cars, the constant sandwiches and beer, country fair after country fair. And very little had Arianna to show for it except survival and proximity to a man whom she adored, but who now no longer loved her back–though sometimes at night she might have been able to believe that he cared. Even there, however, even then, there was not, as there had been in the past, any tenderness, any endearments. It was something else that drew him to her flesh; something Arianna could not understand, and something that Jeremy resented but was unable to break from.

He was her teacher, as he reminded her over and over, almost her creator. Without him she would be merely Polly Smith. Had he never been drawn to her ethereality he would still be the great "Sindbad of the Skies" (which he had been only two short years ago), not the Jeremy Jacobs who was now merely an accoutrement to her performances. She would be Polly Smith, he told her, shopgirl, charwoman, barmaid, scullerymaid, factory worker, or at best, paid slut. She would be, as she should be, in the crowd watching *him*. As she should be, should be. But, human nature being as fickle as it is, as the crowds had begun to thin for "Sindbad of the Skies," they had begun to swell again whenever he had taken Arianna up into the skies with him.

Arianna held and held to the memories of their flights together; flights that had taken place almost immediately after a long season of sensuality in a white room. She recalled Jeremy's perfect profile, near hers, against a turquoise sky, and the crowd growing smaller and smaller below them. That unique privacy, their distance from the world, his heart near her shoulder. She was, in those moments, perfectly happy. Soon, however, he had insisted that she sail alone, meeting her afterwards in the dark anonymity of a small hotel room where he fiercely, and rather sadly, took whatever pleasure he could find.

Once he had accused her of robbing him of the sky. "You've taken the sky from me," he said, "you've made me earthbound. Now I'm concerned with mundane materials; train schedules, patching canvas and silk, testing leather harnesses . . . ." He was wearing black that day and Arianna would always remember his eyes, like two lifeless coals, staring at her accusingly. She had begged him tearfully, then, to come to her, and, as they had in the past, to enter the clouds.

He had looked at her with utter hatred. "You shop-girl, you SLUT!" he had shouted. "You are capable of understanding absolutely NOTHING!"

And that night, for the first time, he had not come into her room at all.

The landlord returned with a strange, heavy mass of meat and potatoes, which he called a pudding. As Arianna attempted first to decipher and then consume it, Jeremy, at last, began to speak.

"You'll be using the parachute tomorrow. I've printed that in all the announcements. There's a flat field, apparently, somewhere in this God-forsaken countryside, and you'll be landing there."

Arianna felt a little lighter. Whenever she used the chute Jeremy visited her room afterwards, and then became almost loving, almost as he had been in the past. Perhaps it was the sight of her falling–separating from the balloon, which had separated them – that excited him. She didn't know. All that mattered was the pleasure of his perfect face coming nearer hers and his broad hands on her skin.

The landlord having retired into the back rooms, and Jeremy having announced his business intentions, the ground floor of the inn filled with an anticipatory silence, which seemed out of place in the gloomy interior. It was the silence of a space that was normally thick with conversation, pipe smoke, and human sweat. The silence of a room surprised by its own vacancy.

"Have you noticed," Arianna said now, "how quiet it is in here? It is as if something is absent, as if something has been shut out."

"Something has," Jeremy replied, but not unkindly. "Listen."

Then Arianna heard the wind, roaring down the chimney and rattling the windows in their casements. It was struggling to get in, in exactly the way a prisoner shakes the bars of his cell when he is struggling to get out. There was anger and desperation in its assault and the suggestion of a refusal to believe that the materials that it attacked were unyielding.

Why didn't I hear this before? Arianna wondered, and as she wondered, Jeremy turned his chair and himself in a counter-clockwise direction, away from her, so that she was left with a view of one of his corduroy shoulders and the even darker shape of his hair against the inn's dark wall.

Later that night, though too early for sleeping, Arianna approached Jeremy's room and knocked tentatively at his door. He slid back the bolt and allowed her to come in. Once she crossed the threshold, she walked over the worn carpet to a red chair near the window.

"You should talk to me," she said. "You should let me talk to you." When he didn't answer her she added, "I still love you."

"Your love is a prison," he said. "I can't get out."

"I don't keep you," she said.

"Oh, you keep me, your delicacy." A mock bow followed this. "I created you and now you keep me with you."

Arianna ran her fingers through the halo of her yellow hair. She understood little of this. Outside the window she could see the moon racing through grey clouds, full, like an alabaster balloon travelling, travelling.

"Do you remember," she asked the man across the carpet, "how you found me? Do you remember the white room and all the white nightdresses and the sheer curtains and those white sheets? Even the furniture was painted white and you said everything around me should be white." She turned to look at him. "Jeremy . . . Jeremy. *How* did you stop loving me?"

"We left the room. I stopped."

"Why won't you leave me?"

"I can't. *You* won't stop."

She stood up and approached him. "I set you free," she said. "Go!"

"I'm not free to," he whispered, turning his face away. "I'm not free. No more sailing for Sindbad. Prison instead for Svengali."

"Come up with me."

"No!"

"Go by yourself."

"You understand nothing!"

Several leaves from some lone tree struck the window Arianna had abandoned, and then disappeared as quickly as they had arrived. A sudden touch of night's fingers against the glass.

"You used to tell me stories," Arianna said.

"No more stories, Arianna."

"You used to love me."

"No more love, Arianna."

"Admit it . . . you used to love me."

"What is memory, Arianna? A reflection of something that is gone . . . gone. *Why* do you insist on memory? There is only this now," he gestured around the room, "this ever-changing prison that you've built for me. Oh, don't look at the walls, Arianna, they have nothing to do with it. Nothing solid like that. It is a prison of light, of ethereality . . . I can't get out."

"You're free to go," she said, nodding towards the door.

"No," he said quietly, "I'm not free. There is nothing out there. There is only this." His delicate features contorted into a look of despair.

Arianna, moved by his sorrow, reached one hand forward to touch the side of his cheek. He clutched at it with one of his own.

"There is only this," he repeated, drawing her down on the bed beside him.

There he made passionate, prolonged love to her, crashing up against her again and again like a ship in a hurricane encountering rocks.

When Arianna awakened an hour later Jeremy sat hunched over a table at the far end of the room, his black hair gleaming in the lamplight. He did not turn around when he heard her stir, leave the bed, begin to dress. He did not turn around when she left the room, closing the door softly behind her.

She knew what he was doing, what he always did after they made love. He was scrutinizing his maps of the polar seas. Tonight, she had noted, as she passed quietly by his table, it was the South Pole he was examining; a contradiction in terms as far as she was concerned. How a continent could be south and cold at the same time eluded her. Nevertheless, back in the days when he still spoke to her, his polar lectures indicated that that particular end of the earth was as bleak and white and featureless and freezing as the other. More than anything Jeremy had wanted to sail a balloon there . . . to disappear into white. Instead, he had somehow evaporated because of her. Or, so he believed, had become grounded, ordinary.

For his sake, in the early days, Arianna had pretended to love the idea of polar regions and, in fact, had eventually in some ways come to do so, because they represented Jeremy. She had learned the names of glaciers and ice barriers and Arctic seas. She had listened for hours while he spoke about polar expeditions and their sad, inevitable ends.

Now she tiptoed down the hall to her room and left Jeremy alone in his. Alone with his isolated, personal interpretations, his calculations concerning ice floes, icebergs, and Arctic air currents, his lists of polar destinations. "Starvation Cove," she had heard him whisper as she slowly, quietly, closed the door, "Cape Farewell, Ice Haven, Fury Strait, Winter Harbour . . ."

The wind woke her, though it had been in her dreams as well, tossing white garments from a long clothesline up towards black chimneys. She lit the lamp and walked over to the window, whose deep ledge allowed plenty of room for both the oil lamp and her own two thin arms. Fierce black outside; the moon was down, and dreadful stars, sharp and exaggerated – little knife-points in the sky. But steady, at least, in the shrieking gale.

It is an interesting phenomenon that the light that warms evening rooms creates a barrier, a kind of blindness, to the differing darknesses outside. It also transforms all windows miraculously into mirrors, so that their function suddenly is to reproduce what is in the room rather than to reveal what is outside it. Arianna, leaning towards the window, then, could see very little of the street below; could see only black, those intense stars, and then her own white face floating in the centre – light, airborne, balloon-like.

Gradually, the thought of a balloon at night began to form in her mind and, as it did, the ominous stars became benign. Sailing through silence into black, with or without moonlight, but with the night wind; a song in the silence.

Enchantment. "Wynken, Blynken, and Nod," she murmured, remembering, just for a moment, something of her lost childhood.

Arianna very rarely became poetic and was mildly surprised that she was doing so now–and even more surprised at the soothing effect it had upon her. She extinguished the lamp. Nothing emerged from the street below. The wind lullabied her, singing:

> *Sail on a river of crystal light*
> *Into a sea of dew*

And then as she sank into sleep it breathed the word *ether* over and over again in her ear.

The next morning. Ah . . . the next morning! As if the wind had forced some magic dust in through the cracks of the windows of this very ordinary inn, miracles had occurred. First Arianna discovered that her window looked out, not to the street at all, but onto a sea of purple heather that seemed to stretch on forever, moving over the swells of the hills under the power of the wind. As she stood gazing at this stupefying phenomenon, Jeremy, as if having undergone some mysterious stage of evolution during the night, burst into her room and looked at her with such affection and longing that she drew away from him somewhat, startled by the change.

"I'm free of you," he said excitedly, "I love you again. I am separate. I am other. I adore you. I'm free."

In his joy he lifted her up and whirled her, in her white nightgown, ecstatically around the room; a small room, but the best in the house and possessing, therefore, two windows. Both of these flashed by Arianna now, so that she glimpsed first the white of the walls, then the purple of the heather, then the white of the walls again.

"You are a beautiful white iceberg," he said, "floating on an Arctic sea under a midnight sun and I . . . I am a navigator on a ship three miles away, looking at you through a spyglass. We are NOT the same because you are THERE and I am HERE! And when you are here I shall be there in order to avoid collision but loving you, LOVING you madly!"

"Oh Jere –" Arianna began. But he silenced her.

"Perhaps I am an aurora borealis," he continued, "and then you can be a white drift beneath. You see how different we will be? How unconnected? How beautiful it will be?"

"Yes," said Arianna, doubtfully, while her imagination for some reason sang:

> *With a clear pure light*
> *Like a little candle*
> *Burning in the night*
> *You in your small corner*
> *And I in mine*

Something else from the mists of her childhood but she couldn't remember where, when, or why.

"Dress!" Jeremy commanded. "Prepare yourself. Something white . . . a white skirt."

"But the trapeze . . ."

"Ah, yes, the trapeze . . . white stockings then, and lots of lace in the blouse. I'll see to the balloon."

And after one, long, passionate kiss, he left her there; puzzled, perplexed, wildly happy, and alone. She savoured each of these states in turn, then flicking open the clasps of her little leather trunk she began to lay out her aeronautical costume on the bed, positioning its arms and legs in the exact gesture she herself assumed each time she dropped through air to earth.

W A L K I N G H O M E through a storm more clamorous than the full force of the rhythm band she remembers from kindergarten, more clamorous than recess in the thick of fifty-seven boys larger than herself, the child inhales wind.

It is everywhere; lifting her small plaid skirt, slamming her schoolbag against her shins, tossing cinders into her eyes, tearing the very important mimeographed home and school announcement out of her hands. Ann fights this turbulence down Greer Avenue under churning September trees which have already begun to throw off their smaller twigs. Some of these sticks attach themselves to Ann's ankle socks. Others ride, unnoticed, in her hair. On either side of the street the square brick Tudor-style houses present a succession of moving walls to the assault of the storm. Ann looks at these as she negotiates the blast, using them for ballast. They slide, like dark freighters, slowly past her. If she keeps moving, keeps swimming through the ocean of air, one of the houses will be hers. She will step inside and the outer storm will vanish. The carpets will not stir, the pleats in the drapes will remain undisturbed.

Above her head, wires revolve like playground jump ropes, sing as though children were playing near them, with them. One snaps and sends a shower of tiny stars down to the unyielding sidewalk on the opposite side of the street where the end of the black cord jumps and jumps like a child skipping rope, driven from within by its own electricity, from without by the fists of the wind. Ann looks at it, amazed by this pretty display of danger and power. She had no idea that the ordinary overhead wires, slung across her street from pole to banal pole, were filled with glittering fire. But Ann knows that fire burns children and she moves away from it, struggling up the cement steps towards her door.

Inside there is calm, her mother's voice and a radio describing the surrounding storm; the velocity of the present wind, the enormity of predicted rainfall. Ann swallows a glass of milk, slowly, filling her throat with the tranquil liquid while her face and body distort on the surface of the electric kettle. Then she climbs the carpeted stairs to her room, where she is greeted by the expressionless glass eyes of thirty neglected toy bears. Ann no longer cares about the bears in whose adventures she was deeply involved just three months ago. She has forgotten their journeys over pillow mountains, their weddings, their birthdays, their illnesses and recoveries. Now what she cares about is a book, its pages and the landscapes created by them. She cares about the androgynous child couple, separation, an early death. She cares about millstone grit walls and casements, rifled tombs and obsessions.

The wind in her own yard is beginning to disengage larger branches from a variety of trees. Downstairs the radio speaks the word "hurricane." By the next morning ravines will have become lakes, cars will have been crushed by maples, electric cables filled with fiery stars will be dancing on the corners of most of Toronto's city streets, and Ann's school will be closed. But she will not care about a natural disaster too close to home to be significant. Ann is storm-driven instead by the distant winds of *Wuthering Heights*.

As the child Heathcliff, a demonic baby god with the sea in his eyes and foreign ports submerged in his unconscious memory, is unfurled from the master's cloak at Wuthering Heights, the wind outside Ann's house flings open the milkbox under the kitchen window and begins to slam the tiny door in a repetitive, disturbing fashion. As Heathcliff and Catherine scramble over the moors or climb to Peniston Crag, the banging gathers momentum, resembles a fist striking a table in the midst of argument – a furious point being made. While Catherine stands all night long, desperate in the rain, looking for the vanished Heathcliff and allowing the weather to infect her with her first bout of dementia, a bridge on the outskirts of Ann's Canadian city sighs and slips quietly into the embrace of a swollen river. Six houses full of children who have never read *Wuthering Heights* follow the bridge's example. Ann does not know about this; nor would she be likely to care if she did know. Catherine is delirious. "Open the window, Nelly," Ann whispers. "I'm starving."

The next morning all schools are closed. Catherine and Heathcliff have reached adulthood. Ann can read all day.

She reads for most of the daylight hours, descending the carpeted stairs, visiting her mother's kitchen for breakfast and lunch. "Are you playing with your bears?" her mother asks and Ann says "Yes," enjoying the taste of the lie on her tongue, not wanting her mother to enter the novel's territory with her – keeping it secret, special, apart. She is a prim child, perfectly behaved, carries her dishes to the sink, smiles at her mother and walks upstairs, step by step, towards the wonderful chaos she has recently discovered.

Outside, the manicured lawn has become a jungle of tangled branches, the flesh of several trees jagged and exposed, the garden earth sodden, tulip bulbs revealed. Inside, the child imagines moors, brutality, passion, fixation. Heathcliff has returned from a three-year absence and is wreaking vengeance on all around him. Catherine is undergoing her final stage of evolution from child to changeling to ghost. Ann skips over the parts she doesn't understand. She understands more than she knows.

By five in the afternoon the dark day grows darker and Ann's eyes are tired. She closes the book and slips it between the mattress and the springs. On her way through the living room she pays no attention to the television, which shows scenes of destruction in flickering black and white. "The wind," says her mother as her daughter passes through the cold television light, "exceeded one hundred miles an hour."

Ann barely hears her. She is taking what she has learned to the basement. Another space.

Upstairs and upstairs again is so extensively polished. Glass windows reflect an interior where everything gleams. Kitchen counter, linoleum tile floors, hardwood around the edges of the living-room carpet slippery enough for skating in socks. Banister for sliding down, had Ann been the kind of child to slide–its rich wood shining, dark, gold. Flat table in the dining room, smaller surfaces of side tables by chairs glowing, dustless, remote. This is the homeland of the cleaning lady: that sad, grey individual who claims the house twice weekly. She arrives dressed in what seem to be her own cleaning cloths, and Ann has often watched her move like a ghost with galvanized pails, from room to room to room.

The moment Ann closes the door to the basement stairs and stands on the third step down, it is clear that she is somewhere else; a location that the cleaning lady never visits, an unpolished region. The rough plastered wall, the painted grey stairs. And, at the bottom of these, the damp smell of the real earth beneath the concrete floor.

Several rooms hunker down here: one for preserves; one for the furnace, that large beast with its boiler; one for laundry; and one that operates as a sparsely furnished, primitive form of recreation room, in whose corner Ann keeps her dollhouse. This elaborate toy, largely overlooked until now because of emotional involvement with bears, is suddenly an apparatus perfectly designed for shrinking the world of the novel into the territory of seven small furnished rooms. Four tiny dolls live there and magnificent dramas are born among them. Tempers flare, furniture is over-turned, tiny pots and pans are hurled against a tiny kitchen counter. Father doll loses his job and sits for days in the living room–a ruined man. Mother doll runs away or hides for hours behind the dining room sideboard while police are called and the two children languish in their beds, wasting away from diseases with names like *calaria* or *malthropia*.

Father doll is angry, violent, he drinks some. Mother doll is beautiful, petulant, passionate. Their names are Heathcliff and Catherine. The children, who are called, collectively, "the children" or, separately, "child," are incidental to the central drama. They are minor characters who, when not dying, are used cruelly by their more interesting elders –forced, for instance, to dust each small superfluous item in the house, or locked outside while their parents make delirious love.

As the days go by, Heathcliff becomes angrier and angrier, finally leaving the dollhouse in a fit of black rage. He goes as far as the laundry tubs where, during a soapdish sail in a violent sea, he is nearly drowned. The next day Catherine, believing him dead, and driven mad by sorrow, spends four foodless days on the roof thereby catching *scandaldralia* from which she surely would have died had not Heathcliff, at the last moment, dragged himself from his own sickbed in order to harangue her back to life. The children, who are mercifully healthy at this time, carry small bowls of hot soup in and out of the rooms of their unco-operative parents.

Involving other children in this play, Ann quickly discovers, is a waste of time. They want to call the adult dolls "Mummy" and "Daddy" and the smaller ones "Susie" and "Bobby." They want to send them to school, or to the kitchen, or to church. They want to sit them down at the table for pleasant family meals; want, in fact, to reproduce the orderly ordinariness of the world upstairs. They have not read *Wuthering Heights*, and when Ann describes the book to them their eyes glaze.

During the weeks and months and eventually years that follow the hurricane, while all around her adults are re-ordering what chaos has done to their world, the doll-house dramas become Ann's secret; her private passion, her miniature theatre which absorbs her, between the ages of eleven and thirteen, for several hours each day. At thirteen and a half, still clinging to the pages of the book, she abandons the dollhouse forever.

But then, is it really possible to abandon such delicious alternatives forever?

ARIANNA'S BALLOON was, of course, white, and
festooned with garland after garland of pale pink roses held
aloft by white winged cherubs, whose toes caressed soft,
unmenacing clouds. The basket was made of the finest
ornate wicker with decorative swirls and scrolls, and was
also painted white in order to be a suitable accompaniment
to the gorgeous globe that surmounted it.

But Arianna and Jeremy saw little of this as they
approached the chosen field at the end of Haworth's West
Lane. Instead, they walked towards a neat, soft, rectangular
bundle, which looked like a multi-coloured packing crate
tied as it was by the thick rope of its own rigging. Beside
this, a sturdy pile of wood and straw awaited ignition. The
quivering air produced by its heat would fill Arianna's balloon when it was unfurled and she, scrambling into the
moving basket, would be hurled aloft at what was really an
alarming rate of speed. After sailing for a couple of miles in
a westerly direction, she and her pretty bubble would part
company as, milkweed-like, she would descend to earth
somewhere between Scar Top Sunday School and the farm
called Old Snap.

The smell of the heather, trampled under the feet of the
crowd that awaited her, was intense, almost intoxicating.
Arianna placed a sprig of it in her hair for good luck and
handed another to Jeremy, whose eyes had already turned
soft mauve, in response to the purple sea that stretched out
from where they stood towards infinity. Except for the
places where they were interrupted by a swath of couch
grass or an outcropping of millstone grit, these tough plants
were evident as the predominant flora of the upper coun-

tryside. In the valleys, however, three oddly shaped reservoirs reflected the sky.

"Jeremy," said Arianna anxiously, "there wasn't anything said to me about water."

"You won't be anywhere near it. Ignore it."

"But I'll know it's there."

"Erase it from your mind. Think white. Think Arctic and all water will be frozen and covered with a soft snow." He looked at her tenderly. "My poor darling," he said and the words were unfamiliar in his mouth.

A sudden blast of heat slapped Arianna's back. The fire roared healthily in the dry breeze. Jeremy walked over to the podium which had just finished supporting the entertainment of the Haworth Wiffen, Waffin, Wuffin and the Keighley Bingem, Bangem Comic Bands, the Methodist Sunday Schools' four tableaux; Britannia and her Colonies, Different Nationalities, Indian Hoop Drill and, in Arianna's honour, Spirits of the Skies, and even now held up the Keighley Board of Guardians and the Haworth Local Council sitting straight-backed and dignified on their wooden chairs. It would take approximately fifteen minutes to fill the balloon, which was now unfurling around the rising heat. It hung, at the moment, suspended from a wire that had been attached to two strong poles, so that it looked like a gigantic piece of laundry flapping on a line. During this interlude Jeremy gave his customary speech on the virtues of womankind.

"Purity," he began, "is colourless, odourless, and, most importantly, weightless. It is silent and it is constant. It is the dewdrop that reflects the world and yet does not interfere with the world except to make flowers clearer and brighter. It is moonlight bathing, perhaps, this very moor on which we all stand on a frosty night. It is the gentle crystals of snow, which can, overnight, change our sooty towns into fairylands. And it is air, the playful breezes that refresh us in the midst of summer heat.

"It is of these things, of these *blessings* that our purest women are constructed and they are capable of breathing moonlight, frost, and dewdrops into our lives if we are wise enough to let them. Consider our modern man, exhausted and disillusioned by the day's labours, returning with aching body and troubled mind in the evening to his own hearth to find this pretty snowflake, this moonbeam waiting there for him, waiting to smooth his brow and ease his soul's torment with her love and dedication.

"Ladies and gentlemen, the delicate Arianna stands here before us, clothed in white, ready to begin a performance, which will, in the manner of your excellent tableaux, act as a symbol of the purity I have been speaking of. She stands there, as I've said, and represents the women; all the pure, unselfish women who daily ease the lives of that poor base animal known as man.

"Sometimes we poor fellows need reminding. Yes, we need to be reminded that without the care and comfort of a pure woman we would be nothing. It is she, after all, who spurs us on to great and noble deeds. It is she who, when we are in the midst of despair, brings to us the moonbeams of hope. It is she who, without a thought, would throw away her own happiness just to see us smile."

A few of the shepherds and colliers and weavers scratched their heads remembering only too clearly Jeremy's treatment of Arianna the day before. Most, however, forgot about it altogether or assumed that they had misjudged him.

Jeremy continued, "And so, my friends, what you are about to see is not simply a young, pretty woman sailing away in a balloon. Oh, no . . . no indeed. What you are about to see is the very spirit of British womanhood ascending to her rightful place with the angels in the clouds. Remote, untouchable, apart. Who are these women who help us, after all, if not angels? Should they not be given the power to fly like other angels? And if this is impossible for all, should not there be one who can represent the rest?

"Arianna Ether has chosen to perform this task, to ascend like an angel to heaven and then, with the aid of this wonder of modern invention, the parachute, to float, sylph-like, back to earth again in order to demonstrate the absolute purity, the *lightness* of the cleansed female soul."

Arianna gazed, as he spoke, reverently at Jeremy's beautiful face. Then she looked, with almost as much awe, at her gorgeous balloon, which was growing larger and larger with the help of the fire beneath it. Already it had begun to tug at its rigging, which was being held down by several of the village's strongest men. Arianna tensed each muscle in her body in anticipation, preparing for the moment when she would have to spring without hesitation into the basket.

"We could call this," Jeremy suggested, "the apotheosis of Arianna." The crowd looked confused. "Apotheosis," explained Jeremy, "means deification, and deification, my friends, means changing a normal human being into a god or, in this case, into a goddess. This is normally accomplished by placing the deified person above the rest of humanity, by placing her in the sky. Shall we deify Arianna? Shall we apotheosize her?"

Jeremy paused meaningfully.

The crowd roared, "Yes!"

"Are you sure?"

The word *sure* was Arianna's cue to sprint towards the basket and scramble inside so that, as the crowd shouted the second "Yes!" she would be launched towards the stratosphere.

How quiet the journey was. Arianna rested her hands lightly on the edge of her basket and looked down at the crowd, which very rapidly shrank to the size of a dark puddle. On the podium, now not much larger than a brown envelope, Jeremy was merely a small dark exclamation point, his face like a distant star. Several hundred handkerchiefs fluttered on the puddle's surface as if there were beams of sunlight dancing there. As always, every single muscle in Arianna's body relaxed except for those areas where the halter for the parachute was uncomfortably fitted.

Below her, the balloon's shadow slipped easily across the heather and the unconcerned sheep who fed there. It broke into angles when it crossed a sheepfold or a stone wall. Very occasionally, it mingled with the shadow of a tree, but not often, for only a few trees survived the harsh climate of the moor and its incessant winds. These winds were co-operating today, blowing Arianna steadily in the direction that she intended to go, guiding her safely over all three of the fearsome reservoirs.

As she glided over these smooth, polished, liquid tables Arianna forced herself to look down at the water and saw, to her amazement, her balloon and a half acre of sky shining up at her. It was, at that moment, as if there were no Earth left at all, only Heaven, and she felt dizzily joyful in the excess of light and air, realizing that for the first time she could see herself the way others saw her; a circle of colour in an expanse of sky. Her fear of water vanished in the serenity of these quiet mirrors and she happily remembered how Jeremy had changed.

She had never felt safer. She thought of the love in his purple eyes, which would be blue now as he watched the sky across which she floated. Seeing the dark, solid shape of Scar Top Sunday School emerging from behind another swell of the moor she examined her harness, its buckles and leather, looked back, once, at the lovely series of reservoirs, lifted both slender legs over the edge of the basket and, in ecstasy, jumped.

The balloon sailed away without its passenger in a westerly direction, its shadow moving past the Old Silent Inn, over sheepfolds, across patches of ling and bilberry. It darkened, for just a second, the dancing water in the beck, extinguishing the blinding gold of reflected sun. It slid over, consecutively, Lower Withins, Middle Withins, and Top Withins – the alleged site of Wuthering Heights. Then, without a single sign of regret, it slipped over the shoulder of a hill and past the monolith that marked the entrance to Lancashire. Eventually it came to rest on the green of the town of Colne, where Jeremy rescued it the following morning.

THERE IS ALWAYS, on the way downtown, some-
one on the street, someone she glimpses through the glass
shield of the car window, someone who can cause Ann to
be surrounded by the cloud of pathos that she has, by the
time she is ten, begun to associate with the enormous, dark
paintings in the city gallery; paintings filled with blood,
lust, wars, and a lively assortment of seven or more deadly
sins and betrayals.

This time Ann spots her on the Toronto street corner of
Church and Dundas: an old lumpy-legged lady struggling
across the street with two full bags of groceries – the word
"lonely" flashing on and off like a neon sign persistently, if
invisibly, above her head. Cars honking her out of the way.

Although she is now six blocks behind her, the old lady
will haunt Ann. Ann knows this because that one glimpse
of the old lady has caused her to sit bolt upright against the
plush slab of the back seat of the car. It has taken her breath
away, has caught in her throat. As surely as if her mother's
car had run directly over both of the lumpy legs, the old
lady has thrown this particular day in Ann's childhood into
a kind of nightmare. Much as she tries to think of something else, Ann finds that her imagination is forced to follow the old lady home; home to her dreary furnished room,
home to her hot plate. Ann has never seen a hot plate but
once whispered, in fear and despair, from the back seat of
the car, "Mummy, where do those old men live . . . the
ones down here with the groceries?"

"Were they sitting on benches in the park?" her mother
had asked.

"No, Mummy, they were walking with groceries and old
ladies do too."

"If they are not sitting on benches in the park then they do not live at the Scott Mission. If they have groceries they live in a room with a hot plate."

The hot plate appals Ann. It renders her speechless with pity. The rooms these lonely beings enter, then, are empty except for one dangerous plate – glowing, hot, offensive. These old men and women take their groceries home, struggle up dark staircases, enter a shabby room and lean, wheezing, against the wall while they regard with sorrow that single piece of burning crockery. Such, according to Ann's imagination, is the fate of the thoroughly betrayed.

Nobody carries groceries on the street where Ann lives. Nobody, Ann is certain, has to spend hours regarding with sorrow that terrifying hot plate. Seldom has she seen anyone over the age of fourteen walking anywhere. The street's outdoor population is composed instead of a row of stately, stationary maples, which in summer interrupt the sunlight that normally pours through the bow windows of the large mock-Tudor houses. Very occasionally, an old lady or two is seen in winter stepping gingerly into the snow from the front seat of a gigantic car while a grey overcoated son or son-in-law holds her firmly by the elbow.

The old ladies downtown have no sons, no sons-in-law. Ann is sure of this. Their pasts contain nothing but a series of brutal departures: sons gone off to killer wars, husbands gone to buy that inevitable newspaper (from which there is no return), hope emigrating to a warmer climate. And then one terrible arrival. The hot plate.

At the Art Gallery of Toronto, one of her mother's favourite downtown destinations, Ann crosses the parquet floor. It squeaks under her feet like the bones of abandoned old ladies, while, on the right and on the left, monumental, dark oil paintings slide in and out of her line of vision. These works of art are full, as always, of tumbling figures set against angry skies and brooding vistas. *Venus Bringing*

Arms to Aeneas, The Elevation of the Cross, Judith with the Head of Holofernes. Such weapons! Such torture!

In the midst of all this adult chaos, Ann searches for the children whose portraits, if not comforting, are at least calm, and Ann has become familiar on previous visits with their small sober faces. How stiff they look in their bejewelled garments, holding a bird or a flower in one raised hand as if to say, "Look, this is what I am . . . destined to fade, destined to fly away." Like the little white tombstones Ann has seen in country graveyards, the ones with a carved lamb or an etched rose, their eyes carry messages concerning removal. "We are gone," they seem to say, "We are gone and we will never come again." *Portrait of a Boy with a Green Coat, Boy with a Dove.*

Her mother thinks these children are cute. But Ann knows better. They are not cute at all; they are terrifyingly absent, as is everything connected to them. *Oh, little boy,* Ann thinks, *where are your curls now, your bird, your green coat?*

Room after room, groaning step after groaning step. Ann and her mother walk and pause and walk and pause. Eventually they reach the end of the last room of the gallery and there, on the far wall, is a large photo mural that has been divided, by some painstaking hand, into thousands of one-inch squares. Hanging directly above this strange work of art, which depicts Christ washing the disciples' feet in fuzzy black and white, is a fabric sign that states OWN A SQUARE INCH OF TINTORETTO! in bright block letters. Ann carries the ten dollars necessary to make the purchase in her little black purse, the one with the small brass clasp and the three pink flowers, because last Sunday she discovered, in the middle of the painted, then photographed, table, something from which all the disciples turned away, busy as they were removing their shoes and stockings for their master's attention. It rests right in the middle of the painting on the white tablecloth and is so flat, so unobtrusive, that you might mistake it for something else altogether. But Ann suspects, Ann knows. And Ann will buy the square inch of canvas that it rests upon as a sort of charm to ward off the possibility of having it foisted upon her when she's old.

She approaches the woman at the desk beside the painting. Her mother hovers proudly behind her.

"I'd like," she says, "to buy a square inch of Tintoretto. That part in the middle of the table. The hot plate."

"The plate . . . ?" asks the woman, surprised. "You are sure that you wouldn't like Christ's eye?"

"No, I mean yes, I'm sure."

The woman smiles at Ann's mother, and says to Ann, "Is this your first art purchase?"

"Yes."

Patting Ann on the head, the woman murmurs, "Congratulations. You are now a patron of the arts."

These glass shields that block the betrayed from contact with the child seem permanent, somehow, as if they have been cemented to her right shoulder. It is odd that in order to visit culture, Ann and her mother must travel into the dark heart of cities, past alleys filled with starving cats, past Indians lounging by liquor stores, past immigrant labourers returning from night shifts carrying black lunchpails. "They *earn* their groceries," her mother says. Past brick walls covered with grime and manholes belching steam to the Art Gallery of Toronto, the Royal Alexandra Theatre, Massey Hall. Near these palaces of the arts there are steamy restaurants filled with tired waitresses and – not too far away – the Victory Burlesque planted, ironically, in the centre of the garment district, as if to advertise the clothing these women shed with such astonishing gestures. Gestures Ann will never see. Past Portuguese gardens that grow sunflowers, beans, and then – miraculously – a small enshrined Virgin. All this glides like a parade by the child's pale face in the window when her mother drives downtown. And then there is *Swan Lake*, Mozart, Tintoretto. Her own Tintoretto. Her own square inch of it.

Now, three years after the purchase, Ann gazes through glass at yet another city's centre: Franco's Madrid. Long boulevards leading to the architecture of Fascism and, snaking out from these, thin streets filled with the small lives into which Ann's tour bus is too large to shoulder.

"There is no poverty in Madrid," the tour guide announces in perfect English, with only a hint of the song of her native tongue. "There are no slums."

As mother whispers, "That's a bunch of nonsense," Ann looks down from her elevated seat, through the window to the sidewalk where an old woman is selling lace to tourists. Does the tour guide mean there are no hot plates in Madrid?

They glide down the boulevard behind polished glass. They are well above the crowd, travelling as if on a low-flying magic carpet towards the Prado Museum.

Though the child doesn't know it yet this is the world's darkest collection. It inspires awe. It inspires terror. The first five crucifixes cause Ann's knees to weaken; her heart to pound. Yellow skin, too many wounds, too much blood, too many women screaming sorrow. And the familiar parquet, platform of the world's great art, sighing and groaning in sympathy under her feet.

Room after room after room of Rubens. Pink and yellow and lavender skin. Eyes and mouths. Then Bosch's daydreams and nightmares. "Mummy, *look*! He has a flower growing *there*! And, *look*! Is that dog going to the bathroom?" The Goya horrors: assassinations, witches' sabbaths, monsters, cripples, and hunchbacks. And then a memory in the making, one that Ann will never shake. Her mother standing, contemplatively, in front of Goya's bloodstained Saturn who is frozen in the act of devouring one of his children. "Mummy, that man has bitten the baby's head off!"

"Goya's vision," says her mother, still gazing at the painting with admiration, "was remarkably dark."

Ann discovers portraits of small people in the next room and senses that, after these statements of brutality, the absent children would be a relief. Entering, however, she is surprised by a collection of dwarfs, each more cynical, more knowing than the last. This is immediacy. They, unlike the frozen children, leap live from the canvas right into the territory of Ann's childhood. Grotesque, accessible imps and elves, behind whom unfurl more and more rooms of chaotic injustices.

Ann feels safe with these lively deformations. "Velazquez dwarfs," her mother whispers, having at last torn herself away from Saturn's murderous activities.

Then, five rooms down, on a facing wall, Ann sees it: a familiar leg, from which is being pulled a familiar piece of clothing. Ann propels her mother straight through five doorways, past the El Grecos, past the Titians, past the Raphaels until the painting is there, directly in front of them. All the disciples, the pitcher, the bowl, the water, the tile floor, the table, the plate – all the details Ann has memorized at the Art Gallery of Toronto since the painting's arrival three years before, after the money was raised.

"Well, I'll be damned," says her mother.

Ann knows now that what she purchased was a square inch of fraud, a square inch of betrayal. Judas, she notices, is a major figure in the painting.

In the hotel room at siesta time Ann takes off her skirt, leans back against the two large pillows she has placed behind her, and searches through her portable Penguin edition of *Wuthering Heights* for a suitable section concerning lies and betrayals: those particular lies, those particular betrayals that affect children. She settles for the part where

Hindley has locked the young Heathcliff in the garret (Ann can see the garret). Catherine tiptoes up the stairs away from the guests who are listening to the Gimmerton Band, and slips out onto the roof through one skylight and into the attic by another.

Ann imagines the roof. It is December. From the roof you would be able to see almost all the way to Gimmerton. Catherine, cat-like on top of Wuthering Heights, would not feel the wind that buffeted her. She would look for a moment towards the sky, see scudding clouds and a partial moon. The wind would force the fabric of her skirt up against her legs so that she would have to fight cloth and wind and slippery shale to get to him – the betrayed one – where he crouches in the dark. She would have to open the glass and drop lightly down to his side. There would be no colour there. The two children would be fumbling, murmuring, grey shadows. From the lower sections of the house they would hear what the pious old servant, Joseph, called the Devil's psalmody; the songs of the Gimmerton Band. Ann can see the whole Gimmerton Band, "mustering fifteen strong: a trumpet, a trombone, clarionets, bassoons, French horns and a bass viol, besides singers." The light of the lamps and candles flickering on all that brass.

Ann can see the whole house now, as if someone had removed a wall, or as if it were an architectural plan. She adds all the detail she can: the fire in the kitchen hearth, the crumbs on the table, the double flight of stairs, and the empty chambers on either side of them. The two children whispering in the attic, heads bent towards one another, their hands touching and separating, touching and separating. Beyond them the winter moors, the rapid clouds, the moon, the wind, the wind. "The Holly and the Ivy," the French horn slightly off-key.

All of this in a Madrid hotel room while in a vast building, in another part of the city, groups of tourists take no notice of the hot plate, dead centre on the table in the real, the authentic, the actual Tintoretto.

ARIANNA ETHER awoke into darkness dressed in her long white nightgown, or perhaps a garment even lighter, so easily did it move around her body. She was lying flat on her back in a place that was soft, yet strong with a strength of its own. She had no recent memories in her mind, only a feeling of being "lighter than air" and a sense of pure well-being.

Happy, happy, happy wailed the wind around her. *Heartfelt hallelujahs*, it added and then, *Hallowed, hallowed, hollow*.

Arianna was perfectly still. Only her eyes moved. There were no familiar walls to tell her where she was. But she found, to her surprise, that she didn't care much one way or the other. She discovered, as she gazed, only the same piercing stars she had seen the night before and a perfume that the wind blew towards her.

Hosanna, hosanna, howled the wind, breathing more and more perfume into Arianna's vicinity. *Heather*, it added, rather softly, nudging Arianna towards recognition of her whereabouts.

"Of course," whispered Arianna, memory creeping back to her, the white wheels of memory creaking, working again with great effort as if throwing off years of rust.

What is memory, Arianna?

"Of course, I fell into the heather." *And there*, she thought, turning her eyes slightly to the right, *is my balloon. How white and lovely it looks against the black, my balloon, and how it waits there for me to climb back into it and return it to him now that he loves me.*

Helium, helium, snarled the wind as if unhappy with the direction that Arianna's mind was taking her. *Hogwash!* it added.

Help! thought Arianna, for it hadn't occurred to her to use her voice. And then, *I wonder what part of the moors I've fallen into?*

Hag, hag, helped the wind.

Well, thought Arianna, *you needn't be nasty!* And then in enormous happiness she laughed at herself talking, if silently, to the wind. And it seemed as if the wind laughed as well in a breathy, sobbing sort of way.

Hello! it suddenly said. Then, disposing of "*h*'s" for a while it made a definite statement, several in fact, in a clear, unbreathy, female voice.

"A hag," it announced, "is not only an ugly old woman much like a witch, it is also a soft place in a moor, or a firm place in a bog. A respite of sorts one way or the other. You are, therefore, lying in a hag – a heathery hag, if you must know – lucky you. And at the right time of year, I might add. One week later! – had you fallen one week later the blossoms, the perfume would be gone. Until next August, of course, which may be sooner than you think."

"What?" said Arianna, her voice rising happily. "This is mad." Single words sighed by the wind she could accept but dictionary definitions were something else altogether. She sprang to her feet, or rather floated, so extraordinarily lighter-than-air did she feel. She whirled ecstatically around in the wind, searching for the source of its voice in much the same way that she had danced, earlier in the day, around and around the room with Jeremy, until she became quite dizzy. Stopping, she used the sight of her balloon for ballast until she had to admit that it was not her balloon at all but rather the full moon which, tonight, had not yet gone down. Turning away from it, but not with disappointment, she was confronted by the pale face and clear blue eyes of a young woman who was almost as thin as herself, but who was dark rather than fair.

"Nobody knows anything," continued the woman, for it was she who had defined the hag. "You see that little knoll yonder?"

Arianna, slightly in shock from her sudden awareness of the woman's presence, craned her neck to examine the spot to which the woman pointed. And there, at the end of a series of billowing hills was a smaller one – rather regular in formation.

"That is Hob Hill," the woman announced, "and you think a hob is a fireplace, don't you? Something you put your kettle on. Admit it, that's what you think."

Arianna nodded, suspecting that she was wrong.

"Wrong!" said the woman. "A hob is a little friendly spirit who slips into your kitchen at night when you are sleeping and helps you with your household chores. Sweeps up, mops down, et cetera. Since he is a little person, his hill, his moor, has to be smaller than these" – the woman gestured around her in all directions – "and so there it is. And if you don't believe me then you are a fool!"

"I didn't say I thought it wasn't true."

"You believe it then?"

Arianna was silent for a moment, thinking. "Yes," she eventually replied.

The woman visibly relaxed. "Well, that's a good thing," she said to herself, "particularly under the circumstances."

"Anyway," she said to Arianna, "let me continue. These hobs can grow, if you want them to, into almost anything that you want them to be. Then, of course, they start changing their names and demanding more space. Space," she repeated, looking around her, "then they need a lot more space."

Spa-a-a-c-e, roared the wind.

"They'll take over anything, everything. I'm sure you know the Celtic rhyme: 'First he sweeps, then he polishes, then he grows up, and demolishes.'"

Arianna didn't, but at the moment felt it safer to remain silent.

The woman was clearly warming to her subject. "After they grow they're not so friendly any more. But they still belong to you. Completely. They are all yours. *He* is all yours." The woman crossed her arms and looked at Arianna meaningfully. "Then, of course, he is a demon – utterly horrifying – but infinitely more interesting, I'm sure you'll agree, than a little elf with a broom in his hand.

"The question is," the young woman mused, "why do one's demons stick to one?" She looked at Arianna closely. "Because," she answered herself, "one has created them, after all, one way or another, and so to them, whether they like it or not, one is *mother*, one is *home*."

After uttering this last word the woman sat on a rock and looked rather sadly towards the village where Arianna had slept the previous night. "Home," she said again, but much more quietly.

Arianna began to feel vaguely afraid. Her childhood, which had begun to nag her the day before, now made a reappearance. She remembered witches and how they were reputed often to live out on the moors, where they collected poisonous herbs and chanted weird words. They had also lived, she now suddenly remembered, in the wardrobe at the south end of her bedroom. Or at least, one had. She could recall every leathery line on the creature's face, every wart. She resembled Aunt Agnes, who came to tea on Thursdays and who disapproved of children's laughter. She resembled this woman not in the least.

Witch, whispered the wind. It appeared to have calmed down somewhat, but, in fact, it was merely taking a rest so that it could gather strength.

From this one witch, this one cupboard, Arianna's childhood bedroom, in its entirety, recreated itself in her mind. The papered walls, the shelves for picture books and dolls. Six pennies hidden in a drawer. Five small white dresses where the witch was. A parasol, much loved. The hobby-horse, a friend during the day, a terrifying enemy at night when he turned from white to grey. The whole world as it existed before her mother died and her father took to drink. Arianna began to visualize a little silver locket that she had forgotten until now. One that, to the child's sorrow, would not open because it was not made to. Just a solid, shining heart to hang, bright, against white cotton.

"I had one that opened," said the woman, "with a lock of my mother's hair inside, but it wasn't as pretty as yours."

Arianna was startled out of her pleasant reverie. "What was that?" she asked.

"I said that my locket opened but didn't have such pretty engraving."

"How do you know?" Arianna approached the woman now and scrutinized her pale face. "How did you know what I was thinking?"

"It was perfectly clear. Your little bedroom and then you, small, trying madly to open the tiny silver heart. It was all right here." And the woman pointed to a boggy area vaguely to her right. "And, I suppose you've been trying to open an impossible heart since then, haven't you? We always do these things at least twice. If at first we don't succeed we become obsessed. It's very simple. What's your name?"

"Arianna Ether."

"Oh, no, it's not."

Arianna confessed. "It used to be Polly Smith but now it's Arianna Ether."

"No, now it's Polly Smith again. You were having some very strong memories. Arianna Ether had very few memories, *n'est-ce pas?* Hard at work in the here and now picking away at some closed heart. Where are we, by the way, these days in the here and now? What year is it?"

"How can it be that you don't know? It's 1900, the turn of the century."

"Well, even that's debatable. Maybe it's the turn of the last century, or maybe it's the turn of the next century, or maybe the centuries have stopped turning altogether. Who cares? Why did I ever bother to ask? Curiosity, I guess. Good thing you are out here. You might have *still* been picking away at that closed heart at the turn of the century after the next."

"That heart," said Arianna/Polly with dignity and pride, "is open now."

"Really?" asked the woman with more than a hint of sarcasm in her voice. "Black hair? Perfect profile? I have my doubts."

"How do you *know*?" asked Polly, "What *are* you?"

"I am exactly the same as you," said the woman, "Look, I'll have a memory and you tell me what it is."

And Polly/Arianna, unpractised though she was, did see a coal fire and an unhealthy little boy sitting near it writing in a tiny notebook.

"The boy?" she asked.

"My brother."

"The fire?"

"Our parlour."

"Then are we *both* witches?" asked Polly/Arianna, horrified at the thought.

"No," replied the woman. "We're both ghosts."

"You mean I'm . . . ?"

"As a doornail." The young woman extended her arm towards Polly/Arianna as if to congratulate her. As if to shake her hand.

It took several moments for Arianna to grasp this information. "It's not true," she said at last.

"Oh, truth," said the woman vaguely, "I'd forgotten all about that. Facts, I suppose she means." Then, looking at Arianna, "The facts are: we're ghosts."

"It's not true. I feel . . . I'm supposed to fall; but the parachute – "

"Didn't open."

"I must get back to him," announced Polly/Arianna, floating as quickly as possible to a standing position. "He'll be waiting and oh, God, he'll be angry. Where's my balloon? What wild wind! Where did it take my balloon? I *must* get back to him!"

Him, him, hummed the wind.

"You mean you want to haunt him?" asked the woman. "Because if that's what you mean it can be easily arranged."

"Yes, that's exactly what I want! I want to haunt him. Haunt him. I want him and I want him to want and to love me!"

Hurly burly, hurly burly! chanted the wind. *Haunt, haunt, haunt!*

"Personally," said the woman, "if you want my opinion, and even if you don't, I think that haunting is a waste of time. Mooning around rather, when there's so much to be done out here. And now that there are two of us there's twice as much. All this sorting and sifting and settling of accounts. Mountains of memory after you're dead!"

"I'm not dead."

"Yes, you are, and so am I. Only I've been dead a little longer."

Suddenly it began to snow – fiercely. The little black village disappeared from sight. Every feature of the landscape was shut out by white. Arctic weather.

"This is my home, where whirlwinds blow, where snow-drifts round my path are swelling. 'Tis many a year, 'tis long ago, since I beheld another dwelling," chanted the woman.

"What's all that?" asked Arianna in confusion.

"Oh . . . just something I wrote."

"Well, it seems quite strange to me."

"Yes, I was quite morbid, really. It's amazing how much I've cheered up since I've been dead."

The wind roared through the two women.

"Do you always get blizzards like this in September?" asked Polly/Arianna.

"Sometimes. But it's not September any more. It's probably, let me see, February. When you are dead, time has no meaning and weather is more capricious."

"Oh, dear," said Arianna, but to her surprise rather light-heartedly, "I guess I really am dead. He was handsome and now I'm dead. What's your name?"

"Emily Jane Brontë. I wrote a book, but I'm not sure that matters. Brontë means thunder in Greek."

"No, it's not," said Arianna, astonished at her own sudden knowledge. "It's not Brontë, it's Brunty. Your father changed his name. Was he a lot like thunder?"

"No . . . yes. Now he is like memory."

"So, if we decide not to haunt, what exactly do we do out here?" Arianna surveyed the wastes all around her.

"We remember," said Emily. "And now that there are two of us we'll watch each other's memories and tell each other stories."

"True stories?"

"Oh . . . truth . . ." said Emily, vaguely. "Whatever you want, I don't mind much, really, one way or the other. It depends on what you remember . . . whether you remember the ideas or the objects."

"I remember him," said Arianna. "I remember hope."

"Yes, memories of hope are good. A beautifully unrequited state and very memorable. You hoped . . ."

"I hoped all the time for a house."

"Oh, yes," said Emily, now surrounded by the spring flowers on the moors. "Yes, I see it. Let's remember houses. We could talk about building them." She hugged her transparent knees in anticipation. "You must tell me the story of that house. You don't still want to haunt, do you?"

"Well, not just yet," said Arianna, who was already beginning to construct the story in her mind. "But maybe this house we never built was already haunted . . . by something."

"Oh, good," said Emily sitting, now, cross-legged at her companion's feet, "a ghost story! I just love ghost stories!"

Ghosty, ghosty, chuckled the wind, and in quite a lyrical fashion for, by now, it was summer.

THE HIGHWAY.

Its arrival in the province has, for Ann, heralded the end of an era. And the beginning of another where four lanes sew the disparate parts of her life together like a long, grey thread. The highway connects everything: the countryside and the city, the known and the unknown. It makes certain of her mother's friendships possible to maintain. It reduces distance to a manageable time frame. It connects the house in the city with Ann's mother's past – a village and a farm in a rural landscape that becomes, with the advent of the highway, a miraculous hour and a half away. An hour and a half of grey speed and you are able to enter the nineteenth century; its general stores, its woodstoves, its large high-ceilinged rooms, its dusty gravel roads.

Ann had been forced, until recently, to carry rural attributes around in her mind in much the same way she carried *Wuthering Heights*, the two melding now and then.

Before the highway, there was Ann's early childhood in the city and a more complicated road to the past: a road made up of the sequential experiences of earlier forms of travel. Ann sitting in the back of her mother's lush, curvaceous Buick, meandering along the old road which turned and dipped and then changed with ruler-straight regality, into the King and Queen Street of one small town after another. Pickering, Newcastle, Port Hope, Grafton – their red brick town halls, their clapboard churches, their five-and-dime stores, their gas pumps which resembled undersea divers. There were spots, too, in the countryside between towns where trees would reach towards each other to make a tunnel through which the car hummed. Then light and shade would flicker briefly on the paper dolls and their wardrobes which Ann had placed on the plaid fabric of the back seat.

Farmers rumbled by in pick-up trucks; twelve bales of hay in the back, a dog beside them, alert, in the cab. Other dogs, too, that leapt towards the car, having crouched in anticipation behind farmhouse shrubbery ever since the appearance of the last vehicle some twenty minutes before. Porch swings, rail fences. Brief glimpses of water: a brook, one river, and now and then the Great Lake itself shining on the far side of an orchard.

All of this seen from deep inside the moving room of the car and through the sun-shot mist produced by the cigarettes her mother smoked as she sat behind the wheel, separated from her daughter by the thick slab of the seat. Ann straddled the hump in the back and picked up the cardboard dolls and laid them down again. Gingham dress after gingham dress. Or she counted horses in disappearing pastures. Or she looked for children of her own age playing near the front stoop of their houses.

Now that the highway has come into being it eliminates the landscape of getting there. Now there is, as there would later be on jumbo jets, only there and here and a swift void in between.

Ann sits erect in the back seat, stunned by velocity as new green-and-white signs announce towns she can no longer see. The bright white broken line, the slick, grey overpasses. Near one of these, but in the world rather than on the highway, a brand new dome made of glass is being lowered by a huge crane onto a brand new Catholic church. This is taking place on the outskirts of a town whose name reproduces, exactly, the sound of the Great Lake's waves tossing foam and pebbles near the shore.

"Oshawa, Oshawa . . . " the child whispers in the comfort of the car.

Like all the other finned vehicles surrounding them, the car slows, and slows again, and finally stops altogether. Ann's mother lights another cigarette, and squinting, leans over the wheel and looks up through the windshield towards the hemispherical blaze of glory that hovers just above its final destination, suspended by a chain from the sky. Ann has both her hands on the rear side window. Then she rolls it down and sticks her head out to see. Oh my Lord!, to *see this*, this glass heaven swaying in the wind, sunlight breaking through it like rain. It is a conductor of the light that blazes down to the surface of the highway.

The overpasses are jammed with crowds of people who gaze like an awestruck primitive tribe or an entranced group of pilgrims at this miracle of light floating in the air. A brass band! Ann is sure there must be a brass band! In her imagination the band is crowded with heraldic horns and she sees sunbathed gold even though there is no evidence of music whatsoever. At the same time she sees, when she pushes her face out the window, only the dome and, for a fraction of a second, the silver glint of a row of automobile side-view mirrors stretching out from her own car. One by one, the little ovoid landscapes reflected there, the little green signs and cement overpasses, begin to pull away and then the Buick in which she sits slides under the concrete bridge and out the other side into a place where no majestic events happen at all.

"Mummy!" Ann shouts, clutching the foam, vinyl, and springs, "Mummy, we have to stop and watch it!"

"Honey," replies Mummy, jamming her cigarette into the ashtray, "this isn't the kind of road you can ever stop on."

Nevertheless they enter, and then come to a stop in the past. Grandma's house, as reassuring as a Bartlett print. Autumnal walks through the blazing maple woods, crackling fires on the two chilly, windy mornings that make up the weekend, evening games of Chinese checkers, snap, old maid. And then, of course, the highway again, the return to the city.

At this point the highway goes bad. The sun disappears, the wind turns icy, the Great Lake is as grey and still and featureless as the asphalt on a four-lane highway. Nothing reflects gold. The outer world beyond the guard rails loses significance. The word "Oshawa" no longer sounds like the currents of a Great Lake caressing its beaches and begins, instead, to resemble the sound of one car after another coming off an assembly line, or the discontented mutters of striking auto workers, or a thousand transport trucks shifting, simultaneously, into fourth gear.

The trouble, for Ann, with having this memory in the future is that it will be impossible to have just the first half of it. The inevitable second part will nudge the first aside, making its presence known before the floating dome can be fully savoured.

Because, returning, they see no hemisphere of glass on its basilica pedestal, see instead an unfinished church, a crane from which hangs emptiness, and enormous glass shards littering the space between the architecture and the highway. Because of this, the whole memory will be broken.

A suitably profound finish to the landscape of getting there. Grey, broken, unstoppable. Adolescence, adulthood, old age.

No more luminosity hovering in the outer world.

And so, the child turns inward. Her grandmother dies and the fist of time closes around the past, but the past is kept nevertheless, like mythology, between the covers of a book. Or like ancestors with names such as Obadiah, Kaziah, Oran, Ezekiel, in a tidy, fenced, nineteenth-century graveyard with a view of rolling hills and snake-rail fences, and no noise at all except the wind moving the cedars at the back of the plot.

After the broken dome, heaven changes. Ann again takes the book down from the shelf. She looks at its cover; a strong man depicted there, growling at the wind, his back to a stunted tree. The wood engraver has drafted the weather so intricately it looks like the sea. Swirling currents lift the man's dark curls. Ann opens the book and turns from wood engraving to wood engraving: graveyards, stone walls, fierce emotion, snarling dogs, landscape, landscape. She begins to read and becomes once again irrevocably lost in that first moorland blizzard. *Let me in, let me in. I've been lost on the moor for twenty years.* She enters, Ann enters the structure called *Wuthering Heights*.

"Oh, Heathcliff, Heathcliff," she whispers in the dark of her own pink bedroom, any winter night the wind chooses to howl through the city in which she lives. "Oh, Heathcliff," she sighs, while her mouth aches with a combination of desire and orthodontia. She is taking small steps, groping, blind, towards weather.

The blizzard she has stumbled into shrieks through the dining room, on whose round rug she often sits reading. It howls around the china cabinet and attacks the sturdy, plump rosewood legs of the table as if, the moment she opened the leaded-glass door of the custom-built shelves to remove the book, she had let *it* out; this beast, this innerness, this otherness. The past. The difficult past.

The events along the road from the valley to the heights.

"WHEN YOU'RE lighter than air," Arianna/Polly said, settling herself into a corner made by the intersection of two stone walls, "then a house can hold you down, weigh you down in a pleasant way, so that you don't float away altogether."

"I suppose . . . " said Emily, doubtfully.

"And, if possible, there would have to be two houses for us. One for the balloon, you see. A Balloon House."

"Was this imaginary house yours or his?"

"It was ours."

"No," said Emily thoughtfully, "No, I think it was yours, but . . . never mind. Go on. Tell me what happened."

"I began thinking about the house a lot when we lived in a white room – a white room in a tourist home right by the sea so that, no matter what, I was always afraid that one wave might wash us away altogether. And I couldn't swim and was very afraid of the water."

Arianna looked at Emily to see if she disapproved of this fear. Seeing no reaction, she continued.

"It pounded, this sea, always, because it was winter and stormy, and its nearness fogged the windows behind the white curtains, making the glass white, too, and shutting the view of the world out. The water was always out there calling and, because of that, the room felt temporary and, of course, what I really wanted was eternity. I didn't much like what the sea was doing to the house where we had the room. I discovered why the term 'weather-beaten' had come into existence. That house was beaten by the weather every day. Eventually, I knew, it would have to succumb.

"All we did in the white room was make love, over and over and over. He was under me and over me and all around me and inside me. There wasn't an inch of me anywhere that he didn't know, hadn't touched somehow. He was only concerned with me as I was then, with the physical details of me and he would want to know nothing of my past; only what I thought, how I responded there and then. He would always silence me when I spoke about another time, by placing his mouth on mine, his body flat over mine, as if constructing a barrier to memory.

"And the sea that I feared got into our lovemaking until at times I felt that he was a large wave crawling up my shore; a wave or maybe a whole ocean, filling the rented, white, temporary room. A white sea that I sailed, dazzled and terrified, because, as I knew, water is heavier than air. I've never been afraid of the air."

"This moor is like a sea sometimes," said Emily.

"How I loved him, though, so that the fear got mixed up with the loving. I navigated him, or tried to: me the only detail on a white sea. Soon, however, I saw that there was never going to be any past; that he had locked it out, had locked out even a past that was connected to us because, in that sea, in that white room, there were never going to be any details. There was only weather, the weather of a featureless sea, and the present, which was skin and hair and bone and pleasure.

"You must know that a sea is unidentifiable, because, despite its waves and white-caps and froth and foam and colour, it really has no identifying details. I could show you engravings or paintings of twelve different oceans – the Indian, the Atlantic, the Pacific – and you couldn't tell which was which because they all look the same. No recognizable features. No details. Just water the weather is working on. No special details at all.

"And, of course, I wanted some. To be able to say, this is us. This is what happened and this is where it happened. I wanted more, I guess, something beyond the white room, though when he was touching me I couldn't have moved to anywhere else. Because I was drowned in him.

"He would have to leave sometimes to do a performance. He would leave, sail his balloon somewhere and return, usually wordless, with a bouquet of white carnations for me and his heart beating like the sea and his breath as deep as the weather. I began to feel *his* eyes staring out from beneath my lids and the world got farther and farther away.

"And so, in time, of course, I wished it back again – just a little, just enough to provide a setting for us to love against. Somehow I thought that unless there was some more scenery, I wouldn't be able to remember our loving. I wanted memory and there really isn't any memory in a white room. A white room has no memory, perhaps, if you want to look at it from that point of view.

"When I mentioned a house to him, or even a journey together, he would become as silent and as neutral as the white walls that surrounded us and I knew he really didn't want anything more, anything else. 'There's just us, Polly,' he would finally say, for I hadn't yet become Arianna, 'just us and your lightness and your whiteness.' But he would say this almost angrily, if I mentioned the house, or at least coldly, without an expression of any kind on his face.

"So when he went off to make money in his balloon and I was left alone in the white room for a few days I began to make the house – you know, to picture it in my mind. At first I just made the inside and it was just about the size of a dollhouse I'd had as a child, with the back missing and the other side not quite real despite its lovely little windows with shutters and its front door with a tiny knocker, because you hardly ever turn it around to look from the outside in.

"I picked out all the wallpapers and the curtains; all the colours for the various rooms. I wanted colour! I refused to have a single white object in the house. Even the bath I had constructed out of cream-coloured porcelain with chartreuse and pink roses painted in it, and green vines. It wasn't a rich person's house, mind you, but it had charm:

lots of chintz in the parlour, though never on a white ground, and lots of odds and ends, bric-à-brac, and pictures. Pictures on the walls, you see, because I wanted *details* . . . to the point where I didn't mind crowding. I wanted lots of objects and I wanted there to be lots of memories associated with those objects.

"Gradually, I became quite happy with it, with all of it. The dining room had Chippendale chairs and silver candelabra. But the house was not too large, not, as I've said, a rich person's house. And no servants because I did want to stay alone with him.

"Eventually, the inside of the house became so wonderful (there were fireplaces in all the rooms), and so full and so furnished (I had those clasps on the inside of the windows – have you seen them? – the ones that look like little hands). . . . I had all the china – a soft blue with peacocks – and all the silver (just plate, I was not ostentatious). After he had been away four or five times I knew that I had finished my house but I couldn't bear to put a front on it because then I'd feel shut out. So I left it open, like a dollhouse, and began to work on the garden. This was nice, leaving it open, because then I could look at all the rooms at once.

"I didn't know anything at all about gardening and I still don't – but that didn't matter because I was able to create the garden finished. I didn't have to plant it, I just had to want it and there it was, just as if some old gardener had been working on it for twenty years. Roses climbed over arbours, iris swayed in flower beds, springs jumped out of little grottoes, vines climbed trellises. I had a boxwood maze, of all things, which led to a small bench (painted yellow, not white), and baths for the birds who, under the circumstances, I was able to choose. And the birds never migrated and all the flowers bloomed at once."

"I hope you changed the seasons now and then," said Emily, "to allow for storms."

"Why, no," said Arianna, "I didn't think of that. Anyway, with the sea right there I had plenty of storms in the white room."

And as they spoke, the season all around them changed again, this time to autumn.

"After those days I spent secretly building the house or working on the garden, he, Jeremy, would come back and enter the white room. He would pull me over to the bed – not roughly – gently, and we would begin again those hours and hours of lovemaking.

"It was always he who operated the door that closed us in together, always he who turned the key; twice, now I remember a double lock. At first I thought it was to keep the sea with its white breakers out, all his bolting and locking, but then I realized, after the ocean got into our lovemaking, that he was really locking it in. And me too. Making me so much a part of him I was swallowed.

"It was then that I started to use the imaginary house to ground me when I thought that I might float away altogether from too much touching. I would visualize some small detail when he caressed my thighs and stomach; an ink stand with two metal deer perched on it, or the inlaid box where the fish knives were kept. And while I moved through swell after swell of pleasure I would have something to hold on to; a rose bush from the garden, or even a common rake. As I melted under him or dissolved over him I would visualize these things – in detail – as if I were drawing them on the white paper of the room. I remember once, when my whole body was aching and aching with pleasure, I became confused and thought the white sheets were the blue curtains of my imaginary house, and I realized that I would have to tell him because otherwise I was being unfaithful: like harbouring a secret desire for another lover.

"And so, a few weeks later, after he'd returned from another two or three days of ballooning, I confessed my pretend house, my play house I called it, taking care not to omit any facet of it, any of my precious details, so that when I had finished explaining he would know it as well as I did. I took him on a sort of tour; room by room by room. By then I'd travelled that route so many times by myself I could actually hear things: how footsteps sound different on wooden floors than they do on soft rugs, the *tick tock* of the clock in the hall and its chime – I don't like the important-sounding gongs that clocks sometimes have, so I was careful to give mine bells. Then we strolled pleasantly, I thought, all around the garden where now I could smell the earth and flowers. And inside again, afterwards, I lit some fires in the hearths of the parlour and the dining room. I was cooking something as well, I was so pleased to have him there, and I could smell the herbs and the meat.

"I finished by leading him up the red-carpeted stairs to the bedroom with its wallpaper and mirrors – there were no mirrors in the white room – and its bureaus and ample bed. Of all the rooms in the house, that was the one I had made for both of us.

"When I stopped talking I realized that the white room was filled with his silence and the pounding of that fearsome sea. He looked at me from across all that and his face was a mask of sadness. He just gazed at me, not with the neutral look that I'd seen before, but with one of real pain. 'You've killed the white room, Polly,' he said to me. 'You created that house and destroyed the white room.'

"That was the first night since I'd known him that he didn't touch me at all.

"The next day I knew that, by telling him, I'd put the front on my house – that the inside was no longer open and that somehow I'd built a wall around the garden and its gate was closed as well. The sea roared outside the white room but even when I rubbed a clear spot on the glass I couldn't see it because there was a fog. Horns and bells in the distance and the packing of suitcases inside the tourist home. Within a week or two I was sailing in the balloon with him, and he'd changed my name to Arianna.

"As for me, I took all the love and affection I'd had for the imaginary house and gave it to the balloon and sailing it and the details of the landscape underneath it.

"And for a little while, when we were working together, we had some details, we had some memories. But he was always unhappy, always silent, and eventually he stopped ballooning altogether to manage my career."

"Oh, my," said Emily, "Yes, I could see your house clearly, and I could see the white room as well. How strange! I seem to think that the white room was his invention as much as the house was yours. He may have imagined the whole thing. I was right, you see, about the house being all yours. It was yours in a way no real house could ever be. How easy it must have been to transfer that ownership to the balloon. You must have loved your balloon."

Arianna nodded silently, sadly.

"Yours was a very civilized house, I must say. The house I built wasn't like that at all. Its energies were not contained in the way yours were, they were always bursting free. But the white room – maybe I know about that too, maybe I could tell you! But first I want to tell you about the house I built, and I wonder what you will think of it. Look up there!"

Emily pointed a vapour-like finger up towards the summit of the highest of the swells that surrounded them. On it stood an old black farmhouse in very poor repair. Near its walls, outside its doors, a few chickens were doing their best to scratch at the earth in the same strong wind that, in an instant, had carried both Emily and her friend much closer to the structure.

"There are trees here!" said Arianna, surprised.

"Only two," replied Emily, leaning casually against one of them. "Please look at that," she said to Polly/Arianna, holding one thin hand towards the view.

Rolling down from where they stood was billow after billow of moorland; black heather in the dark light (for now it was November) crossed, now and then, by a slate-grey cliff or a patch of orange ling. The moors appeared to go on and on forever, as if they were out of control and couldn't stop. Above this strange, endless expanse, walls of fierce clouds trailing scarves of rain. And behind them, the odd straight sword of light, thrust down by the winter sun.

Both ghosts were silent for several minutes, maybe hours, maybe a season or two.

"Oh," said Arianna at last, "I think maybe this is frightening."

"Awe-inspiring, not frightening," Emily said quietly. "Not nearly as frightening as a closed, white room."

"All this wind!"

"Yes," agreed Emily, joyfully.

A T T H E A G E of fifteen, Arthur Woodruff becomes obsessed with Tintoretto, for several reasons. The first and perhaps the least important is that when herded, along with thirty of his unwilling classmates, several blocks south-east from Harbord Collegiate to the Art Gallery of Toronto, he is, if not impressed, then at least surprised by the size of the Tintoretto there. While most of his friends move, snickering, from naked woman to naked woman, Arthur paces back and forth in front of the Tintoretto until he feels he has walked the marble floor, patted the stationary dog, exchanged pleasantries with Christ, and cast one or two suspicious glances in the direction of the turned back of Judas. You can move around in this painting and Arthur, at fifteen, needs that. He finds himself becoming gradually enchanted by the canal at the far end of the tiled room and by the three trees that are revealed by three arches. He finds himself becoming more and more interested in the white towel that one of the disciples has draped over his arm like the maître d' in a high-class restaurant and by the white, apron-like cloth that Christ has tied around his waist like a fastidious housewife concerned about spoiling a new skirt.

In fact, to the adolescent Arthur, Christ looks as if he were preparing, not to wash the disciples' feet, but to scrub the floor.

Arthur quite likes the floor. Although he sort of wants to swim the waters of the distant canal and walk across the distant hills, more than anything he wants to click his cleats on the marble-tiled floor and, while he is clicking them, to pace out the carefully measured perspective the artist has painted there.

He is bored, almost repelled, by every other painting in the gallery, even the ones with several pairs of breasts to ogle. The women seem to him simply fat and he prefers his girls long-thighed and thin. He prefers, he believes, for he hasn't much experience in the field, that female flesh be one consistent texture and colour – unbruised and undimpled – and if it is not depicted in that manner then he doesn't want it there at all.

After his class is dismissed, Arthur takes the news of the painting home with him to the apartment above his father's laundry and dry-cleaning business. The painting is enormous, he tells his Italian mother. It includes all the disciples and all of their stockings. The word *Tintoretto*, repeated by her tongue, sounds musical, almost perfect, and they laugh together when she tells him that *tintoretto* means "little dyer of cloth" in Italian, because that is one activity in which Arthur's ordinary Canadian father engages in his purgatory below. One of the worst, though most encouraged activities because of the extra fee. It is right there on the sign that announces WOODRUFF'S DRY CLEANING AND LAUNDRY. In smaller letters, added almost as an afterthought, is the sentence WE DYE ANY FABRIC. Arthur's father, then, with his wounded leg, his ordinariness, his boring, repetitive war stories, is a *tintoretto*. Arthur loves it. It adds a touch of theatre, a touch of the exotic, to the steamy, claustrophobic earnestness of his father's profession.

That is the second reason for the obsession.

The third is dictated by his Italian blood, which has a tendency to dance, regardless of how he tries to repress it, sentimentally in his veins, as it does in the veins of his mother. She has filled their apartment with plastic, illuminated shadow boxes depicting *The Last Supper*, or *The Bleeding Heart of Jesus*, or angels speaking quietly to dark-haired children. She wears crucifixes and says rosaries. She prays in dark Catholic churches at dawn for the health of her husband, the welfare of her child. She weeps often: with joy, with sorrow, with resignation. When Arthur takes her to see the painting she weeps for its Italian-ness, its religious subject matter, its glimpses through arches of landscape she knows she will never see again. Arthur adores his mother at these moments, adores the tears that she weeps so easily.

But there is another aspect to his blood, an aspect that keeps the dancing, sentimental Italian element severely under control. His father's stiff repression. His father's almost military fear of emotion. His father's withdrawal to cold neutral places after a day involved with the heat of cleaning other people's soiled belongings. And so, even while Arthur adores his mother, he shrinks from the intimacy of the moment, in love and in terror, speechless and removed. In mid-adolescence the battle is over. His father's blood has won.

To overcome this rush of love and fear he jokes with his weeping mother. "Look, Mama, look at Christ with his apron on and that big tub. Maybe he isn't washing the disciples' feet at all. Maybe he is dyeing the disciples' socks. Maybe Tintoretto made Christ a *tintoretto*!"

His mother weeps with laughter. Arthur stands apart from her, smiling vaguely, attempting to enter the cold marble of the painted room.

By the time he is eighteen, preparing to enter the University of Toronto as a scholarship student, his destiny has been determined by his obsession. His father, suspecting a scholar, perhaps even an artist, in their midst, has given him a small room behind the laundry, for a study. More like a hallway than a room, it contains one window, through which Arthur can never see because of the steam that continually coats it. Still, the room seems cool and clear compared to the laundry itself, and Arthur withdraws there in the evenings after lectures and on weekends after several perspiring hours on the pressing machine.

For the first few months he makes repeated attempts to wipe the fog from the window with a borrowed piece of laundry. He tries all fabrics from rayon to terrycloth. The only result of this small task is that the world outside is changed to a blur of smeared colours. Then gradually, gradually, the window returns to its original state of opacity. There is something satisfying, something comforting about this – this useless attempt to let his vision out and let the light in, and Arthur experiences a mild delight while engaged in the activity. He watches, with pleasure, as the sharp edges of Lee Wong's Groceteria and Schendell's Used Furniture become blurred, dissolving into soft, abstract, pastel shapes. Believing that he wants to be a painter, he attempts to store visual experiences of this nature in his memory. After a few months, however, he leaves the window alone, resigns himself to the moist, close environment, and forgets altogether that the colours and shapes of the outside world ever held his attention at all.

By now he has learned, by borrowing the cumbersome art books from the Central Library on College Street, an enormous amount about Tintoretto; about his ceilings and scuoli and about his life; about the art and the art world of sixteenth-century Venice, its rivalries and vendettas.

On the wall of the steamy little room he paints the words "Il disegno di Michelangelo e'l colorito de Titiano," words he has learned that Tintoretto had inscribed on the walls of his sixteenth-century studio. But Arthur hates Titian – colour or no colour – imagining him a wildly jealous man, unable to cope with Tintoretto's superior talent. Arthur believes, utterly, the legend that states that Titian expelled Tintoretto from his Venetian studio upon discovering the extent of his young pupil's genius.

It is Tintoretto's character that Arthur is beginning to admire at this point, even more than his achievements. He loves the concept of the passionate inner man combined with the practical outer one, who even as a boy could undergo such an unjust dismissal and still admire the man who carried it out. A man who in an era of studio-trained artists was himself, of necessity, self-taught. The son of a simple dyer of cloth.

Many of the Tintorettos that Arthur sees in the books he has borrowed are filled with wild activity. Cloth and weather, cloth and wind. This is interesting, because nothing at all appears to disturb the atmosphere of Arthur's first Tintoretto at the Art Gallery of Toronto. It hangs, serene and slightly pompous, covering a full wall with static heaviness. Its very lack of movement is in direct contrast to the only other Tintoretto reproduction available in the gift shop – *St. George and the Dragon*

Arthur has pinned *St. George and the Dragon* up on his wall. He spends hours studying it, trying to decipher its messages. In the foreground of the painting a menacing, hysterical princess is thrust towards him by something she is trying to escape from; her voluminous clothing struggling with her away from threatening weather, dark landscape, and the languid corpse of a young, nude man. She wants out, she wants to be away, and at certain moments, when Arthur has looked at the painting for too long, he fears that she wants him.

What she appears not to want is Saint George himself – a small horseman in the background who is engaged in the act of spearing a timid, lethargic dragon. The dragon is not nearly as frightening as the emotions of the princess. Perhaps she has not even noticed Saint George, so driven is she by the demons that seem to live with her inside those yards and yards of pink silk.

Arthur is only a student. He knows next to nothing about women. But looking at the poor, dutiful, underrated saint, and then at this huge whirlwind of a princess, he is certain that the story is all about her.

By the age of eighteen Arthur has read Ridolfi's strange, antiquated biography of Tintoretto no fewer than ten times, making use, at last, of the small amount of Italian his mother had coaxed into his memory when he was a child, and making use, also, of his mother to help him translate the difficult passages. It is in this small book that he learns that Tintoretto, deprived of a studio and live models, constructed miniature rooms filled with tiny wax figures. Rooms with little windows cut into them and candles placed outside them so that the artist could examine the effect of a low sun streaming into a room, or could study the dispersal of light in religious miracles. He constructed luminous, three-dimensional worlds so that he might represent them two-dimensionally on canvas. Arthur learns that the apprentice painter hung small wax angels from his studio ceiling so that he, squatting beneath, could draw the human figure floating over him. Arthur covets such an environment. Oddly enough, it is not the canals, the romance, the splendour of sixteenth-century Venice that he wants. Only the calm interior of a young man's studio, its tranquillity – the hand-made angels turning on their threads, the flickering candles throwing golden light, the small room full of static religious subjects. The artist himself moving in an orderly, quiet, daily fashion, away from the bustle of crowded studios, towards greatness.

When Arthur was perhaps ten years old, his mother placed a plaster-of-Paris *Last Supper* on a shelf above the television. There it remained, unchanging, as Arthur grew.

Now, at eighteen, he begs it from her, takes it down to his narrow room, and places it in a cardboard box from which he has removed one side, and into the walls of which he has cut three or four windows. Arthur turns off the lights, covers the foggy window with borrowed dirty laundry, and lights a candle.

From the ceiling, like lumpy pink fans, hang rubber dolls that Arthur has collected over the last few months from Queen Street junk shops; the cardboard wings he has made for them droop listlessly from their plump shoulders. For the moment these are ignored, as Arthur focuses his attention on positioning the candle outside the four-inch window. Then, kneeling so that his eyes are level with the small sculptural group, he contemplates the room he has created.

Into this room streams a shaft of yellow, unearthly light. One half of the face of each disciple is illuminated, orange, except for the garish features of Judas. His head is turned towards the window, towards Arthur, towards the candle, away from Christ, whose vaguely menacing face shines like a partial moon in that company. The colours of all the painted clothing – the hideous turquoises and purples – are deepened, enriched, by the tint of fire. Arthur lights another candle and places it behind the rear window he has cut into the box.

When the light moves into the room from the rear window the *Last Supper* amalgamates, becomes an ugly lump, resembles a poorly constructed artificial mountain. Personality disappears. Judas, Peter, John, Jesus, Timothy, Andrew melt into a meaningless mass of flesh and clothing. So much clothing, obscuring everything beneath. Arthur thinks of the canvas sacks on wheels that his father pushes through the humid rooms of his shop, the endlessness of it. He thinks of the bolts of silk that Tintoretto's father dyed, over and over, during long sixteenth-century workdays, he thinks of the riotous clothing attached to the princess on his wall.

Arthur lights another candle and places it in front of the grouping just beyond the territory of the box. His own face leaps into startling life, lit from beneath. Above him, still ignored, the round undimpled bellies of rubber dolls shine, orange, in the light.

When he illuminates the west, the final window, all the disciples come back into amazing focus. Christ's clumsy plaster-of-Paris hand becomes eloquent, its gesture profound. The unexceptional plaster robes worn by everyone in the room now evolve into something magnificent, something which Arthur knows the great masters referred to as drapery.

"Drapery," he mutters, looking around his narrow dark room at the barely discernible bundle of soiled laundry he has crammed into the window and at the trail of shirts and vests he has dropped carelessly across the floor. All these years the clothing that has come into the shop, other people's laundry, has been drapery; something gentle, boneless, something that falls over, that transforms the frame beneath. "Drapery," he whispers again, the sound of it suddenly sanctifying his mother's tablecloths and curtains and pillow slips and coverlets, his own jeans and T-shirts, his father's profession, the dirty laundry on the floor of his bedroom.

Arthur runs out of his room and into the front of the shop, gathering silk now (Tintoretto – little dyer of silk): women's undergarments, the smaller the better, to drape over his dolls. Unconcerned by the sexual significance of these small pieces of cloth, unconcerned by the fact that they are nylon and not silk at all, he drapes the panties over his naked rubber angels and the larger swaths, slips and half-slips, over any object in the room: two chairs, one stool, the cardboard room, his piles of books. He lights the remaining seven candles, positions them dramatically to the left of several draped objects and, reaching for his sketchbook, ink wash, and sanguine Conté crayon, he begins to draw.

Four hours later, Arthur's father puts down the sports section of the Saturday paper and leans inquisitively forward in his chair. His eyes dart suspiciously around the room as his nostrils recognize smoke. Following the smell of burning rubber, burning nylon, down the narrow staircase, he moves towards the room at the back of the shop.

Behind Arthur the reproduction of *St. George and the Dragon* disengages itself from the lower of the two thumb-tacks that fasten it to the wall and curls upward in the heat. First the frantic woman disappears, then the corpse, then the tiny knight and listless dragon. For a few moments, before the complete episode bursts into flames, all that is visible is the turbulent sky.

But Arthur, facing in the opposite direction, does not see this. He is too busy with the flaming drapery, too busy trying – as his father sees when he opens the door – to put the fire out with his bare hands.

ANN'S MOTHER is brushing out her daughter's hair, preparing her for the dance in the Presbyterian church basement.

In the face of this dance, this reality, which looms as large as a freighter in the harbour of her imagination, Ann is unable to exchange her auburn curls for the preferred long black curtain of hair. She is unable, too, to exchange her grey pleated skirt and cashmere sweater for a wind-tossed dark cloak, dampened by rain. The failure of her imagination, at this point, appals her. As she looks out the kitchen window she sees only the back of the neighbouring house on Glen Grove Avenue, several fruit trees whose leaves detach in a light wind, Toronto autumn twilight, and her own garage. Tonight is her first dance. She is fourteen.

"Sit still," her mother says.

Ann stiffens the muscles in her neck against the pull of the brush. Everything around her is in sharp focus; the waxed linoleum, the glass-covered kitchen clock, the ungainly handle and buckle lock on the refrigerator door, one knife and one fork on the gleaming kitchen table. She is terrified, practically paralyzed. After the torturous brushing of hair Ann will be forced, by her mother, to eat. Then she will be forced, by her mother, to go to the dance.

"Aren't you going to have supper?" she asks, now.

"Daddy's coming home later."

"*Daddy's* coming home *tonight*?"

"You knew that," says Ann's mother, tying a ribbon in Ann's hair–which has grown, under the attentions of the brush, into something resembling brown candy floss. "Business," she explains.

Sometimes Ann's father inhabits a territory called Ungava, a vast trackless region in Arctic Quebec where there may or may not be minerals. Sometimes Ann's father inhabits a territory called "the bush," the middle north of eight out of ten Canadian provinces, where there also may or may not be minerals. Sometimes he inhabits a region called Bay Street, where he attempts to convince millionaires that minerals exist in the other two regions, whether they do or not. The territory that he rarely inhabits is this kitchen, where Ann is experiencing a terror of anticipation concerning a church basement. Though graced by a startling imagination, (as evidenced by his belief in invisible minerals), and given to spectacular appearances, in bush planes, near the docks of Ann's various summer camps, Ann's father is neither vain nor showy. He prefers the midnight chill of an Arctic tent or a cabin overheated by woodstove to the comfort of wall-to-wall carpets and French Provincial furniture. He is hardly ever home.

"Does he . . . did he know about the dance?" asks Ann.

"I don't know. . . . " Ann's mother is removing a tuna fish casserole from the oven. "I don't think so . . . why?"

Ann does not wish to risk the possibility of the spectacular appearance of a bush plane on the church lawn. Once, her father buzzed one of her backyard birthday parties and five little girls ran tearfully home.

"Oh . . . nothing," she says.

She closes her eyes tight, inhales the fishy odour of the casserole and attempts to be Catherine preparing for the arrival of Edgar Linton at Wuthering Heights. No banal bush planes there, buzzing doggedly through wind. There, financial security rides up from the valley to the heights in a stunning leather coach, pulled by charcoal-coloured horses. The calendar on the wall would not reveal her father's itinerary (Ungava, Goose Bay, Yellowknife), would sport instead a series of grim black crosses made by Heathcliff on the days that Catherine had not spent with him.

And Heathcliff, himself, would be brooding about this; in candlelight, in firelight, in moonlight. But he could never successfully brood, Ann knows, under the fluorescent light over this kitchen sink. Sink light, thinks Ann, attempting to banish it with her imagination.

But it is no use. Fear causes even the vaguest of animals to pay attention. The outer world has never been so clear.

Ann is afraid of two things: one is a certainty and the other is almost a certainty. She is afraid that there will be no one resembling Heathcliff in the church basement – a certainty – and she is afraid that no one will ask her to dance. Her mother, driving Ann through the autumnal streets that lead towards the dance, is afraid of something else altogether.

After she has stopped the car near the church door she looks directly into her daughter's eyes. "This is your first dance," she says.

"Yes, mother."

"I want you to have this pepper pot." Ann's mother removes a brass object from her handbag.

"It belonged to my mother and now it's time for me to give it to you."

"What's it for?"

"It's in case any of *them* get out of hand."

"Out of hand?"

"Yes . . . in case one of *them* tries something when he is walking you home. Or," she adds thoughtfully, "in case someone else tries something if no one is walking you home."

Ann examines the small metal object. "It's very pretty," she says.

"Then all you have to do," her mother continues, "if one of them tries anything, is open your purse, take out the pepper pot, unscrew the lid, and throw pepper in the jerk's eyes."

"All right," says Ann uncertainly, "but what exactly is *something*?"

"Oh, you'll know something when you see it," Ann's mother assures her.

Ann stuffs the pot in her new purse, opens the car door, places her loafers on soggy leaves. Heart pounding, she looks towards rectangles of light at lawn level. This is a church. She already feels like broken glass.

"Go on," her mother says with a dismissive wave of her left hand, "you have to start this nonsense sooner or later."

Before she turns to walk away, Ann looks at her mother's face framed by the open car window. "The pepper pot," she says, "did you ever use it?"

"No," replies her mother, starting the engine, "unfortunately."

Ann endures exactly half an hour of the church basement. As expected, Heathcliff is not there and, as dreaded, she is not asked to dance. Outer life is at its worst and most vibrant as, one by one, the girls she has been pretending to engage in scintillating conversation are lured away by sweaty-palmed partners. Ann studies a Bible picture on the wall behind her. This was once, after all, her Sunday school, though the fact of this hideous dance will banish those memories for ever. A few lambs, Jesus, a bunch of boys and girls. Suffer, little children.

When she can bear it no longer she leaves the basement and walks the residential city streets. Unwilling to go home with her pepper pot full and failure written all over her face, she eventually decides to walk all the way up Yonge Street to the highway. This takes over an hour and as she walks, the landscape of the moors returns, reassuringly, in her imagination. Heather shivering under wind. Hearts cracked open. The weather and the landscape a suitable reflection of a province in the mind.

When she returns home Ann will tell her mother and her recently arrived father that she has had a wonderful time at the dance. She will invent suitable partners and name songs. What she will not tell them is that, standing on a cement overpass, looking down at insignificant cars, she had opened the pepper pot to the wind and black snow had scattered into the night.

What she will not tell them is that she has decided to spend a lot more time with Heathcliff.

EVERY DAY Arianna had risen at six in the morning, made a lunch of bread and cheese, and left her father's rooms and her father snoring on a daybed.

The London she entered, then, was dank, dark, and mostly foggy. Gutters filled with trash and horse dung. Noise, pandemonium of dark rattling carriages and no accessible sky. Angry horses snorting steam. Here and there the ridiculously bright, almost garish colours of a flower-seller's cart set against the grey.

Arianna had wondered occasionally, vaguely, where the flowers came from, what enchanted land was capable of producing days filled with growth and colour, and whether this might be the same land into which her mother had disappeared.

Her mother, the absent flower.

Each morning she proceeded along slimy streets, past seedy pubs, and towards a nauseous-green door, which led her into her place of employment: Furnell's Fabric and Furnishing, its dim lights, its freezing or sweltering conditions. Presently she seated herself in front of that menacing little black devil, her sewing machine. It was, and she seemed to sense this, evil in the flesh: naughty, dark, shining, busy. Its cogs and wheels and endless supply of thread represented to her the interminability, the dailiness, of her employment.

The machine itself was always seizing two disparate entities, stamping its tiny silver foot on them and then sewing them, inexorably, together. Whir-r-r-r, chang, chang, chang. And Arianna's own muscles operated this. Pump, pump, pump on the decorative wrought-iron pedal, all day long. Her thin hands, like two pale spiders, moving the fabric up and over and through, up and over and through.

All around her, stationed at their own personal whirring black demons, were replicas of herself: pale, young women whose spider hands darted over grey or brown broadcloth. They kept their heads bent, their eyes cast down; and they looked, sitting in their straight rows, like one woman at a sewing machine, reflected to infinity in a fun-house mirror.

Except that Arianna sported quite unruly, curly, blond, almost white hair and in that sea of black, brown, and grey heads hers stood out like a new shilling. As if it were a lamp, the only source of light, if you ignored the sooty windows, in the factory.

"So where did you, how did you meet him? I can see that it is inevitable – you'll insist upon talking about it sooner or later."

Emily and Arianna were floating up the perilous path towards the height of land known as Ponden Kirk. Sleet was making its ferocious way down the valley towards Haworth but by the time the two ghosts reached the top of the cliff it would be spring again.

"I met him in the factory."

"Factory – ?" Emily glanced in the direction of Ponden Mill where even now hundreds of men, women, and children worked at looms. "I thought you were a balloonist."

"Oh, that . . . I told you . . . that was later."

"All right, in the factory . . . "

"I'll never forget the day – "

"Don't be so sure . . . but go on."

"I was working as usual on grey broadcloth, making winter capes for gentlemen, not paying any attention, when I reached down for more fabric and pulled up a smooth swath of scarlet. I looked around the room and discovered, to my amazement, that everything had changed. The grey interior of the factory had become enormously festive. Some women held turquoise, others yellow, still others red like mine."

"Why?" Emily motioned for Arianna to join her in her favourite spot, under an outcropping of granite. They could see almost all the way to Keighley from there.

"God," said Arianna, remembering vividly now, "looking back, it seems as if all that colour was an omen of change." She settled into the hollow beside Emily. "It was balloon silk. The factory had received a contract to make three balloons."

"And?"

"And one of them was for Jeremy Jacobs . . . the 'Sindbad of the Skies'!"

"Was he there with the silk?"

"Not that day. That day we all fought with the silk – it was slippery, you know, hard to manage. We had to learn how to handle it. But a few days later he arrived – I suppose to inspect the work in progress. He told me that he spotted me right away. Something about a shaft of pale sunlight breaking through the sooty window and illuminating my hair. I remember that I looked up from my machine to see this astoundingly handsome man standing in the aisle staring at me. And then when the shift was over, there he was, waiting at the factory door. Somehow it was that simple. We just . . . walked away together."

"To where?"

"That first day? All over London, it seemed. Mostly to clothing stores. He said, I love you but I hate your grey clothes. You should be dressed in white! And then he bought me seven white skirts, seven white blouses, white ribbons for my hair. I followed him around like a household pet. I felt . . . stunned . . . somehow . . . drugged. I never returned to the factory and I never saw my father again. The next day we took the train to Dover, where we rented that room I told you about."

"Didn't you feel like a fallen women?"

"On the contrary, I felt lighter than air. For a while. And then I felt like I wanted some detail. That was what ended it. Or part of it . . . but I already told you that."

"I think I like trains," said Emily suddenly. "Sometimes I drift down to the station at Haworth. I like the steam and the energy. They are like weather. Some of them are named after winds."

"On the train he sat across from me and just looked at me and told me to do certain things so that he could watch me doing them. Look out the window, he would say, or, Read this book. Put your chin in your hand, lean forward, lean back against the seat. Then, after each change, he would look at me with utter adoration. No one, absolutely no one had paid that kind of attention to me before."

"And you did those things?"

"Instantly."

"Why?"

"Because he told me to."

"He told me he would look after me, completely, that I would never have to worry again." Arianna paused. "About anything." She watched the moor turning violet, autumn approaching again. "But it wasn't true. Eventually I started to worry about him . . . after he changed, I mean." Arianna was silent. Then she grabbed Emily's transparent sleeve.

"Heavens! Can't we slow this down? I was just getting to enjoy the heather and now, I can tell, it's November. November, by the way, was terrifying in the white room."

"Yes," said Emily, "we can slow it down. We can focus in and that slows it down. Or we can haunt, which means that we have to enter that time."

"Can we haunt him now? Can I haunt him now?"

"He's gone. Soon he will freeze to death on an ice floe in his Arctic sea. Or starve to death. It doesn't really matter which. Perhaps it will be both. Anyway, he will be perfectly preserved up there. A solid block of ice. But dead. And there will be no spirit floating around either, as far as I can see. He'll probably go to Limbo. But why was November so terrifying?"

"The promenade was deserted. So was the tourist home. The sea was dark green, or steel-grey and threatening. Jeremy was there all the time. There were no balloon trips. Once he covered me, buried me, in white feathers and then he dug me up again. Feathers floating all over the room. And the wind rattled the window panes. Once it was so stormy and windy, there was seaweed stuck to all the glass in the morning. He started to draw me with white chalk on black paper. Jeremy will be dead?"

"Yes."

"I knew that. Should I be sad?"

"No."

"No . . . I don't feel sad."

"Why should you? You're already dead."

"Ah, yes, I'd almost forgotten. Anyway November was terrifying because of the dark. Jeremy had some theory that he was the dark and I was the light – the light part of him perhaps – I don't know. He dominated, and as it grew darker he dominated more."

"Did you fight?"

"Never."

"You should have fought and fought and fought. Love should be angry, otherwise there is no ferocity. And then it just doesn't matter. It could be anyone's love affair, any ordinary person's love affair."

"How do you know this? You never had a man."

"Listen, I've been inventing angry love affairs since I was nine. It was my life's work. Who needs a real man? They're all so unpredictable and they never get angry at the right times or say the appropriate things. They only interfere with the inventing. Anyway, one thing I know for certain: all love affairs are pure fiction and if two people are imagining the same love affair it just gets too complicated. Every love affair I ever invented was filled with lies, betrayals, lust, double-crossings, madness, imprisonment, and death. White feathers! Hrumph! How banal! But I like the sea part and the seaweed on the windows. As if the tourist home had gone for an ocean voyage while you were sleeping or as if it had been attacked by the sea. The trouble is I've never lived near it, the sea, that is, but I don't think you can enter the sea when you are angry. You can't participate. You can only stand and stare at it or float over it in a boat or swim in it with long, graceful strokes. Therefore I prefer the earth, the moor, where you can run and run and run. Away. Towards. It doesn't really matter which."

"I never really ran anywhere," said Arianna, "except over to the balloon on the word 'sure.' "

"What about walks by the sea? Surely you and Jeremy took walks by the sea."

"Not often. Outside the room he would become strange . . . distant; as if, as if he were having a problem with space. Nothing locking us in together. Which is odd, now I think about it, because space was already his profession and later became mine. But not until after he changed. Then, after that, we were always sailing away from each other."

ANN'S LONG voyage to the rented room.

There are midnight skies and suggestions of a meteor shower. This is summer: heat, and strange inexplicable lightning.

They had known each other superficially for some time; had attended the same parties, taught at the same college, moved in the same circles. Still, they had never spoken, at least not intimately, and when they touched hands, or kissed in the perfunctory way that acquaintances do, it had been awkward, a collision, something to be pulled away from quickly, with embarrassment, before one moves on to the next meaningless greeting.

They are out on the lawn, in the still, dark, humid air, smoking; their cigarettes like signals from separate boats, distant from each other on the Great Lake. The roar of traffic from everywhere else in the city a muffled sound that surrounds but does not involve them. Inside, someone at the party shrieks with laughter – a single voice in a sea of voices – and then thunder, far off.

He says, staring straight ahead, "I'm going away now." And then there is the thunder again, the artillery.

A breeze moves into the lush, well-manicured vegetation of the Rosedale back garden. And from somewhere, probably a mundane car lot, a searchlight appears in the sky, and begins to compete with the lightning.

Ann knows that he is not speaking to her, is barely aware of her presence, that he is drunk and on the edge of self-argument. She lights another cigarette, and waits.

"I'll be back in six months."

She has never, since the hurricane twenty years ago, thought of the city's trees, those plump familiar maples, as ominous. But now, abruptly, they seem so; their shapes like Goya monsters pulsing, reluctantly, into life against the unnameable colour of an urban night sky. What meteor shower could penetrate this unpredictable lighting, she wonders, and all the rest of this activity, all this artificial illumination?

"If I come back in six months," he continues, "at least then I will have done what I must. I must go away."

Ann searches the sky directly above her head, the only uninfected area – if you ignored the airliners – where the stars have enough dark to shine. She remembers her first star and what a disappointment it was after the solid yellow five-pointed drawings in books. "*That's* a star, Mummy?" she said, after being allowed to wait up for this vision one night, when she was three. "Is that all there is?" "But look," her mother said, "there are hundreds and hundreds of them. They are small because they are farther away than you can even imagine. But if you could get closer, then they would get bigger. They are the farthest away things that we can see."

And here he is, Arthur Woodruff, art historian, talking to himself about being far away. Explaining the necessity to the night. Unaware that she is listening, letting the subject of distance enter her preoccupation concerning the meteor showers, the lightning, the earthly searchlight, the maples, ominous under the touch of sudden troubled weather.

"And then I'll come back," he says.

Ann listens to the swelling whir of the cicadas, unsure whether or not to include them in her catalogue of weather. What insects hum around the wind-blasted walls of Wuthering Heights? Insects are so stubbornly seasonal they must have, in some way, been invented by barometric fluctuation. Should they not then be, by rights, on those moors in droves? She imagines Heathcliff gloating as a cloud of locusts moves down the valley towards Thrushcross Grange and then Catherine emerging dark, triumphant, from among them.

"Yes," he says, "I am going for six months. . . ." He pauses, lights another cigarette, flings his glass into the lily-of-the-valley, and quite savagely shouts the word, "AWAY!"

Ann has seen him now and then, aloof and brooding, in the halls of the college. A Renaissance man. The art historians, she knows, lecture in the dark, lurking by their slide machines, gazing in the golden half-light thrown out by projected images of Crucifixions, at the backs of their students. They recite dates. They speak of influences and the birth of perspective.

"Can I do it?" he wonders now, in a gentler, more reflective tone. "Can I go?"

Ann's ideas of travel have been formed by one European voyage with her mother and by that slow, stately journey to the country, before the highway, by everything encountered along the way, by the presence of the Great Lake out the right-hand window of the Buick, by the small towns through which they'd passed, by the little old ladies with flowered hats and lace-up shoes she'd seen there, making their daily trip to a series of similar general stores. That and the hard road, the sad heart of Wuthering Heights; the cumbersome books she studied and taught. It was as though her life were being lived, uncomfortably and secretively, inside the great, dark, rattling carriages of nineteenth-century fiction.

"If I go," he says, "I'll be gone." He clasps his hands behind his back. "But in six months I'll return."

Impatient suddenly with the party, her escape from it, and this man's insistent subject matter, Ann surprises herself by shouting at him from across the garden, "Then what are you going to do about it? Why don't you just go?" She immediately regrets this challenge she has flung into the darkness. It is not like her to give advice. The word "go" hovers uncomfortably near the lawn chairs, or seems to, so fixed is Ann's gaze upon these neutral objects.

As Arthur walks towards her, across the grass, his face is illuminated by sheet lightning. She will always remember this: the white mask, startling and disembodied, the dark suit he is wearing blending with the night. He kisses her once, roughly; then, standing back he holds both her hands and looks through the dark directly into her face. And she sees him, even without lightning, and all her indifference evaporates. It changes, in a second, into something as huge and monstrous as the swaying night maples. The shock of this silences her and she will never be able to speak of these first moments. She takes them, private, into herself, shares them with no one. They are the first signs of raw materials she will need to keep near her, the small bits of fabric she will use, their patterns ripped so haphazardly they are impossible to identify.

During the next six months Ann begins her book about weather – the notes for it – which she hides in various places all over her apartment: under rugs, behind radiators, inside slipcovers, so that years later, cleaning, she might come across a yellowed slip of paper that would say something like, "west wind, 70 references; north wind, 92 references. East wind, south wind, nothing."

She begins to pay attention to the skies she sees in paintings, photographs, and travel posters. Visiting her mother, listening to stories of the past, she asks, "What was the weather like?" Ordinary conversation, at the post office, in the grocery store, becomes charged with meaning; "Hot enough for you?" or, "What crazy weather!" She collects odd names for certain seasons: *dog days*, or for strange meteorological regions: *horse latitudes*, *the Bermuda Triangle*.

And all the while she is building a man, a partner in storm, creating the idea of him in his absence. She selects certain images from her childhood: a shard of broken heaven near the highway, the wind of the disregarded hurricane pushing against the walls of her house, the grimace on the face of a faintly remembered saint in a dark, kept painting. That and the sound the page of a book makes as you turn it to discover sorrow immodestly disclosed there, and how you take the sorrow from it and preserve it more carefully than your own happiness.

She grafts all this to the fractional collision in the garden, carefully constructing its significance over and over. How he stumbled against her and then vanished. How he spoke of being away and then thrust his hands through the dark to meet hers. The stars her mother spoke of speeding towards proximity and then exploding into invisibility. The perfect balance of *here* and *gone*, dramatized in a Toronto back garden in thirty startled seconds.

Then she takes her construction and superimposes his shadow over everything else she does, so that in a way he is always with her and the engineered idea neatly precludes any expectation about the actuality of the man in her life. The energies of what might have been expectation are directed towards the beginnings of her book about weather –a subject she was introduced to by a woman who has been dead for over a hundred years.

Ah, Emily, she thinks. *Oh, for a walk on your moor now that I have something to take there with me; a male face disclosed by lightning, a searchlight, a star.*

And the shock of unexpected touch.

"I LOVE A ROOM that is full of wind," said Emily, "a room that *moves*. Papa never let us have curtains, which would have been perfect, especially light curtains, because the windows there could never keep the wind out, never! Even as it was, even though we were clothed in woollens, our skirts moved in the air while we stood utterly still. We were besieged, you see, by something other, something outer, regardless of how we were sheltered. But in spring Aunt and Tabby aired the house–windows open–and everything flew. Once we chased one of Papa's sermons around the house, up and down the stairs, through the parlour into the kitchen, and rescued only the last page before it was sucked into the fire. 'Our God is a consuming fire!' the last page began and we laughed and laughed. Papa, too, and Branwell laughing, almost hysterical, his red curls tossed by wind."

"I was never happier than when the wind was in the house – unless it was when I was out of the house myself, in the wind. The only thing that could have moved me more would have been to haul some of the stars I saw from my bedroom window into the parlour in the afternoon. Or snow. To freeze the interior, to make it polar, to change everything to white. To have icicles."

"At night sometimes my mind went white, as if it had become a white wind. Howling."

"Have you ever howled, Arianna, at the moon, at the wind, at the moors? You should have howled at him, tossed your anger out to the sea. You should have let the wind into the white room. "If you couldn't move him, you might, at least, have moved the room."

"Where is he, where is he?" wept Arianna, "Why do I want him?"

Waste, waste, waste, whispered the wind.

"All this wanting is a waste," said Emily. "And I thought you'd stopped."

"So did I," said Arianna miserably.

"Why want?" Emily continued. "Enjoy desirelessness. Such is oblivion. This wanting will pass. And yet . . . and yet Catherine would never rest in my book. She scratched and clawed and wanted and haunted. Poor Heathcliff. How weak he was and how weathered by her wanting. 'I'll never rest!' she promised. But how elusive she was. Just beyond his grasp . . . always. She was shameless. A shameless, shameless ghost! Always a ghost – a wanton shadow. Ah Heathcliff, she would sigh, and then evaporate! Take any form! he cried. So she became invisible out here in the landscape. Ha! Such forms! He couldn't see her, so he wanted her, which was what she wanted! They were engaged in a never-ending circular argument. It was their chosen vocation."

Hallucinate, hallucinate, howled the wind.

"Their whole love affair was an hallucination! I never really let them touch–except once. One desperate embrace. But by then she was dying. And on purpose! To make him want her! Her death swallowed him whole. The new form she took–that of absence–obsessed him."

"Who is Catherine?"

"Someone I invented. And in some ways she was the invention of someone else I invented and he was her invention. *I* invented them so that they could invent each other."

"He invented Arianna Ether," said Polly, becoming for the moment Polly, "but then he didn't want her."

"He was afraid of the second invention. He invented the white girl too, though, and he wasn't afraid of her – Polly Blanc, Polly Blank. Who was she, anyway? An evanescent creature. Pure fog. He could walk right through her. Listen, once in the book I have Mr. Capital H – Heathcliff, *He*,

Him–bribe the sexton to open Catherine's coffin eighteen years after her death. 'It was her face yet,' he comments and then, 'It would change if the air blew on it.' So he closes the casket – quickly. A little air, a little exposure in his presence and *it* would change. The face, the person would evaporate. He *knew* that; so did she. Absence was essential, after childhood, to the hallucination. Desperate departures, absences, reversals, withdrawals – the ongoing war. A permanent state of unfulfilled desire. And, weirdly enough, longing itself was what they desired. Mr. Capital H gave a long melodramatic speech about Catherine's ghost, her well-honed haunting skills. Moaning and complaining and writhing and loving every minute of it.

"If you must haunt, Polly/Arianna, then haunt well – although I still maintain it's a waste of time. Never reveal yourself completely. Just when the haunted one believes in your presence – disappear. Never let him see you whole.

"It's good to be a ghost, Polly/Arianna . . . you can use absence to a marvellous advantage."

Six silent months in Ann's tidy kitchen where tea towels hang – clean, motionless rectangles – from a gleaming metal bar; where the only change in temperature is the heating and cooling of the pristine oven that warms single portions of frozen food; where Ann sits at a small, unstained table, marking the papers of students who do not share her passion for *Wuthering Heights*, or where she sits, as she does now, working on her book.

She has just written a paragraph on rain. "Weather has come right in through the window," she has stated, "in the form of driving rain at the time of Heathcliff's death. He has *finally* (she has underlined the word finally) opened the window. He has opened himself. He has let himself out and he has let the weather in."

The first ring cuts right into the middle of a mental picture Ann has constructed of a casement window swinging free on its hinges. With the second ring the window slams shut, and the landscape begins to fade, hill by purple hill.

She carefully caps her fountain pen. She walks across the bare floor. She answers the phone.

"I'm back."

"Yes."

"I went away and now I'm back."

"Where did you go?"

"Venice."

"Why?"

"Tintoretto."

Ann gasps. She remembers the square inch. "You're sure," she says now in confusion, "that it was Tintoretto? Oh, God," she murmurs, "Tintoretto."

"The drapery," he explains. "And the angels," he adds.

"What?"

"It doesn't matter. We'll go for a drive. You'll come with me for a drive. Is it okay with you?"

No, thinks Ann. "Yes," she says.

"Well, it's not okay for me," he says. "This is not okay with me. This is a disaster for me. I can't do this."

"All right," says Ann quietly, amazed at her disappointment. What is a disaster? she attempts to wonder. But she knows, she knows.

"I'll be there in fifteen minutes. And we both agree to one ride together: the first and the last."

"Yes," says Ann.

"We'll drive, we'll talk, and then we'll go back. And that will be that."

Jesus, thinks Ann as she replaces the receiver, I knew exactly who he was. He didn't even have to identify himself.

Although she has been on the phone for only a few moments, the afternoon has turned to evening, and when she returns to her page she has to light her kitchen to see what she has written.

Ann is speechless in the car, overcome by a combination of anxiety and expectation. They are driving the highway, fast; green signs blurring past the side window she has turned towards. He is talking.

"Look," he says, "I'm not in love with you. I just really desire you but I'm not in love with you. What this is all about is that I want to go to bed with you."

There are ugly subdivisions now all along the highway where it once was green. Ann wishes that she were a child again, that she had brought along her paper dolls to distract her. Ann wishes she were a paper doll. Then she could change, in a second, into something else – or someone else could change her by folding paper tabs over her cardboard shoulders. She could change into a girl going to a ball or into a cowgirl dressed for the rodeo. They are nearing the airport. She could change, she remembers, into a steward-ess, or a shipboard nurse. What she wants now is to change her mind about this man with whom, she realizes, she has inexplicably fallen in love.

"And," he is continuing, "if there is any chance of you falling in love with me then we stop right now."

Ann notices the sky above the highway darkening, turn-ing asphalt grey. "I won't," she says to him, twisting in the seat to examine his profile.

"I'm in love with someone else," he says, staring fiercely ahead. "We have a wonderful, warm relationship."

Ann knows he is married. She hates the word relation-ship; the way it sounds in his mouth. She watches the flakes of snow melt on the windshield of the car, the dancing swirls of white on the road ahead. She understands that until now this has been a summer road for her. Weather and the highway have not yet come together in her life. He has turned on the windshield wipers and the headlights, for now it is getting quite dark.

"This is bad weather and it's getting dark," she says. "We should be going back."

"Back!" He throws both hands off the steering wheel and brings them back down again in a slapping gesture. "Back? We never should have come out here in the first place. This is crazy." He shakes his head. "We must think of a place to meet, somewhere out here on the highway. Just once and then *never* again."

"We should be driving in the other direction," Ann says to him. "We are too far from the lake."

"What has the lake got to do with any of this? We could meet here." He jerks his head in the direction of one of a series of highway hotels.

"I'm used to the lake on this highway," says Ann. "It was always there, on the right, whenever we went anywhere." And then she adds, for no reason, "And it was always on the left when we came back."

"It would have to be during the day," he remarks, becoming fractionally calmer. "I'm always at home at night. Tuesday, I'll meet you on Tuesday."

By now the wind has lifted the accumulating snow off the surface of the highway so that, mixed with that which falls from the sky, it becomes a new texture, ghost-like, around the windows of the car. The atmosphere becomes exaggerated, confusing, unclear. Except in the closed cab of the moving vehicle where a man and a woman are locked in together, locked in a prison of speed. There, tension hangs in the surrounding air with knife-like clarity.

"You could cut it with a knife," Ann's mother always said about tension in a room, or about silence. Her grandmother, on the other hand, used knives to describe velocity. "Quick as you could say knife," she would confide. Vanishing acts were usually associated with this modifying clause. He left the room, he ran away, he was out the door, he hopped a train, he jumped the crick, he was over the wall, he was into the lake . . . quick as you could say knife. The glint – the brief, bright flicker of the blade – enters Ann's mind now as the storm grows stronger around the car.

They turn down the Gardiner Expressway towards the centre of the city and the change of direction relaxes them slightly. They begin to talk about weather; about how to drive through storms, about snowploughs, about runways in airports, which are heated from underneath in order to melt the deadly ice, about the ropes that are tied between houses and barns in Saskatchewan so that farmers visiting cattle will not be lost in the ever-present blizzard. Ann describes to him a small set of snowshoes she had as a child.

By the time they reach her street, however, they are silent again and Ann's heart has begun to pound disturbingly.

His expression is grim, cold. He turns this mask towards her as she prepares to leave the car.

"We'll meet on Tuesday, then," he states, "at that place."

Ann steps into the six-inch snow on the sidewalk and bends at the waist with her hand on the open door. "The Tintoretto," she says, "the one at the Art Gallery?"

He nods impatiently.

"It isn't real."

"I know," he says, throwing the car into gear.

Looking at the two long tracks the vehicle leaves in the fresh snow on the street, Ann realizes two things: that she has agreed to meet him, and that during their ride through the storm they never touched each other, never even shook hands.

She stands perfectly still for a while. The blizzard thickens around her.

How strange her apartment seems in the late afternoon light. The sun has made one last appearance, dazzling behind the still-whirling snow. Ann stands stupefied at the window, taking in white and gold and several other subtle prismatic colours. Every object on her windowsill is clothed in this new light; her antique bottles and telephone insulators and jars of stones collected from the shores of the Great Lake. Pale pastel statements, unobtrusive, the only parts of her observable from the outside. She becomes in her imagination, for a moment, someone walking down the sidewalk looking at her window. Ah, they would think, someone quiet lives there, someone from whom we shall hear very little. Like the soft brown woollens that she so often chooses to wear, the objects in her windows cover her, revealing very little of her interior in the window's small theatre with its opaque curtains. How still everything has been, everything continues to be on that stage, how silent and unmoving. Behind her, rooms unfold with absolute calm. The shining surface of her kitchen table, the cutlery, unmusical and unshining in the dark of the drawer, the clean undented fabric of the pillows, her skirts hanging, lifeless, in the closet. The small amount of jewellery she owns has been carefully placed in a velvet-lined box with a closed lid, sleeping in a place where no light visits, where no flames glint from its few facets. It has been so easy to put everything she owns, everything she is, away, out of sight in drawers and other dark locations, revealing only smooth stones and soft wool and opaque glass to the world. And it has been so easy to keep that world out.

Even as she stands in its light, Ann knows that the window is keeping the weather's energy apart from her. Abruptly she wants the storm's sharp breath to disturb the air and touch her skin. She removes the glass bottles, the insulators, and the jars of stones from the little wooden ledge and puts them behind her on the floor. *There is only myself at the glass now*, she thinks, *this person that I am. Myself and fabric*. The delicate gauze curtain echoes the white, sun-shot particles of snow. The wind slams hard against the invisible barrier she has come so close to. Her breath fogs the surface as miniature drifts gather in the lower corners of the wooden frame. Quite suddenly Ann grasps the curled brass pulls and forces the window up and open, experiencing, as she does, the shock of frantic currents on her stomach, breasts, neck, and eventually on her face. The burn of sharp snow on her cheeks and eyelids.

She stands transfixed for several minutes, allowing the storm to assault and caress her. Then, with the wind still in her face, she backs up ten paces to watch the weather enter her rooms and as she watches, one curtain disentangles itself from its sash and rises, triumphant, sailing on the back of the wind, with air, snow, and sunlight all around it.

She sees the curtain dance into life, shaken by the teeth of tempest. The fabric snaps, then billows, then snaps again, straining outward from its valance, a celebrant of pure energy.

This is what Ann wants, what she will get from him, what she will become in his presence.

A curtain responding to storm.

Early the next morning, while Ann is dreaming of torna-does – tiny ones that carry dollhouse furniture carelessly around and around in their wake – the shrill ring of the phone awakens her.

"I've just spent a sleepless night," he informs her, "I can't do this."

Ann's room is frigid, her casement flung open. There is a sizeable snowdrift on her bedroom carpet but the sky beyond the partly opened bedroom window is pinkish and calm.

"Where are you?" she asks.

"It's not that I don't . . . Jesus, it's just that I can't. This will be chaos."

Ann's mind goes numb. The receiver is so cold her breath is causing beads of moisture to form on the plastic. She can't speak. The room begins to tilt. Her body, so powerful in the evening storm, feels small now, insignificant, the body of a waif. The body of one who has been brutally abandoned. Already, she has been abandoned, unworthy of even the mildest snowstorm.

She places the telephone politely, quietly, back on the hook and rolls over to regard the wall.

One hour later, with tears in her eyes, she staggers across the room to close the window.

Two hours later the phone rings again.

"It's me. It's all right now. I'm sorry. Could we still meet?"

"Yes," she says, and then she adds: "Please."

In her mind's eye the curtain awakens, twitches under the touch of air. Lint rises from it, magic dust in a shaft of sun.

"Was there something wrong?" she asks. "What was wrong?"

"Oh, nothing." He is casual now, relaxed. "I'm just nervous."

Ann inhales deeply and falls with full lungs sideways onto the pristine coverlet that lies across her bed. She laughs aloud, feeling as she does so the exact location of pure oxygen as it makes the long red tour of her body.

She spends most of the rest of the day writing in her notebook. Unable to leave or re-enter the room in which she has experienced this first bout of suffering, she leans in its doorway with her notebook and fountain pen, recording the cloud formations that pass by the bedroom window.

"SOMETIMES MAKING love is like a terrible accident," said Arianna, "and then, afterwards you are shipwrecked, broken."

"Left for dead," Emily continued, "on some God-forsaken beach, ruined. Imagine a man entering the Arctic or gone for a soldier, flinging himself away from this terrible twinship, away from this daze of completion into the raw, open awakening of the severed self."

"Terrible twinship," repeated Arianna, "we were a terrible twinship. Sewn together, bound together, chained together."

"Together," said Emily. "Consider the pronoun *we*. How does one take it apart to become *I* and *thou*. Each is shipwrecked against the other until all the shared furniture tumbles together in rooms. Everything is a maze of oblique angles – tables and chairs pushed against a door, wedged under the latch to keep the world at bay. Suffocation. Claustrophobia. You can't get out and life loses interest in you."

Arianna watched the shadows of clouds gallop like herds of swift animals over the moor. "But sometimes," she said, "making love is so soft, so easy, none of the room's furniture comes between you."

The ghosts were drifting along the old Roman road that led past Lower and Middle Withins. Smoke from the chimneys of the Old Silent Inn and Ponden Mill in the valley scattered over the moor.

"Do you know what a *hig* is?" Emily asked.

"No."

"A hig is a short, dramatic bout of bad weather – here and gone in an instant. A sort of tantrum – an outburst of the elements. Sometimes making love is like that."

"Yes," agreed Polly/Arianna. "Sometimes it's like that."

T H E R O O M , when she enters it, is dark and closed and still. They do not speak to each other.

Mouth approaching face and hair. His skin is warm, supple, under a starched shirt. And then there is the smell of him: some herb she doesn't recognize, the essence of his unfamiliarity. That, and the rough texture of his woollen jacket near her face. This other body. This other heart and pulse. He touches her, from the beginning, with his whole body. The long hard thigh muscles, the face against her ribcage, her neck, her inner thigh. His shoulder moving across her breasts, a wrist resting gently on her throat.

He does not seize but pours over her. There is nothing here that is grasped for or clutched. He slides the backs of his hands across her stomach, his face between her jaw and collar bone. The sheet wraps around one ankle. Various objects in the room tumble and disappear. The ugly hotel light blurs and darkens.

"Why Tintoretto?" Ann asks, later.

"Because he was alone."

"But his family . . . that daughter."

"He learned alone, without workshops. Without painting backgrounds for some other artist's commissions. Without, in the beginning, models."

I am alone, thinks Ann. *Is he alone?*

"When I was younger," he confesses, "I used to believe that Tintoretto was my great-great-grandfather, or several more greats than that. Then, quite suddenly, I knew he was no relative of mine. Though I hadn't been to Italy yet."

"Tell me about Venice."

"It is bubbles and blisters and walls warped by water. It is sinking and dying. So-o-o-o beautiful. The city weeps. It is, somehow, my landscape and yet . . . I can't get hold of it, can't quite bring it into focus."

Ann moves one hand lightly, cautiously, towards his thigh and he watches her.

"My landscape," she says, "is the moors . . . West Yorkshire, though I haven't been there. I would like to buy air rights to those hills . . . to purchase their atmospheric conditions. I feel possessive about them. I want them to be all mine."

"Brontës."

"One Brontë. Emily. One book."

"*Wuthering Heights.*"

"Yes. How many Tintorettos? How many paintings?"

"One – or at least one at a time."

"Which?"

"At first it was *St. George and the Dragon*. Do you know it?"

Ann does not.

"There is something terribly the matter in the painting. The woman – the princess – has just had some earth-shattering news and she is trying – I'm convinced of it – to get out of the painting."

"Pardon?" Ann laughs.

"No . . . I mean it. She is quite frantically trying to escape."

"From the dragon?" Ann is recalling the myth.

"No . . . the poor dragon, he is not even remotely menacing." Arthur places his hand, lightly, absently, on Ann's arm. "I'm quite serious, she is trying to jump off the canvas. You see – there is something terribly the matter, something that has nothing to do with the dragon and I can't – couldn't ever – figure out what it was."

"You said 'at first.' Is there something else . . . some other painting now?"

"Many. But, yes, one. *The Temptation of Christ* in the Scuola San Rocco in Venice." Arthur squints his eyes as if he were studying a painting. Then he opens them wide. "The devil in that painting–I just thought of it–is dressed in the same pink silk, the same drapery, as that princess."

"A devil in pink silk. How strange!"

"Yes, exactly."

Later she feels his body grow tense beside hers. "I have to go."

She rises immediately, unable to bear the repetition of the sentence. Suddenly she can hear the tick of his watch. The chill of the room reaches her.

"You could, you know, have come to my place."

"I would never do that." Now he is busy, hurried, angry. "I don't want to know about that."

"But it's fine, I . . . "

"No. And we must not meet again; at least not for a long, long time. We want to end this, not escalate it. We want to get this out of our systems."

Stricken, Ann gropes for her clothing, turns in her pain away from him, dressing quickly. The garish colours of the room snap into her line of vision everywhere she moves. She avoids her own eyes in mirrors. He is buckling his belt.

There is failure here and she can see it in the tawdriness of the room's furniture, in the rumpled sheets. How dreadful, she thinks, this is, this desire for something not mine. One glance towards his preoccupied gestures. He is drinking a glass of water as if she were not there, as if she had never been there.

Outside, winter has taken hold with a grim silence. Nothing moves.

The stationary knife of frozen air, his voice cutting into her ear, saying, "We must not . . . we must not."

But they do.

As the months go by Ann is stunned again and again by her meetings with Arthur, finds herself staggering down hotel halls, not knowing how she got there, where she has parked her car, how she will escape, how much longer she will live. Everything is geometry, tilts at odd angles to a ground no longer horizontal. Her life becomes a series of doors that slide shut or click closed, whose locks must be constantly examined for safety. The rest of her days evaporate into a sequence of barely remembered landscapes glimpsed from the windows of a car racing at impossible speeds down an eight-lane highway. Her handbag is littered with crumpled tickets given to her by oddly gentle policemen who examine her face and ask if there is anything that they can do to help.

But she inhabits a region where no help is possible. On the other side of doors she collapses into a great lake of flesh, a lake so huge that from its centre no shore is visible. Having nothing to do with the way his mouth moves over her, her conversations with Arthur concern the wings of angels, the expression of prophets, the creation of scaffolding, painstaking sixteenth-century labour. They delight her with their whimsicality and annihilate her with their lack of relevance concerning his feelings for her. Occasionally he brings news of his daily life. We have bought a new car, he says, or, we are looking for a new apartment. Simple statements with the impact of the blow of an axe. The enormous reality of the rest of his life slams against the walls of her brain, and then she must hurl herself into the privacy of the painfully bright bathroom in order to regain her balance, her belief in gravity.

In the bathroom, clutching the cold sink, she looks at her own face in the mirror, sees twisted features and the burning eyes of an animal left for days in a leg-hold trap. She must leave him, must leave the room, must never return. It's not so much that she doesn't want to see him again but that she doesn't want him to see her as she is—so mutilated, so exposed, so open to the pain he unwittingly inflicts. She knows the word "we" coming from his mouth will never include her, can never include her. She is a river of flesh to him, a river whose source is the room. She is born there. The room's borders are the limits of her existence.

She leaves the bathroom and is, in seconds, awash in his embrace. He is hers again, she is certain of this. She would lie beneath the wheels of a thousand freight trains for twenty minutes of this pleasure, this troubled storm of blindness and forgetting. His mouth, silent now, draws her toward him, his body cracks her open and certainly there is lightning and thunder, the tempest she has always wanted, the hurricane: its power, its devastation.

He falls away from her into sleep and she watches several dreams flicker on his face like the shadows of leaves on the grass. "I love you," she whispers into an ear deafened by dreams, her planned flight obliterated, broken.

Leaving the room, the lake of flesh, she drives her car back into the city and the vehicle is now a cage, its speed and direction locking Ann away from Arthur.

Anyone who glanced into the cab of this car would see a young woman speaking to no one. But Ann is not speaking to no one, she is speaking to Arthur, engaging him in a one-way conversation to which there are no answers, a conversation that even lacks questions. She is making a series of announcements. "This is the way it is . . . ," she begins, "there are no memories beyond you. Everything finishes with you.

"Your face in my hands," she says, "you in the room. I'm not leaving you. There is no weather without you."

Meaningless landscapes slide by the windows. She is already waiting for the next time.

"I ONCE WENT back," said Emily, turning her transparent face towards Haworth. "I didn't exactly haunt but I went back and looked around."

"What was it like?"

"Just the same. Utterly different. I was there. I was a child."

"How was that possible?"

"Oh . . . you can haunt the past if you want to. We've transcended time. Odd . . . I was always trying to do that while I was alive and now that I'm dead it seems so ordinary. Ordinary, but all the same somewhat interesting."

"What does transcend mean?"

"I'm not sure after you are dead."

"Well . . . you went back and . . . ?"

"I had been remembering it, the day-after-day of it, out here all by myself. Silently, when I was alone, before you fell in. When I was alive I was always longing to be out here on the moor tramping around with the wind. And suddenly here I was, my wish granted, for eternity. Knowing this I started to long, once in a while, for the parsonage where I lived all my life. So I decided to haunt a little, even though, for me, it's quite out of character. Longing for something that you once had is a mistake because the pictures in your mind are never the same as whatever it is you are longing for. Memory puts gauze over it, makes it look prettier. Then, when you return, you notice the small ugliness in a way that you never did before. Maybe the mistake is the return."

"If I were to haunt him it would not be possible that he could be ugly. He was beautiful."

Emily rolled her ghostly eyes, deciding to ignore Arianna's illusion. "It was Tabitha who frightened me the most," she said.

"Tabitha?"

"Tabby. She was our servant . . . but more than that really. We adored her. A great lump of fat she was who smelled of baking bread and potato skins. Her face, you know, was like an enormous Yorkshire pudding; the same colour and texture, the same creases and folds. I lurked around in the kitchen and she didn't even notice I was there watching her. Grown-up, dead, and haunting. A ghost in her presence and she ignored it! Even though she was the one who was continually filling our little heads with supernatural nonsense –

It was far in the night, and the bairnies grat,
The mither beneath the mools heard that –
I put that in my book: one of her songs. A lullaby."

"I can understand why she frightened you."

"No, no . . . those were my favourite kinds of songs. What frightened me was that I couldn't see her whole. I mean each detail, each large, small, dark, light detail was of equal importance. Nothing receded and nothing predominated. There was no depth and no distance to her. None at all. Nothing clustered together into a mass. Every particle of her being made a separate, disconnected statement. Do you remember how, when you were alive, if you looked at a tree you saw a tree? I mean, you didn't see each of fifty thousand leaves extending from its own personal twig or stem. Well, and I'm warning you, when you haunt, it's the leaves and the stems and the twigs that you see. For some reason it's impossible to bring the whole tree into focus. It was the same with Tabby. The hairs on the ends of her warts, the enlarged pores of her bulbous nose, a string of saliva between her upper and lower teeth became just as important, just as demanding of attention as her kind eyes and clean apron . . . which, because of all this intensification, I found wasn't nearly as clean as I'd thought. She was really made up of a collection of tiny uglinesses. I couldn't bear to be around her. And perhaps it's true . . . perhaps the spirit really does abhor the flesh because, when I saw myself as a child, I found that I was ugly too. I had a cold and the area around my nostrils was inflamed. My fingernails were cracked and filled with coal dust from playing near the fire. My hair was dirty, my shoes were scuffed. Oh, Lord . . . the world is filled with such squalor!"

"You mean we can haunt ourselves?"

"Yes . . . but believe me you wouldn't want to. There is dirt everywhere. Nothing is pure."

"What else did you see?"

"Glances."

"Glances?"

"Yes, the way my sisters looked at each other, secretly, and with envy, blood lust–even hatred."

"But they were just children."

"So was I. And I was the most pulled in, the worst of the secret haters. It was very plain. I never looked anyone in the eye, but I scrutinized them, investigated them, when they weren't looking at me, and with a ruthless coldness. And I thought that I loved my family. In fact I thought they were all that I loved. Looking at my dirty little face and suspicious darting eyes I realized it was only my own imagination and my brother Branwell that I loved. And how jealous I was of my imagination: that tiny, detailed, horrifying world I carried with me everywhere I went. My treasured, invented nightmare, my darling pain. It locked me carefully away from other people; even the other people that I believed I was close to. But it opened me up too, and set me loose in places no one could have believed I would ever be able to visit."

"What places?"

"Kingdoms. Bright kingdoms of the heart, which were built of terrifyingly clear palaces–some of ice, some of glass. Dusky, empty kingdoms whose architecture had crumbled

and whose inhabitants were ghosts: much more complicated and interesting spirits than we can ever hope to be.
Claustrophobic kingdoms where everything rubbed shoulders with everything else. Forests you couldn't move
through, impassable streets, clogged sewers, and bestial,
multiplying populations. In those kingdoms everyone,
everything collided and embraced and wrestled and seethed
and grew into and out of everything else. Melting kingdoms
where steam was the only weather and the roads bubbled
and the destinations dissolved and the lovers washed over
each other like waves and disappeared down drains. Kingdoms of eruption where everything vomited something
else."

Emily smiled, remembering. "But, you know," she said,
"I never imagined this tranquillity, this fluidity. This kingdom of absence we inhabit now."

A N N   K N O W S she would never be able to sit, working on her book, in one part of a house while Arthur inhabited another; would never be able to say to herself, rooms away, *Those footsteps downstairs are Arthur's*, and then continue to use words describing another subject altogether. She would, even after exposure to the dailiness of him, be thrown by evidence of his presence into the same state of red alert that she experiences now when she is near him: each of her senses tuned to high frequency, her radar picking up moods that haven't even reached him yet, that are still two days, two weeks, or sometimes even months away. She, who so rarely sees him, is aware, from great distances, of how his feelings toward her shift and change.

She is, when they are together, so tremendously awake, her ability to concentrate so focused on the moment, that she takes all the superfluous details of their meetings home with her; the pile of the terrycloth hotel towels, the cracked rubber of the insulating lining of the curtains they must pull in order to ensure privacy, the small triangle of dust that a maid has overlooked on a plastic telephone, his cufflinks and her earrings, thrown like dice onto a bedside table. These trivial particulars move out with such precision it is as if he has brought all of the perceived world with him into the room so that there is a barrage of stimuli springing, at his touch, into life all around her. And she, newly sighted, taking it all in, taking it all in. Unable to keep any of it out. Unable to sort or classify; unable to say this object should be carefully scrutinized, this object glanced at in passing, that ignored altogether. So she takes home all the details that move out from him and she takes him home as well: not just the way he approaches but also the way he moves away from her. She can recall, at any moment, the way he rises abruptly, changes the angle of his gaze, the tilt of his head; or the way he changes, quite suddenly, the topic of conversation.

She takes all of this home to her empty apartment and there attempts to sift it, wanting to pan for gold, wanting to let the ordinary slip back into life's stream. She wants to choose perhaps one or two words, a glance, a specific touch to keep. But this is impossible. The fool's gold of the attached details clings to her memory with as much tenacity as the rare gold of emotional response. She hoards it all.

Over the months, he has used no words to describe his own response to her. She must read his face, his body, to assess the climate of the affair and she must, always, use her powers of prediction concerning his future changes of mood, his reversals, his subtle denials. This is how obsession is created, she thinks: by the other's unwillingness to be known. The mystery, the secret that he keeps from her while exposing her, constantly, to the fact that they are inexorably joined. Two adulterous lovers tied, back to back, in a purgatorial eternity. What does he return to, and how can she know that, and how could she interpret it were the information suddenly within her grasp?

He does not want to be known – at least by her – does not wish to submit to her scrutiny. Short allotments of communion. Dark acts in hidden places. She is becoming almost familiar with the way he touches, then releases her, practically propelling her back into a world in which he has no function. The world outside. Ann thinks about all of this while she rides the subway or walks the halls of the university, or even when she is driving her small red car towards the limits of the city – that no-man's-land. The only acre that is theirs.

Now she watches him walk across the rented room, reach into his discarded jacket and pull out a package of cigarettes.

He lights one and returns to her, pulling his knees up as he leans against the wall, resting the ashtray on his stomach.

"What are you thinking?" she asks.

"What am I thinking? I'm thinking about Tintoretto's use of lightning. Most of his paintings appear to be illuminated by lightning, so that, if you look again, you are afraid that they might have returned to darkness."

"Lightning Tintoretto."

"Yes, but that term's a reference to his speed of execution. I'm talking about the way the painting looks hundreds of years later. As though you might blink and it would be gone."

"And are you thinking about any special paintings?"

"Yes. Have you seen a copy of it, I wonder?" The smoke from Arthur's cigarette has moved halfway across the room. "There is this most wonderful angel swooping down with a tray–looking just like a garçon in a French café–delivering the bitter chalice to Christ in the garden at Gethsemene. And all the drapery is practically transparent, edged in blue and white, illuminated by lightning. In fact, the drapery almost *is* lightning. Imagine a French waiter with wings clothed in lightning."

"Tell me more about it. Is there landscape?"

"Ah, yes, there is often landscape. Odd, that, because apart from gardens there is no landscape in Venice. Everything is built, architectural. And Tintoretto never left Venice. Why then all this landscape?"

"What is it like? Describe the landscape."

"Maybe it's not landscape. Maybe it's skies and weather."

"I love weather. Tell me."

"The illuminated angel casts his light on everything: on Christ who wears red, on the sleeping apostles, and on this very stealthy procession of soldiers who are creeping in on the left. The marvelous thing is the way the landscape is just suggested by all the leaves glowing in the reflected light of the angel and the chalice. The soldiers have no landscape, neither do the disciples, but Christ has these luminous leaves."

"We have no landscape."

He moves away. "I don't want to talk about that."

"We should have some landscape."

Silence.

"Tell me about another painting then; one without landscape."

"There is *Jacob's Ladder*." Arthur visibly relaxes. "A really disturbing architectural painting. The ladder is a stone staircase – spatially confusing because of the weird perspective he used and even more confusing because the painting is on the ceiling. The angels in this painting, the way they come down the stairs, they look like Broadway dancing girls: like Rockettes."

Ann laughs, recovering from rejection.

"The whole thing could be a stage set. Tintoretto was not above resorting to the blatantly theatrical."

"What about God the Father?"

"Oh, he's there – a wispy pink cloud at the top of the staircase. Utterly upstaged by the angels. And Jacob. Jacob has his face averted as if he's trying to ignore the whole event – as if he's embarrassed by it."

"All these ceilings. I'm amazed that you don't have a permanent bend in your neck."

"You don't need to worry about that. When you go into the Scuola San Rocco . . . where all these paintings are . . . they give you a mirror."

"A mirror?"

"Yes, a mirror to look at the ceiling."

"What are your favourite, *who* are your favourite figures in the paintings?"

"Angels."

"Not disciples . . . not pink, wispy God-the-Fathers?"

"No, definitely angels because of the light that is in them, the light they cast, and because of the drapery."

Ann looks around her at the sheets, the rough sea of the untidy bed. This, too, is drapery.

"Do you have a favourite angel?"

"The one who tempts Christ in the wilderness. I told you about him before."

"But you said the devil did the tempting."

"Yes, but Tintoretto makes the devil an angel – androgynous–and with such a face! A face filled with sorrow and compassion and hands filled with wholesome bread. The most beautiful eyes. The tempter has the most beautiful eyes and the eyes are filled with tears."

Ann is silent. Then she speaks. "I wish . . . "

"Don't wish." He turns his face away, examines his watch. "I have to go."

"Where are you going?"

"I have an appointment." He is dressed, has disappeared before she can tell him what she wishes. She wishes she could see the paintings. She feels that they might be a map of him; all of the hidden places to which she can't travel. She will see the paintings, she decides, some day . . . with or without his permission.

In the evenings, after she has seen Arthur, Ann reads the words of Thomas Aquinas concerning angels. Angels, the old saint tells her, are composed of action and potentiality. Their bodies are made of thick air. Many of them cannot be in the same space. The motion of an angel is the succession of his different operations. The motion of the illumination of an angel is threefold: circular, straight, and oblique.

Light. Heat. Motion. The beating of wings in an otherwise still room.

The Venetians sometimes called Tintoretto "Thunderbolt." "Brontë" is the Greek word for thunder. There are connections everywhere.

Ann wants to see Arthur's burning angels, the light that is in them. Ann wants to see herself, aglow, in the light that Arthur's angels cast.

"MY HOUSE," said Emily, "began in the grate of our parlour, which at certain times was my whole world. You see, we stayed there most of the day acting out wars and passions – great military campaigns on the carpet. Whole continents in a woven rose! We children shared a single fused mind for hours every day. We all saw the same fantastic histories. We had collective hallucinations! It was like spontaneous combustion!

"We would work at it and work at it – destroying cities, destroying marriages, building and then demolishing empires, causing the most unlikely people to fall illicitly and disastrously in love with each other. Finally, it would become so interpersonal, so complicated, that my brother Branwell would shout, 'Time, gentlemen, time!' And he would have to practically bellow to be heard above the din.

"And then we would each take our little lap desk down from the top of the piano and write quietly for an hour or two."

"About your play?"

"Yes, sometimes, our invented lands. But as we grew older we sometimes became more private . . . to have something of our own.

"At first, before those special kingdoms that I told you about, the place I called my own was *Parry's Land* – a great Arctic continent – pure white – like that room, and named after my favourite Arctic explorer."

"Arctic!" gasped Arianna. "How he loved the Arctic! He wanted to balloon there."

"I know that. He will . . . now."

"Oh."

"But that's not what I want to talk about. My house began in the grate, the fireplace; it began while I was listening to the wind and looking at fire and stone. I thought about how the stone hearth shelters and contains a fire, like a house would, but, regardless of all that protecting and sheltering, the wind works on it anyway. Really, there is nothing you can do to keep this wind away from the fire or anything else. It gets in everywhere."

In . . . in, sang the wind.

"But I'd never seen it put the fire out. It never managed to destroy it. So I invented a house that contained fire and I wanted both the house and the fire to be worked upon by wind. Wind. Fire. Stone.

"I wanted a house with a fire inside and a storm outside. But since I, myself, was inside when I began all this, I started with the idea of flame. Then, suddenly, the flame became a person—two, in fact, two flames lapping at each other but never joining to become a single flame though they shared the same stone hearth and were a party to the same storms. You know how when a flame is strong enough the wind feeds it? These flames, these people, were nurtured by storms. They needed them and they knew it.

"Which is why, when one of the flames descended into a house in a sheltered valley it began, slowly, to die. But that house, that sheltered house, I built a little later.

"I began, as I said, to build the house as a result of looking at the fire and, of course, I built it with words. In the very beginning fire was fire only, had not yet developed into personality. So I talked about it and talked about it. Made it stir shadows in the corners of dark rooms, made it reflect in pewter dishes and silver jugs and in the polished surface of an old oak dresser. It seemed, suddenly, to be the only source of light in this cavernous dark room—the *house* as we call it here—the place where people really live in a dwelling.

"One moving orange light, reflected on surfaces, but shut out of recesses. Then, I thought, would these shadowy places in the house be empty? And as I thought this, my dog, Keeper, groaned and twitched in his sleep, lying by my left foot, and I knew that the shadowy corners of my house would have to be filled with dogs."

"I had a dog once," said Arianna. "A French poodle whom I called 'Montgolfier.' He was so adorable. He often flew with me . . . just a little thing . . . a toy French poodle."

"A French poodle," sniffed Emily contemptuously, "is *not* a dog!"

"Oh, really?" said Arianna, offended and coming to Monty's defence. "Then what exactly is it?" She crossed her arms, stood up very straight, and looked sternly at Emily.

"A French poodle is a piece of frippery. A vain, stupid, overbred, hothouse flower. That sheep," Emily pointed to a woolly creature who munched near them, "has more brains than a French poodle and six times the character."

"Monty was very good-looking and he was *brave* . . . unafraid at a thousand feet. He even parachuted! The crowd loved him!"

"A bauble, an ornamental affectation! Keeper would have swallowed your Montgolfier in one bite and would never have thought of him again unless, of course, his artificiality caused him to have indigestion."

"Then Keeper was cruel and wicked."

"Oh, yes," said Emily proudly. "And strong and fierce."

"All of the children at the fairs and picnics could play with Montgolfier."

"None of the children could have played with Keeper."

"Why would you want to keep a dog like that?"

"Why would I want to keep any other kind? Listen. Keeper was not fickle, he loved only me. His attentions were never diverted. You wouldn't see him fawning and cowering before any other individual. He wouldn't have taken a table scrap from anyone else. He was that sure of who he was and who he belonged to. He was proud and

completely faithful. Who wants a dog who could be any-
body's dog?"

"Who wants a vicious, snapping beast who can only show
kindness to one person?"

"I do . . . or I did . . . " Emily paused, tired of the
disagreement, and looked towards the heights. "My house
wanted those kinds of dogs as well, so I filled all the dark
corners with them. They were . . . savage."

Arianna shook her head.

"They were so savage," Emily continued, "that they
attacked any intruders, and to them, all non-residents and
guests were intruders."

"Could they be called off?"

"Yes."

"By whom?"

"Oh, I'll talk about him later."

"He," said Arianna, as if the masculine pronoun could,
for her, conjure only a single image, "never liked Montgolfier much. But by then he didn't like me much either."

"But he still touched you?"

"Yes, because he said he could do that with indifference
as easily as he could with love."

"And why did you touch him?"

"Because, like your Keeper, I was unable to be distracted
by anything . . . anyone else. Except my balloon, sometimes, and the landscape that moved beneath it."

Both ghosts were silent for a few moments. Several seasons passed. Then Arianna spoke again.

"You see . . . I was like your dog – not in temperament
– I didn't attack intruders, but in fidelity, in a fixed state of
mind. Would Keeper have abandoned you if you had
stopped caring for him? I doubt it. I couldn't abandon
Jeremy, though I often wished that I could at least want to
abandon him. I simply couldn't. My mind, my heart,
wouldn't let me. I was trapped by my love and so was he.
That was what he hated most of all – being trapped by my
love."

"He isn't trapped now," said Emily. "The Arctic is the
landscape of the self, of the naked soul. It is what the inner
landscape looks like when everything beyond the self has
been discarded. Imagine, everything that moves up there,
everything alive, is white: for camouflage, for safety. The
self would be the only visible detail in that landscape. What
a place to visit! I pretended to visit it so often that eventually
I started imagining dungeons instead. Invisible bears! Invisible birds! Eventually, I wanted my terrors to be visible. I
wanted to see the chain on the wrist *and* on the wall. God!
Imagine floating into white!"

As she spoke, a swift blizzard swept fiercely through the
valley below them, buffeted both spirits briefly and disappeared over the back of the hill they stood near.

Emily smiled at Arianna. "How I love storms," she said.
"I simply adore weather!"

White . . . white, wailed the wind.

"Balloonists are not too fond of storms, not too fond of
wind. Especially unexpected wind." Arianna watched one
of the twisted trees near the old farmhouse bend, like a
dancer, at the waist as the weather manipulated it. "Is that
what happened to me? Was it the wind?"

"No," said Emily evasively.

"Well, what did happen to me?" asked Arianna. "How
did this happen to me?"

"Slowly and painfully, like all falls. The actual physical fall
seems to me to be just the final moment of a much larger
fall, don't you think so? One of my characters, for instance,
tumbled from the house I built up there, into the safe valley
and the house I built down there. I wasn't nearly as interested in the second house, by the way. I mean the storms
weren't as violent and there were too many trees."

"I'm not too fond of trees either. Have you ever seen
what a tree can do to a balloon?"

WHAT IS ANN leaving behind in order to embrace at last the weather of *Wuthering Heights*?

Finally, it was only questions: the questions people ask habitually on phones. *Are you there? Where have you been? Are you all right . . . is everything all right? Is there any chance? What are you doing now? What's wrong? Can you speak? Can you talk to me? Can we talk?*

Ann, shivering in phone booths on the edge of the highway, asking those questions. *Where are you? What is wrong?* Heart pounding like thunder. *Is there something wrong?*

"No . . . yes."

"What is wrong?"

"Nothing."

What she will remember forever is the oddness of the last room, for she has come to believe, after one and a half years, that every hotel room on the highway is exactly the same. Then suddenly there is this oddness, this difference. This sense of something slightly askew.

He opens the bed, as always, as though it were a door, a grave, a theatrical curtain to be swept aside. They lie together, removing their clothes, each other's, speechless. His hands in her hair. They make love and tell each other stories and make love again. Then she speaks, her mouth at his neck. Knowing the answer. Fearing the answer.

"I told you I'm not in love with you," he says.

She has never wanted to stop, has wanted to fling her quiet self, always, right into the centre of the blizzard and all the high and low pressure areas that cause it. She has learned that weather happens to you and around you with ruthless detachment. It even happens without you. It just doesn't care.

"I feel most ambivalent when I leave here. It's very difficult to go back."

Ann senses the wind, the fir tree tapping against the imagined mullioned window. "Let me in, let me in, I've been a waif for twenty years!" She says nothing. A blanket of snow covers her. And yet she is, she realizes, so naked. How has she let this man make her this naked? They were standing on a hill once, a year before. There was a hill, then half a mile of forest, then that same highway–the one that roars like a fierce river behind plate glass now. The view, however, was wonderful. From that distance the Great Lake appeared to be pure and uncomplicated. From that distance it was possible to believe, even though you knew better, that the water was not poisoned. And possible to believe that the noise of the highway was merely wind tossing leaves around on forest trees.

It was their first, their only, their last landscape. After that they withdrew into rooms together at places along the highway. "A long road and a sad heart to follow it. We have to pass by Gimmerton Church along the way."

He is still talking. "I've never been in love with you. Perhaps I've merely succumbed to your demands."

A jet plane screams over the hotel – an alarm flung into the room. Pandemonium, chaos, panic, fire, police!, thinks Ann. Arthur leans casually over her, reaching for an ashtray. Then he moves abruptly away.

Ann rises from the bed and walks across the room into the bathroom. The water pouring into the tub sounds like the highway. Immersed, she silently mouths the words: *distance, detachment, casualty.* She closes her eyes and sinks further into the liquid warmth, the convenient noise. Trying to wash the last afternoon away.

When she re-enters the room he has dressed. He has closed the bed, perhaps as a last, casual kindness to her. As if the

tangled sheets could speak of an open wound and the proximity of the weapon.

The whole room between them and this is what she sees:
her own clothing, scattered; bright bits of fabric that have
to be collected again in order to assemble the self, in order
to depart. She dresses facing him so that he can see each
gesture; each movement is a message from her heart's dark
garden. Knowing that from this room on, each day is a day
after.

Buttons that lock her body away. Soft and hard fabrics
that cover the heart. She visualizes every piece of clothing
he has worn over the months: the woollens and cottons,
the leather belts, the colours of socks and ties. But today
he has dressed while she was in another room. Away from
her.

There is no mirror in the room. Until now Ann has
believed that every space they entered contained a mirror.
Now there is not even a possibility that she can glance into
a reflection to reassemble her own poise, her own sense of
decorum. The room reflects nothing.

Where the mirror should have been there hangs, instead,
a print of a Brueghel landscape. A landscape for lovers such
as themselves, a landscape for lovers lacking setting. For
lovers lacking love. Hunters in the foreground and in the
distance, ice, and those who skate there. Ann's own heart
booming like ice forming on a winter lake at midnight. The
spring, the thaw, a long, long way off.

She sees, across the room, the thin spear of glass that
shines through the slightly parted curtains, and the one
shaft of light that comes in from the world outside. One
cold blue blade of winter colour that has lain between them
and that now cuts the room, the afternoon, the moment,
into two brutally detached parts.

For weeks afterwards she will try to reconstruct the last
room, try to imagine the ring of her phone call or the thump
of her fist on the other side of the door. *I've been out on the
moor for twenty years.* The ringing and knocking – sounds of

her wanting in, echoing through the still space, and she hadn't entered yet, would never enter. "In, let me in!"

Still, it is the winter landscape, filling the mirror's absence, that she will remember most vividly. The flight of dark birds against grey sky, and one of the hunters, his back turned, walking towards the frozen pond, the ice-bound sea. He, she thinks now, does not notice the colour of his shadow on the snow. To his left there is a fire that has, also, not caught his attention. She will not remember exactly what it was he had killed, only that the hunt was over, that something lifeless was slung casually over his shoulder, that everything was frozen, and that he was walking way.

What Ann does not see in her memories is Arthur standing near the door of a hotel room from which a wounded woman has departed, his mind a vacant house. A weapon that he hadn't known he'd carried had been called into action with such ease it was as though the act had been committed while he was glancing out the window or straightening his tie: the words merely those of a popular tune one sings quietly while performing daily chores.

And now she is gone.

Arthur, standing on the inside of the door Ann has closed, reads the Hotel and Innkeeper's Act seven times, smiling at the peculiarity of its language. Then he reads the emergency procedures in the event of fire. Do not, he wants to add to the end of the list, attempt to put the fire out with your bare hands.

He examines the palms of his own hands, the strange smooth texture of them. The polished skin there is like that of a child, only smoother, rosier. With the nails of one hand he rakes the palm of the other while he reads again all about closing windows, identifying exits, and the final, desperate act: wet towels along the crack at the bottom of the door.

He believes that he feels nothing.

He took his palms to a fortune teller only once, as a kind of practical joke on the world, on himself. But the visit turned out to be even odder than he had anticipated. After looking at the shining skin for a long time the old woman folded his hand in both of hers and raised eyes full of compassion to his.

"You have no story," she said. "You can touch, but you can feel nothing."

It wasn't strictly true, of course, He could hold a pen and pencil, forks, knives, spoons, steering wheels. The musculature was intact. It was the finer sense of touch that eluded him: the difference between cotton and silk, between a tulip leaf and a blade of new grass, between different grains of wood, ebony, and ivory. The weight of various kinds of paper confused him and sometimes when he was writing he would mistake vellum for bond. That and extremes of sensation. He could not, with the tips of his fingers, feel the painful cold of ice or, ironically, the burn of fire. Snow, because of its weightlessness, his fingers couldn't recognize at all. It was, to that small area of his anatomy, non-existent.

He has told Ann none of this, has hidden his palms, concealing them, after years of practice, with such skill that she never missed them. He touched her with his body, his mouth; caressed her with the back of his hands. Later, when they lay together, quiet and close, he allowed his hands to curl naturally, near his body or hers, like those of a sleeping child.

And now that she is gone, his hands feel nothing and his mind is a vacant house full of instructions for surviving fires.

Close all doors, close all windows, his inner voice announces, do not panic. Identify the nearest exit and leave the building as quickly as possible. Walk, don't run, it adds.

But he is in no hurry to leave the building. He wants to fill the empty house in his mind with objects from this ordinary room. It is suddenly of great importance that he remember every piece of furniture here, that he imprint their shapes, their odd angles, on his memory before they are consumed, forever, by his permanent absence. The phoney Danish chair near the window, the metallic base of the desk lamp with its on/off switch. He looks for a long time at the pattern of the spread. Why all those flowers? He scrutinizes the room service menu, the list of available blue movies poised on the television set.

In the open closet hangs his own tweed coat looking calm and comfortable as if it were familiar with the room. Near it the hanger from which she snatched her jacket still twitches slightly as if touched by a barely perceptible breeze. What was the colour of the cloth, he wonders, and he wishes, just for a moment, that he had turned towards the closet while the woman was still in the room, to see the two garments hanging there side by side.

He paces out the length of the room and then the width. Then he begins to play a distance-guessing game with himself, pitting himself competitively against the size of the room. The closet, he announces out loud (and only the room is listening), is seven feet across. Then, using his own feet, he measures eight.

One for you, he says to the room.

He waits until he has won the game five times before he attempts to guess the distance between the bed and the door. First, lying on top of the spread, he describes the space across the floor, verbally. It isn't such a long way, he whispers. Just a few steps. As a child he would probably have been able to leap from here to there. Hadn't he once won the long-jump at his school's field day? He imagines the cheap carpet blurring beneath such an act of speed and wonders if he could leave two footprints on the pile. Has she left footprints? What colour were her shoes? What was his longest jump? The distance to the door, he now believes, would be the same as his longest jump. He wants to win this one. He wants to humiliate the room.

He, who has always made the arrangements for this series of rooms, now finds that he can remember nothing of the others. Or even if there were others. Perhaps it was the same room, this room, over and over. Or perhaps he has been with her in rooms all over the hotel. If it were the same room then the distance from the bed to the door would be constant and this time would be like all the other times. Nothing would have changed and he would still feel nothing. He would still want neither to know nor to be known.

He rises from the bed and, turning, smooths out all the creases that his body has made there during its brief stay. He erases the hollow his skull has made in the pillow. It is the third time in a matter of hours that he has performed this ceremony but he has already forgotten the other two. He moves over to the large window and returns the curtains to their original, half-opened position. He was wrong about the size of the windows, but it doesn't matter. Nothing matters. Glancing around him quickly, he is relieved to discover that the room holds no evidence of his presence and no evidence of hers. It is as if it had remained locked and vacant all afternoon. As if no one had ever been there at all.

He is suddenly in a great rush, recalling a paper he must finish on Tintoretto's *Ultima Cena* in the Church of Santo Stefano in Venice. He wants to spend a long time discussing Tintoretto's visual interpretation of the word *ultima*: how the disciples at the table fade away into darkness, into absence, the table being placed at such an angle that it is being thrust away from the viewer towards the land of never again.

Arthur removes his coat from the closet and steadies the swaying hanger with his unfeeling hand. Leaving, he closes the door firmly behind him. He has won his contest with the room. He no longer cares, no longer wants to know anything at all about its secrets, about the distance from lovemaking to the door.

The following days pass like thin black trees beyond the dirty windows of Ann's car. The traffic of the world. She drives the city streets making a senseless series of right-hand turns, noticing grey slush and raw, torn construction sites. Harsh reality at a stop sign. Life after the room.

A life filled with detached wires and empty-handed postmen who carry no messages. A life in a winter country where no one requests your address or suggests that you look at the moon. Nothing, Ann now knows, will move closer to her than one desperate winter tree bending in a wind that has blown arbitrarily, casually, in her direction. The earth ragged, ripped open. Out. There. Where the cold is.

She decides, in that moment, to do her very best to leave the highway, the city, the country. She buys a one-way ticket: a one-way ticket to the Brontë moors.

"A rough journey and a sad heart to travel it," she thinks now, again on the highway, but this time leading to the airport. In her heart that same blizzard. In her luggage *The Life of Emily Brontë, Emily Brontë's Collected Poems, Wuthering Heights,* an air ticket to England, and her own unfinished manuscript, tentatively entitled *Wuthering Heights: A Study of Weather.*

PART TWO

The Upstairs Room

And a Suspicion, like a Finger
Touches my forehead now and then
That I am looking oppositely
For the site of the Kingdom of Heaven –

– EMILY DICKINSON

"LET ME IN, let me in . . . . I've been lost on the moor for twenty years."

Then the glass shatters, the arm extends past the window's teeth into the warmth of the room. The little cold hand that brings a sample of weather with it into the claustrophobic interior. The shards of glass on the dusty blanket. The delicate, damp, determined hand reaching forward. One man's hysterical, murderous fear.

"I'll never let you in, not if you beg for twenty years."

The wounding. The wrist attacking broken glass. The only evidence of this frantic attempt a blanket soaked with blood. And even that an hallucination.

"Let me in," thinks Ann, "I've been a waif for twenty years."

She has brought Arthur with her. A part of him has accompanied part of her into this strange geography.

Ann sits, now, out on the West Yorkshire moors on a rock, under a leaden sky and thinks, *I'll never be free of this.* She thinks, *let me in, let me in.* She who has only recently managed to get herself out.

She has memorized the words of the first scene in *Wuthering Heights*. She cannot shake its weather, cannot stop responding to the descriptions.

"Merely the branch of a fir tree that touched my lattice as the blast wailed by," and "the gusty wind, the driving of the snow." *I was*, she thinks, *mistaken. I was misperceived as a harmless piece of vegetation tapping on the glass that separated us.* The word "merely" bruises her. The words "detected the disturber" bring tears to her eyes. *I was a disturber,* she thinks, *then more than that . . . and then the full fury of the nightmare was upon him.*

It is as if thinking of that early scene at this moment, when she has left Arthur and has dragged her limping self out into the weather, identifies it, surely, as his; as if he had taken one of his immaculately sharpened pencils and had drawn a fine line beside the passage to bring it to her attention. "Look, here we are, you and I," he might have said, "This is the nature of our relationship: you trying to get in, me trying to keep you out. The war, the constant war between us."

She rises now to continue her walk on the narrow path that crosses the moor. Now and then she passes an abandoned farm whose buildings are so black they appear to have been burnt by a mysterious, indifferent fire. From their glassless windows hang the frail lines of broken mullion. Around them, like soft grey clouds, lurk clumps of empty-eyed sheep. Ann has already seen several rotting carcasses, remnants of those animals who, for one reason or another, were unable to survive the winter. Unable to survive exposure.

The thing about weather, thinks Ann as she climbs a wooden stile over a drystone wall, the thing about weather is that you either embrace it or you shelter yourself from it. Either way, it can extinguish the flame, with wind and rain on the one hand, or, if you run from it, if you hide in a closed space, the fire suffocates from lack of oxygen.

God, this sky, she thinks, *this uncertain earth*. Her feet slide on mud and press into boggy places. Overhead marches platoon after platoon of clouds bringing who knows what kinds of storm fronts, snow, or hail, an abrupt change of season. Bringing, for certain, nothing soft or warm. A consecutive series of polar statements.

She passes the Brontë waterfall, which has become a meaningless trickle since the reservoir was created late in the last century. She crosses Sladen Beck. *There is water too*, she thinks, *and it changes with weather*. The rain begins and Ann opens her black umbrella, which is almost immediately snatched from her by the wind. She pauses momentarily to

watch it tumble over the heather, a wounded bat trying
unsuccessfully to reassemble the mechanism necessary for
flight. Then she laughs aloud. Perhaps out here everything
will be blown away from her and she will return to her
rented cottage and eventually to Canada, light, unencumbered, without any burdens at all.

Top Withins, the rumoured site of Wuthering Heights,
is still three miles away. "A rough road and a sad heart to
follow it." Ann trudges along in the rain, letting it touch
her bare hands and face, watching the clouds carry curtain
after curtain towards her. Ghost magi bringing swaths of
dusky silk. All around her, wet heather shivers under air
currents and sheep feed on couch grass. Ann feels the
sweep, the rhythm of walking settle into her limbs. Her
strides become longer as if her legs have begun to grow.
Her hips ache with new energy.

By the time she reaches the height of the moor, the ruin
that purports to be the home of Heathcliff, every part of
her that is not covered by her anorak is soaked through.
She is enveloped by weather and her skin drinks moisture.
She is bursting with something resembling hope, resembling joy, and she turns to face the landscape, the open
miles of view that the weather caresses without comment.
And then her small body; alone in enormous space, the
only heartbeat in a sea of dark hills.

"Open, open, open!" she shouts into the wind, swinging
her arms in circles from her shoulder joints. "Space," she
cries. "Air!" Angels, she recalls, have bodies composed of
thick air. The wind assaults her with magnificent indifference and she inhales all of it that she can, loving the touch
of it on her scalp when it lifts her hair, the itch of its sleet
upon her cheek. She believes that the wind has moved past
her inner ear, has invaded the folds of her brain and is
polishing them with a great, cold, cleansing roar. Planets
whirling out of her sky into some other destiny. Every root
of each low scrub plant straining towards ether, towards
freedom.

Then Arthur speaks in her memory and Ann's arms fall to her sides. "God damn him," she mutters, his remembered words pulling her back to the rooms along the highway. Aware of her solitude in the somber landscape, she straightens her spine and raises her voice. "God damn him!" she announces to the miles of heather.

And then she is shouting again: "I want him to want me! I want him to want me! I want him to want this!" She gestures wildly towards both earth and air. "Why can't he want *this*?"

She begins to run, escalating her descent from the heights; hills becoming a brown smear on either side of her. Magically, when she slows to a walk, wet heather bursts into colour, prismatic, under the touch of the sun.

Just before she leaves the moor for the day, Ann finds the umbrella that the wind snatched, broken against a stone wall. Twisted spokes, torn fabric. She leaves it there. It is an artificial form of shelter, after all, which has been mutilated, far beyond all hope of repair, by all this wonderful weather.

And even on dark days Ann awakens to an infusion of light in the cottage she has rented in Stanbury. Designed as a workshop for an eighteenth-century hand-loom weaver, her bedroom is surrounded by windows through which light blasts, and around whose panes creeps the persistent wind.

Everything in the room trembles under the influence of currents of air; the papers on the desk, the thin curtains, even, during the day, Ann's cotton nightgown where it hangs from a hook on the door. At times this odd interior wind is so strong it ruffles the pages of *Emily Brontë's Collected Poems*, which Ann has left open on her night table.

After four or five days Ann is obsessed by the wind. It both pleases and perplexes her. It scatters the mail that the postman leaves at the door, dispersing her one link to her past, her real life. It encourages or kills her difficult coal fire – the only source of heat in the cottage. It rattles at the coal cellar door at night like a vigilante group demanding entrance. It blows into her dreams.

When she walks over the moor the wind causes a knife of pain, straight through her neck just below ear level. It makes all the bracken and bilberry and heather swell and undulate, as if some unknown substance beneath the earth's surface had just reached boiling point.

Each day Ann walks on the moor, mostly across Sladen Beck and along the footpath that leads into Haworth, home of the Brontës. She enters the village through the graveyard, which surrounds the parsonage where her subject lived her weird, closeted life and scribbled her dark book. The cemetery is crowded with green-black stones and filled with the noise of angry rooks who croak, "Wind, wind, wind!" in outrage and panic at Ann's approach.

She is propelled by currents of air into the parsonage museum through the gift shop. This space Ann ignores: its Brontë calendars and bookmarks and cookbooks and paperweights – although, she muses, she could use a paperweight now to protect pages from the advances of wind.

She walks through the rooms of the house; each space put to death and then preserved as a museum. Glass cases. Emily's writing desk, Charlotte's shoes, their juvenilia, the dog Keeper's collar–too large for an ordinary dog and made out of shining brass. The view from each window includes tombstones, then the chimney pots and shale roofs of the little town.

When Ann arrives at the parsonage library, she asks for the diary that was kept by the stationer who sold Emily Brontë her writing paper. In it he reports, combining gossip and legend, some of the writer's activities: the time she rescued Branwell from flaming bedclothes, the time she removed Keeper from the throat of another snarling dog, her ability to bake bread, read German, and shoot pistols all at the same time. None of this describes weather; but weather exists, Ann believes, in levels of engagement. Ann wants to solve the problem of how a woman so withdrawn could also be so engaged with life. Heathcliff, she has decided, was the moor, and Catherine, she has even more recently decided, was the wind.

Their relationship caused storm.

"P A P A , " S A I D Emily, "I am remembering Papa. Papa reading the *Leeds Intelligencer*. Papa dining alone. Papa taking down the curtains. Papa climbing stairs. Papa in the morning wrapping flannel round his throat. Papa's Bible readings."

"Papa," Arianna echoed. "Papa staring at the wall. Papa and his bottle. Papa talking to the voices. Papa sleeping in the afternoon. Papa's face like a grey mask. Papa's hands shaking."

Emily turned her eyes towards the little grey village in the distance. "Mama died," she said, "and Papa never mentioned her. Someone, Tabby, I think, told me that he cut the arms off her best silk dress. I imagined her armless, then. A woman without arms: one who could not sew or draw or write or cook or hold me. I imagined that she died from severed arms."

"Mama died," said Arianna, "coughing in the morning. Horses stood outside on the street and stamped their hoofs. Then they carried her away. Papa returned with a bottle. He never looked towards the window. He spoke to voices that I couldn't hear and there was no light around him. He would never draw the curtains back, open them to morning."

Emily stood knee-deep in heather. "Papa feared fire and so there were no curtains. I imagined rooms of flaming fabric: all the drapery ablaze and Papa's furious shadow growing on the wall. Papa loved guns. He taught me how to shoot, standing near the back wall of the graveyard, firing at air. After breakfast Papa told me stories about harpies, about the love-talker, about silkies. Papa said the word 'Ireland' and his face changed."

"Papa only spoke to voices and a bottle. Sometimes he sang, weakly, songs I couldn't hear, singing to the bottle, holding it in the crook of his arm as he might have held a child."

"Papa never held us. He delivered sermons, shot his pistols out naked windows, daydreamed fame for Branwell, took his meals alone."

"Papa drank a river of whisky, swallowing his nightmares."

Emily lifted her pale hand and touched Arianna's shoulder. "Every nightmare Papa ever had," she said, "came true. He taught me how to shoot a pistol out towards the moor. He said that we were murdering the wind."

ANN DECIDES that today she will walk the Ponden Kirk; that great outcropping of rock that so often sheltered Heathcliff and Catherine when they were children. Peniston Crag, Emily Brontë had called it in the book.

She sets out from the cottage by way of the narrow, walled road that climbs towards the moor. Black stones tower on either side of her, a light mist softens the view, which at this moment includes only the dark quarried walls and the pot-holed, sloppy asphalt that barely covers the track beneath. Shrinking puddles here and there reflect the sky, in an unusual manner, for the weather has turned surprisingly dry; and the atmosphere above, and hence on the surface of these small enclosed bodies of water, is bright blue. Beyond the tall drystone barriers Ann hears sheep nudge and push in a determined attempt to claim another square inch of grass. Occasionally, a desperate bleating cry floats over the wall, for lambs have been born in great numbers over the last few weeks and they all seem to suffer from some form of inexplicable terror.

The road tilts forward, becoming steeper, like a black banner swaying before her in a parade, and still Ann's vision is arrested by walls. But the wind has reached her face and she identifies, a quarter of a mile ahead, the stile she must climb to reach the footpath on the higher ground. When she steps up and over the little ladder, the sky and the earth burst open all around her, more startling, more wonderful because of the restricted approach. "No trees!" she whispers, astounded as always by this phenomenon.

Beyond the curve of three solid hills Ann can see the granite cliff, and she leaves the path, which by now is almost familiar to her, in order to move, magnet-like, towards its metal. Her boots are drawn towards the centre of the earth by oozing marsh and pushed away again by springy turf. She remembers the scene where Catherine and Heathcliff run all the way down from the Heights to Thrushcross Grange and Catherine loses her slipper in the bog. Ponden Hall, the supposed site of the Grange, sits now on Ann's right, a small dark rectangle in the distance, surrounded by the leafless tangle of the valley trees. It is still inhabited and sometimes, returning from the moor in the late afternoon, Ann has seen lights appear in its tiny far-off windows, one by one, as if an interior fire were moving from room to room of the house. The cry of confused infant sheep is carried by the wind from behind a small hill, and then grouse, invisible, deep in the grass, calling, "*Go back, go back, go back!*"

Going forward with difficulty in this trackless region, Ann sees a wide pillar of smoke bubbling from behind an abandoned farm and wonders if here, as in other obscure regions, the Tierra del Fuegos of the earth, there are unaccountable fires. Fires that spring into being for no reason, as if they were the vocabulary of a landscape whose passions must speak, can no longer keep silent. Secret deathless fires, spontaneous and inexhaustible. Ann thinks of the bog-burst she has read about, which almost swallowed the Brontës in their infancy when they were out walking. Walking a century ago where she is walking now. She believes in the bog-burst, believes that there are moments when the calm earth loses its composure: begins to mimic the violence at the heart of weather.

Arthur's absence flickers for several minutes in her own heart – a geographically remote, inexplicable fire – and all she had wanted him to feel burns there.

Ann skirts a broken wall, keeping close to its flank in order to avoid a marshy area to her left, carefully stepping from tuft of yellow grass to tuft of yellow grass; mind in the rooms along the Canadian highway, eyes on the Yorkshire ground. She is, therefore, face to face with the man responsible for the smoke before she has a chance to change direction or to let her shyness compose an acceptable space between them. Acknowledgement is now necessary – unavoidable.

"Here now," he says automatically, "don't go that way. I've got it going nicely there."

As he speaks Ann notices a perfect square of fire, the size of a suburban lot, burning behind him, and how his face and hands are blackened by smoke.

"Why," she asks, surprised at her own inquisitiveness, "are you burning the moor?"

"For better growth later in spring." He looks at the sky for a moment as he speaks, then at Ann. "They . . . ," he tips his cap in the direction of a far flock, safely gathered on a distant hillside, "they prefer newer grass. Not that it should matter to them then, or now. Walk over there. It sometimes advances fast . . . though it will stop, for certain, at the bog."

Ann notices the bright blue eyes . . . startling in the midst of the blackened face.

"I'm black as coal pit," he admits. "From the burning," he adds, awkward in the face of her scrutiny.

Ann looks back to the escarpment she has been trying to reach. "Can I get there from here?" she asks, pointing.

"Not without ruining your boots in the bog you can't. And what is it that brings you out here running with the wind? You aren't hunting grouse, or rabbit, that's one thing sure."

"I'm trying to reach Ponden Kirk."

"What on earth is the purpose in that?"

Ann confesses her fascination with the Brontës and the grass-burner's eyes glaze slightly. Tourists for him have become, over the years, a form of litter on the moor. They rarely appear, though, in this season.

"It's research," Ann says in self-defence, sensing his disapproval, wanting to justify her presence in his territory.

"I myself," he says, "have spent my time without searching, so could not be persuaded to begin re-searching." He pauses for a moment, awaiting her laugh. When it doesn't come, it is because Ann has missed his humour, not because she has rejected it. Unaware of this, he turns again towards the practical, the native giving advice on the peculiarities of his own geography. "Well, you'll have trouble searching today," he comments, wryly. "The top there will still have ice. And you've taken the wrong track, that's the truth. In fact you've departed from the track altogether. You should have turned right at Middle Withins – the last farm – and now it will take too long." He consults his watch. "Dreadful and dark by five-thirty today. Excuse me." He hastily rakes some of the burned grass back into the flames and, as he turns, Ann sees that the hair on his head, which she had assumed to be dark is, when untouched by smoke, in fact very fair, perhaps even white.

Returning, he regards her with humour. "It wouldn't do to burn the full moor," he says, his eyes smiling as he uses her words.

"So you are making better grass for the sheep?" Ann finds herself wanting, for reasons which elude her, to continue the conversation.

"Did I say that?"

"Yes, you said your sheep prefer newer grass."

"They would like that, they would, that lot." He jerks his head without averting his eyes from her face, towards the flock. "That lot, as I said, would prefer newer grass. But the truth is they're not mine. Wall's down as you can see." He looks sadly at a pile of dark stones which have tumbled, over the winter, from the jig-saw linking of a drystone construction.

"You're not a shepherd, then. Just a grass-burner?" This is Ann's own attempt at humour, and it is greeted with precisely the same absence of laughter.

"It were scandal to be just that," he announces, annoyed, not at all amused by her question. "I am a moor-edger, a carpenter, and a mill worker, a weaver. And it were real pity that I were not born a scholar like some." Here he looks at her with disdain, then turns his head away to supervise the smoke.

After a few moments he looks at her again. "Your holiday cottage," he says, "I fixed it. The walls and the windows. For all that you have me to thank."

"I love the cottage," says Ann, hoping to mollify him, overlooking altogether the fact that he knows where she lives, the location of the door she stepped out of only hours ago. "What is a moor-edger?" she asks.

"I'm an encloser. I push the moor back where it belongs and then I wall it out. So that I can grow something out here—something to eat, or, depending on walls, something for the flocks to eat."

"How do you have time, working at the mill?"

"There is no more working at mill. Mills closed last year all up and down valley and those that didn't will soon. So some of mills' weavers, the fortunate ones, return to the hills where they might have stayed in the first place for all the good it did them to descend into the valleys and attach themselves to machines. Clogs to clogs in three generations."

The moor-edger is silent, both hands resting on the handle of his rake.

Ann, almost embarrassed, whispers, for want of anything better, the words "dark satanic mills" and the smoke-covered man whispers the words "William Blake," cutting into her statement almost before she has finished uttering it, startling her, for she has already constructed a persona for him. The simple moor farmer, the mill worker, the uneducated; one with no access to words.

" 'Mock on, mock on, Voltaire, Rousseau. Mock on, mock on: 'tis all in vain. You throw the sand against the wind, and the wind blows it back again.' " Now there's something for you scholars to think about."

"That's Blake?" says Ann uncertainly.

"Himself," sighs the moor-edger with all the resignation of one who spends time trying to reclaim unclaimable land. He looks to the west, whence the wind today is hurtling—

carefully reading the light and the dark, the end of one performance, the beginning of another.

"You'd best return to the cottage now," he says softly. "Bad weather on the way and early nightfall. Besides," his eyes smile again, "mist comes down, or snow, and then there's Heathcliff's ghost."

A few paces away from him, Ann stops and shouts a question back across the wind. "You push the moor back?" It is as if she doesn't quite believe him; as if he is inventing his own activities.

"Yes," he calls across a sea of moving grass, "either that or it advances into the reclaimed land." The wind lifts his hair. "There's no stopping it, the moor."

Ann begins the return journey to the cottage. Ponden Kirk, forgotten for the time being, grows smaller and smaller just above her left shoulder. Above her right the weather advances like a stealthy, murderous army. By the time she reaches the enclosed lane it has begun to snow. The wind becomes muscular, aggressive; its hands flat against Ann's back. *Moor-edger*, she thinks. The term has an oddly horticultural flavour, suggesting flower gardens, weedless and raked gravel paths; seems unsuited to the smoky man whose musical speech and clear eyes are staying with Ann as she walks. That and his easy humour, what she was able to understand of it. She laughs a little as she remembers one or two of his statements. The sheep weren't his. "That lot . . . ," he called them.

Behind the walls the white animals are bleating, calling each other into a firmly packed cumulous formation, grouped to meet the storm.

In unity there is strength.

I think that I shall never keep, muses Ann, while the wind parts her hair into two equal portions at the back of her head, *a thing as stupid as a sheep.*

From the other side of the wall the adult animals demand safety, shelter. The lambs are quiet. Their panic has subsided in the face of focused fear.

"IN ALL THESE love affairs the loved one becomes the prison of the lover, Arianna."

"You mean the prisoner?"

"No . . . no, I mean the prison, the dungeon. The loved one starts to acquire architectural properties; so much so that the bars the prisoner looks through could easily be the loved one's ribcage and the lover knocking like a heart trying to break free. Each is held captive in a cage of the other's bones. Each claims to be the heart. Each denies being the prison. And the terrifying truth is that the heart and the cage need each other for survival. Without the blood there is no bone. Without the rib there is no heart. I wrote a lot of poems about dungeons; the great dark inner caves of the loved one where the lover exists chained to the wall, powerless."

"I told him that he was free."

"But he wasn't free and neither were you. You were each imprisoned in the dungeon of the other."

"I couldn't leave him."

"He couldn't leave you."

Two lapwings dropped from the sky, flying in a synchronized trance. They sliced the phantoms in half at waist level and disappeared behind the adjacent hill. Emily scanned the sky for more birds, and then continued, "My brother looked for prisons, I think. Some people do, you know. He searched for prisons, hoping that they would break his spirit: that wonderful, hilarious, awkward spirit that I loved so well. It wasn't so much that he was trying, all the time, to break his heart, as he was trying to imprison himself and to break his spirit. The married woman he supposedly loved had little to do with it really. She had to have the knowledge of her cage of bone so that he could lock himself inside it. After that she could go where she wanted, do as she pleased, because he trapped himself inside a prison of her, where he was busily breaking his spirit."

"Did I break Jeremy's spirit?"

"No . . . yes . . . not on purpose."

"And your brother – was his spirit broken? Did he succeed?"

"Ah, yes. He succeeded absolutely . . . brilliantly. 'Tell me about this married woman,' I would say to him, and, you know, each time I asked him, his reply was different . . . no . . . not his reply, exactly, it was the same in tone. Each time I asked him, *she* was different. And as he became more and more ill, *she* became, to my mind, more and more interesting.

"The first time he told me about her she was a saint . . . a paragon of virtue, clothed in modest grays and browns, her eyes cast down, her hands folded on her lap. But it was as if he were aware that this was not a suitable prison for someone as wonderful and terrible as he, and so he drank and brooded and raved and came up with something better.

"The next time he described her, her hair had changed from brown to black; her dress was satin, peach-coloured, I think. She had a band of black velvet wrapped around her throat. She was tall – she had been small before – and she had abandoned the needlework and charitable acts that he claimed had previously occupied her time. Now she played some kind of musical instrument, something foreign and exotic – a mandolin, if I remember correctly – and on this musical instrument she played nothing but songs of lamentation and farewell."

"Jeremy did not sing songs," said Arianna/Polly. "There wasn't much music between us."

"Just before he died, Branwell described his married woman one last time. By now he had not seen her or communicated with her for over a year. 'I am dying for the love of a woman whom I find impossible to interpret,' he said. 'Have I told you about her?'

"I said that he hadn't, because I knew that, by now, she would have altered drastically. And she had. Now she was silent and motionless and reaching for him only with her eyes, which he said were just like his eyes. Her hair, which was red now, hung loose. She was brooding, resigned, dying for love of a man whom she found impossible to interpret. She drank and took opium and wrote long, desperate, undeliverable messages. She had shut everyone else out of herself.

"Branwell's true spirit-breaker, his perfect prison. An exact reproduction of himself one week before he died."

FROM THE COTTAGE windows, Ann has a view of hills criss-crossed by drystone walls, the buildings of a few dark farms with names such as Slack Edge and Old Snap, Ponden Mill – now a craft shop and tea room – and, at the bottom of the valley, the Old Silent Inn. Behind the cottage, like two large parallel snakes on either side of the road, winds the village of Stanbury: a series of attached weavers' cottages now converted into modern dwellings, one school, a small church, and two pubs. Above all this, the brown stain of the moor spills over the wide, gentle hills, which hold firm under vast, changeable skies.

It has been snowing for three days and the view is temporarily eliminated, the wind driving walls of white across the top and down through the valleys. Drifts crawl in under Ann's door and do not melt in the cold interior. She takes the scuttle and descends the stairs to the cellar. The scrape of the shovel on the stone floor and the roar of fresh lumps of coal pouring onto the fire are the only man-made sounds inside the cottage. Ann is making new forms of conversation. She performs a task and the cottage responds with the rattle of spoons in a drawer, the creak of an opening door, the purr of a boiling kettle.

She has not stepped across the threshold for three days and she is developing a personal relationship with each of the details of the cottage's interior. As all but one of the remembered faces from her abandoned life fade, the little china figurine on the mantel, for instance, or the quilted hen that serves as a tea-cosy, gain power, become almost as important as similar objects were to her when she was a child. And then she realizes, for the first time, how alone she was as a child, and she knows that her reverence for often-touched objects – objects that are both familiar and dependable – is growing as a result of her solitude here in another country.

And she is cold. Her fingers are aching, then numb–even when she pulls the chair in which she sits as near the glowing coals as safety permits. She warms her hands on teapots, stretches them towards the hearth, places them between her thighs when she sleeps, but they remain two unco-operative, icy appendages. She searches clumsily through her copy of *Wuthering Heights* for descriptions of cold, its persistence causing her to give it the literary attention she is now certain it deserves. She remembers the cold outside the rooms along the highway and sometimes she remembers the cold inside.

The wind that comes in under the door, that slides around the windows, attacks her ankles, and shinnies up the inside of her jeans. To the delicate china lady on the mantel Ann says, "If you are this cold and there is wind everywhere there's no stopping anything." She apologizes to the plump motherly hen when she removes her from her warm post. "Sorry . . . but we all share now. Yes, it's share and share alike." "Dear Arthur," one of her many unsent letters begins, "I know more and more about the cold now. I know even more about cold than you." When bent, in a trance of conversation, over a letter to him, she mouths the words she is writing. As if she were speaking to him directly, as if he were locked with her inside the cold house.

She attempts to continue her work on the varying climates of *Wuthering Heights*, but the contemporary storm distracts and confuses her, and her sentences change before her eyes into pleas for Arthur's attention. Heathcliff's statement to the child Hareton, "And we'll see if one tree will grow as crooked as another with the same wind to twist it," is repeated in the sound of the coal she is constantly pouring into the small hell of her fire. "Arthur," she writes, "I have twisted towards, away, from your fire. You put the storm in me. I am a wind, shrieking!"

On the morning of the fourth stormy day, the wind outside the walls and the wind inside the cottage begin to converse in a jumble of words that Ann can decipher only at intervals. She sits near her now-grey hearth clutching the quilted hen to her chest, while whispers, moans, and laughter reach her ears, and then the hot, combined breath of a man and a woman, one inside, one out.

Ann knows the sounds: the rustle of clothing being discarded, a sob, a cry, the soft, purring noises a hand makes when it journeys over skin. *How can this be?* she wonders, *one of them is out, the other in*. The persistent noises of small animals attempting to make homes in earth, the insistent sounds of the separate each, straining to enter other. Winged lovers beating and beating up against the mirror of their opposite selves. Prisoned inside walls, locked behind doors, together and apart from each other. The storm has given birth to a disturbance of lovers who have now entered Ann's cottage.

And it is she who is apart.

They are everywhere Ann isn't. She can hear the woman brushing her hair in the next room, electricity snapping in the cold surrounding atmosphere. She can hear silk garments slide on and off her body. She knows when he has turned away from her, has become distant, silent, brutal. She can smell the herbal garden of him.

At night the lovers come subtly closer, all the while holding on to distance, as if Ann were a ghost of whom they are, as yet, unaware. They are beside her when she sleeps, moving and moving on the edge of her dreams. The woman weeps in the dark sometimes and the man strikes invisible matches to look at her more carefully, to scrutinize her suffering. But when Ann reaches for them they have descended the stairs and are murmuring, agonizing in the kitchen. Ann hears the male voice articulate the word "can't." It spills into her ears like coals onto a fire. And then the woman's words: "Don't leave me, don't leave me." The walls echo, change the lovers' language. "Leave me, leave me!" they cry, or, "Don't, don't."

In the morning light, the cottage is an enormous furnace,
a heartbeat, the furniture throbbing. The wind inside is
pleading, *Please, please* . . . . It gasps, its tongue a flame.
The lovers are in the coal cellar, crashing up against granite
walls. "Oh, my God," Ann whispers, "they have become
one." Yes, they have become one during the night and the
new beast they are is prowling. Ann hears it groan and pace
and sigh and lick its wounds and she knows she must find
it and set it free. Its huge violent body is seeking space,
needs to burst out into the open. But still it eludes her. She
spends the day pursuing it from floor to floor. No longer
quiet, it howls in corners and scratches on the other side
of doors. "My God, Arthur," Ann writes, "the beast we
were is *here*, but I can't find it!"

Let me out, let me out! the animal growls, always on the
other side of walls that Ann can't see through. Frantic, she
runs in her nightgown from room to room to room.
"Where are we, where are we?" she sobs, "I want to let us
out!" Rooms whirl around her glowing, pulsing.
"Arthur," she scribbles, "you have to help me get it out
. . . otherwise the monster will be everything. I want to
force it out, to push it out. Yes, yes, I want to lock it out,
to keep it out."

The hearth inside is grey and cold. The storm outside
settles.

The beast is asleep. Ann crouches under an eiderdown near
the mantel and waits for the monster to reawaken. But only
stillness surrounds her, stillness and pain. The immobility
and torture of a blade wedged between the ribs and a heart
frozen in the midst of seizure.

She cannot move.

She dreams of the dark Venetian paintings of Tintoretto,
the reproductions Arthur showed her; of the painted, rug-

ged faces of apostles and the soft features of angels. She sees wings like fronds of palm leaves set against skies alive with lightning. She dreams of Velazquez's portraits of dwarfs, of a long hall filled with small, intense men. As she walks the marble floor beneath them they increase in size until, she suddenly perceives, they are no longer dwarfs, but giants, a gallery of giants–the last a Norseman with a broad high forehead and fierce blue eyes. The painting bubbles into life and the large man is shouting, calling through canvas. His hands appear, slapping up against the flat, framed surface. "Let me in!" he is bellowing as the gold frame turns to painted wood and the dark oil to glass.

Rising from her chair Ann staggers past tilting furniture, turns the bolt, lifts the latch.

She feels the beast slip past her body, slide around her legs, taking its leave of her as she opens the old oak door.

"When I was alive," said Emily, "there was this important moment and that important moment and long, eventless seasons in between when I was vague and unfocused and wandering. I'm speaking of externals, of course, when I speak about moments – those circumstances from the outside that force themselves upon your attention. The ones that choose you: love, birth, death, and one parhelion, and a bog-burst. And the once or twice when I was away.

"I never wanted to be away. I wasn't much interested in change. I flourished in the empty times and in the familiar open. I hated the closed-in foreign places, the palaces of instruction, time tables someone else had constructed. It *is* wonderful to be dead, because nothing ever happens – except this barrage of seasons, and then you falling in here. I'm really very comfortable with this. I've never liked it when things were taking place. I didn't want anyone to be born, to burst uninvited into my world. And I didn't want death to tear my few companions out of it. And I certainly didn't *ever* want to fall in love."

"But, Emily," said Arianna, "you're not telling me you lived without love?"

"The trouble with falling in love is that it is really born of a perverse desire to invent the plot of your own life story, to make it episodic. Life should be plotless – none of this and-then-he, and-then-he nonsense. Besides, being in love is really being in a state of rage; it is furious, it is an extended tantrum. Surely you, of all people, should know this."

"But I was never angry with him."

"Ah . . . but how angry he was with you! There is always,

believe me, anger involved, as I think there should be. And then there is the accompanying dreadful collection. There is certainly always that as well."

"The dreadful collection?"

"You know all about that."

"What *are* you talking about? Emily, I have no idea . . . ."

"I'm talking about the *everything* of the outside world that gets drawn into the love affair. It is like a whirlwind sucking the world's objects, the world's events into its chaos until nothing has any meaning any more except in relation to it. The world's inhabitants, its architecture, its seasons, its weather patterns gain significance only in that they represent the mood of the love affair. A combination of blindness and scrutiny sets in. Focus and then expansion. And then the leaf falling from the tree is no longer a leaf falling from the tree. It is another addition to the dreadful collection.

"In my book, Mr. Capital H announces that the whole world is 'a dreadful collection of memoranda that Catherine did exist' and that he has lost her. Her features are reflected in the flagstone floors; her moods, her capriciousness, in the winds that assault his house. His walls keep her out! His windows let her in! Her whispers follow him, but he can't make out what she is saying. A piece of coal shifts in the fire. She is Flame! He can't touch her. She is the smoke that scatters down the valley. She is the news from afar carried on the lips of gypsies and she is the trinkets they sell him from their carts. The creak of their departing wagon wheels – her complaints. He cannot eat, but he tastes her. She monopolizes him utterly. Everything that exists is a message from her. He carries her in his sleeves, his pockets. He wears her like a medallion next to his heart or like the band inside his hat that circles his brain. He breaks a goblet and *her* bones shatter, *her* blood spills. Her eyes stare out beneath his lids. He takes her on unimaginable journeys, so unimaginable even *I* dared not describe them. For three years she existed in landscapes she would never see, never visit. It is unthinkable! Better to be dead, to be cast into this calm sea of eventlessness. Better to be here where these seasons hurling themselves down the valley towards us are merely seasons. Oh, no, Arianna, I never wanted to be in love. It's devil's work. And you *do* understand what I'm saying."

"Yes, Emily, I do understand what you're saying."

HOW SLOWLY, slowly the world comes back. The view from the upstairs window is at first a simple abstract study in black and white: flat, far away, indecipherable, or sometimes, on the edges of either end of sleep, misinterpreted, mistaken for the view from the window of an airplane or from the porthole of an ocean liner. Ann, her cheek resting on her flattened hand, tends for now to ignore it, to content herself with touring, from her pillow, the continent of her night table. Great full hours of exploring between hours of engulfing sleep; sleep that forces itself upon her, first liquefying, then absorbing her like a sponge.

On the night table there are books, two books now: the Brontë poems and the Bible. Two books about weather, too many books about weather, thinks Ann vaguely. Right beside the books is a teacup covered with – violets? forget-me-nots? – which sports a hairline crack as proudly as a fat lady with a brand new incision. "Tell me about your operation," Ann whispers, sleepily, to the curvaceous china.

The little lamp, also very pretty, with daffodils and a short fringe on its shade, does not now shine, nor should it, with the sun pouring onto it and then reflecting with alarming brilliance from the plastic container adjacent that holds the antibiotics. "Ann Frear!" the small plastic-covered sign announces, "four times daily!" and then, like the author's name at the end of a famous quotation, the words "Dr. Nussey." It is not, however, Dr. Nussey who administers the medicine in the mornings and evenings and who asks her if she has swallowed her pills during the day. There is a large man who materializes and disappears, who brings tea in the little plump wounded cup and who, in the beginning, brought the celebrated Dr. Nussey, with his needle full of sleep. The beast crept out; the dark absorbed Ann; and a man, scrubbed clean, walked into her illness. John Hartley, moor-edger, grass burner, healer of the sick, mender of broken cottages.

Beyond the static drama of the night table and then the large man's odd appearances, there is nothing. The day is empty, for Ann, of any form of completed thought and she falls asleep again and again from sheer lack of interest in her own listless attempts to piece together shards of fragmented memory. How, she wonders vaguely, did I come to be here lying in a bright upstairs room, exhausted by illness, and presided over at intervals by a gentle man who sets fire to the landscape?

"Will you eat some soup?" he asks, or, "I've brought you some of Mrs. Arkel's cakes, will you eat one?"

He comes and goes, a large, pale, friendly apparition. He is sometimes scrubbed so clean after a day of work that Ann cannot quite believe in his paleness, the fairness of him. The large bones and broad forehead. The huge hands holding a slim, silver spoon or a delicate bone-china teacup.

"Now today you look almost well . . . three steps back from the grave." John smiles, his paleness almost dark beside the dazzle of the windows. "Shall I read, then . . . some of the psalms?"

"You are trying to convert me."

"No . . . but you see, the first clear sentence you said after the needle was 'let's talk about the weather.' "

Ann does not remember this. "Maybe I've changed my mind," she says.

"Ah, no . . . not you, now you'll want it more than ever. I'll read some of the psalms and let you listen. Then you'll have your weather – descriptions of weather – but the language telling it will be calm. Weather for those weakened by weather."

"Do you go to church?"

"Yes, I'm one of fifteen or so in village who attend." He looks at her to assess her reaction. "The singing," he explains, "I like the singing. Also I pay my debts to the over yonder and the hereafter by keeping God's bride standing."

Ann is silent.

"God's bride . . . the church. I do repairs."

"I went to church when I was in the country with my grandmother." Ann remembers a red brick building, her grandmother's funeral. "It seemed right, there. Old ladies in flowered hats, stained glass, squeaky pews. And yes, the singing. In the city, church was something different. I don't know . . . " she trails off, sleepily.

Outside, moor grasses are pushing their way through heavy, melting snow. Several lapwings sail under the swaths of blue. Hills cartwheel close beneath an assault of light and withdraw again into shadow when clouds pass.

Ann relents and John picks up the book. Throughout the late afternoon and early evening the languid diction of the tormented scribe moves like a river from John Hartley's mouth through Ann's brain; the lyrical lift of the broad Yorkshire accent caressing gentle syllables. The hills beyond the window darken. Approaching night and receding snow. There is no need for Ann to speak, no need, in fact, for her to listen except in the way that one listens to music, allowing it to wash over the ear and the heart. The references to weather catch her attention, like a dragline hook in underwater weeds, pulling and then letting go. She has no need now for the complexities of content, the snares of meaning. Only his man's voice, the music of it; the pure sound of the words, empty of narrative. The repetitious references to weather tugging and letting go, tugging and letting go. The gift of speech, the times of sleep.

Awake, psaltery and harp,
I myself will awake early

Evenings later, Ann is downstairs by the fire and John is finishing the last five chapters. Gone are the supplications

and agonies, the bouts of God's angry weather. Gone are
the hailstones and bolts of barbarous lightning. The scribe
has been touched by quiet flames, the calm earth. He has
forgotten his enemies. He is healed, roaring with pleasure
and gratitude. The words are beautiful in John's mouth,
words like *everlasting*, *upholdeth*, *sanctuary*.

> *He giveth snow like wool: He scattereth*
> *the hoarfrost like ashes;*
> *He casteth forth his ice like morsels, who*
> *can stand before his cold?*
> *He sendeth out his word and melteth them;*
> *He causeth his wind to blow and the*
> *waters to flow;*
> *He healeth the broken-hearted and bindeth*
> *up their wounds.*

At the close of these words John closes the Bible and
looks at the floor. "Well . . . now that's done," he says.
"Now tha'll manage."

"No," says Ann, straightening suddenly in her chair,
sensing his leave-taking. "No . . . come back tomorrow,
please. You could tell me stories. I want to hear you talk
about this landscape."

It has only been dark for an hour or so. Advancing spring
and lengthening days.

"I want," says Ann, "to hear you talk about the sky."

T H E S K Y I N west Yorkshire is never still, never relaxed. It is caught, by those who gaze at it, always in the midst of either a subtle or a blatant act of transformation. Just when you think that you have read its messages and understood them perfectly, the wind shifts direction or changes velocity. The sun appears on a hill two miles away, abruptly disappears from there and flings itself, with no warning, into a beck ten feet from where you stand. The surrounding air chills or warms for no apparent reason, taking directions from a sky that can only be described as manic-depressive, or at the very least unpredictable.

Waiting for John in the evening, Ann stands by the window and looks out at emptiness and stars, the sky showing, briefly, her jewels in the dark. The snow is gone, except on the very tops of the swells, for it has been raining, constantly but unevenly, for the past few days, and the moor has become one dark, motionless, almost imperceptible sea. Now it is cold, clear: black with stars and a moon. And wind.

"We're cursed and blessed by the wind here," John has said to her.

She waits for him, waits to hear the sound of his boots on the path that leads from the village to her cottage door. Her new friend. This giant who, with huge ministering hands, has pulled her back so gently from the abyss, who has taken on, so effortlessly, the responsibility of her weaknesses.

"How did you find me?"

"I came looking . . . it were sort of research. And you with pneumonia!" He throws his hands into the air in astonishment. "I just came looking to see how you'd weathered the storm."

Ann imagines him during the day in his carpentry shop, or in the village chapel; places she has never been. But she does not try to visualize him working on the moor where they found each other – not with his face disguised and blackened and his body ringed by fire. She associates him with the light that warms, not the flame that burns. The bright comfort of the upstairs room, his paleness and shock of white hair. In her imagination his shoulder is always touched by sunlight, softened by the dust on a nearby window pane. And the sword of light is, in this picture, celebratory, ceremonial: nature making John one of her knights. Or even God, that weather-maker, placing a handful of light near his neck.

He has walked into her life and has brought with him no tension, no discomfort. Her muscles relax in his presence, her mind untwists, pretence evaporates. Sometimes he is just a voice and Ann can barely perceive him where he sits in the opposite armchair near the fire: his white hair tinged with orange, the wonderful rhythms of his speech washing over the furniture of the house.

"It were good," he says, "when I were a lad growing up out on t'moor edge. When I came into t'village I couldn't settle; I still can't settle because of the congestion."

Ann laughs. The population of the village hovers somewhere around three hundred.

"I'm happy for the farm," he continues, "though some lads go mad living out on moor. Mad from loneliness."

Ann loves the word "lad," the way it sounds near the fire. There can be nothing wicked about a man who uses the word "lad," nothing unnatural. The clarity of such a man is astonishing; as if these simple words he uses are a microscope directed at his heart and placed there for the purpose of total revelation. He speaks and she comprehends and the world around her becomes rich with light.

He is like large windows in a house; as generous with his distribution of sun and moon and stars as the upstairs room: the place of her recovery.

Ann remembers that once, before she became ill, she had returned from the village in the evening to find that she had left the cottage lights ablaze. The upstairs room glowed like a giant's lantern, flinging light into the dark sea of moor around it, scattering it over drystone and gravel, moor-grass and mud. Ann was forced, at that moment, to look past the image of Arthur's face that she carried constantly in front of her, forced to admire the upstairs room. Its curtains open, its contents revealed, and all the cold surroundings bathed in its light.

"I have these stories from my father," John is saying now. "He would say them in the evening after the walk up from the mill and after our tea. The farm growing heather and he working in mill, as I did myself not too much later."

Ann wants the stories. "Tell me the stories," she says.

"One at a time," he announces.

"One at a time," she agrees.

"And the first will be a story about the earth. I'll not speak about the sky until last so that you'll continue to allow me to return."

Ann laughs. She settles back into her chair. She listens.

"If you would content yourself with strolling in the valley below instead of seeking wind and illness on the moors above, you would have already seen the spot. And you would have wondered and perhaps you might have asked. John, you might have said in that sad, slow way of yours, John, I've seen a grave in the valley with its own little wall. And there's no church nearby nor any other headstones. John, you might have said, tell me about that.

"And so I shall, though you haven't asked, for your not asking is born of innocence and not lack of interest.

"And I should turn out the lights, for my father, who told these stories, was right economic, as he had to be. 'We can talk in t'dark as well as in t'leet,' he'd say, having finished the milking of the five cows, he and I, by the light of one candle. We hadn't the gas in yet at the farm though there were a huge gasometer at mill – Grief Mill – where he worked and where I used to work, down there in the same valley that I'm speaking of. Though now it's just black walls and rust and ruin."

John rises and reaches for the lamp. The room is suddenly clothed in a rust colour thrown from the coal fire, as if it had undergone the same ruin as the described mill. Oblivious to the altered atmosphere, John settles again in the chair whose slipcover flowers have changed into dark, floating, organic shapes.

"Across there is Oldfield village and there you can see his house." John gestures towards the solid wall of the cottage's windowless back. "It stands just there," he points, a seer staring through walls. "His name were Jack Green and he spent part of his life fabricating forests."

"Here?" asks Ann. "What happened to them?"

"Not here," replies John. "And what *would* happen to them I wonder, this being one hundred and fifty year ago? I imagine they would grow higher, if they grew at all, which is unlikely in this climate. A short forest, in that time, if it were growing at all, would certainly grow to be a tall forest. And now I'll tell my story – the one I heard as a child. 'Wilt tha' tell of t'owd black stone?' I'd ask and after that there would be no more questions." Here John looks meaningfully at Ann but in the dimness of the room she does not read his gaze.

"I thought it was about forests."

"Now I'll tell t'story," John repeats. He looks towards the fire and begins:

"Jack Green were rich man's gardener, and south of London to make things worse: in Devon I think it were. He were what you would call these days a designer of the land or what my father called one who tried to do God's work and very nearly succeeded – building hills and lakes and, yes, making forests. Thousands of acres these men in the south own and they want their forests changed all the time to suit their whims. So Jack Green was the man they most often called when they wanted new forests created or old forests altered or whatever, for Jack Green was a man who could coax forests, charm them like. He were right seductive with a tree, were Jack, and it was said when he was walking in woods, trees would fling suckers out toward him as he passed or bring forth saplings right at his feet – even in winter. But there is a price to pay for attempting to do God's work, my father always said, and an even higher price for almost succeeding."

"Do you believe in God?" asks Ann, curious.

"I believe in weather and in belief. You believe in weather and in questions. There should, at this point, be no more questions.

"Let's see if we can picture Jack Green, happy as a healthy lad, playing with rich man's acres. For that was what he was doing – just like lads in village play with dirt and puddles, making battlefields and oceans for their soldiers."

Ann's dollhouse and laundry tubs, and the long province of the floor in between, flicker in her memory.

"There he would stand," John continued, "probably right on the edge of some forest he was planting and charming – the great house like a battleship behind him – and he like as not never even invited for tea, knowing rich men, and some, though not all, of their wives. And probably he'd spend time walking back and forth through his infant forests, enjoying young beechwood and sycamore just brushing his thighs – it were so high, maybe, this forest."

John raises his large hand six inches above the place where his knee bends over the chair. Ann sees the light from the fire catch in the golden hairs on the back of his wrist.

"Would he touch the young trees? Yes, I think he would, but gently, gently, so as not to damage the delicate veins that young leaves have. They bend in an instant and crack in the fingers. A seam of wet green appears and then you've killed a leaf. But Jack wouldn't do this, not Jack. He would caress his trees softly and coax them.

"He didn't plant rows, not Jack. He planted in the manner of God. Sometimes saplings, sometimes seeds. Willow, linden, balsam, ash, birch, walnut, juniper, cedar, poplar, elm, hickory, sycamore were some of the trees he caused to come into being. He'd draw them first on map paper, shading in the wooded areas that he wanted to make. He'd shade them in until they looked like thunder clouds all over the thousands of acres that rich men own. It was said of him, he said it of himself, that he knew one thousand, five hundred different shades of green. And he knew exactly how to place one of these shades against another and how much to use of each and all this would be surrounded by the various greens of grass.

"He loved doing this. He loved bark and twig and root and limb and leaf. And he loved gesture. Gesture he loved the most, for each tree had its own gesture. And Jack's trees, because of the speed at which they grew, changed their gestures like moods, like states of mind.

"Sometimes, when working the land farthest from the house, Jack would pretend to be the wind. A man capable of reaching the heart of a woman like you was Jack, pretending as he did to be the wind. He'd run, right swiftly, through a beechwood forest, circling some trees three times, passing others right directly. And as he ran he stirred up the air so much even the trees became confused and believed he was the wind and trembled their leaves and swayed their limbs accordingly. Or he'd twirl around and around and around in a clearing so that four or five of his forests blurred past him like cars on the motorway – but prettier – a regular smear of greens – the different greens of the trees."

John pauses at this point and, seizing the poker, rearranges several large, glowing coals in the grate.

"It was said," he continues, "that she was tall and thin and straight and that Jack used to see her, now and then, bending over roses in the garden closest to the house. Her hair was black and thick and her brown eyes sloped down at the corners so that even when she laughed she looked sad. And puzzled, as if she didn't quite know why she was sad – which she probably didn't – being a rich man's wife and all her wants provided for. Jack must have admired her, admired her beauty and her grace when bending over roses, but he would never have dared to speak to her, she being a rich man's wife and also confined, it would seem, to the calm, cultivated gardens from which one picks flowers for the house. And Jack all the time busy with his forests, making them grow and being the wind in them.

"Then one day when Jack was causing an ash grove to come into being, concentrating like, so that the saplings would happen just so, as he'd planned and drawn them, she came bursting out of a more mature forest to his left, weeping and wearing green and not noticing Jack at all until he caught her arm as she rushed by. She had been strangely moved, you see, by departing from the great house and from her flower garden and through curiosity visiting one of the forests that Jack had planted, or that he had caused to plant itself. She had seen that each gesture of each tree was different and that these gestures could change before your very eyes, so that the trees seemed to be either reaching towards her or pushing her away. On the edge, you see, of either embrace or denial. Some of them appeared to be beckoning with great longing, others seemed to be poised for attack. All of them were responding to her presence. She was drawn towards the trees and terrified of them all at the same time. She felt that if she stood still she would grow roots and sprout leaves – would become one of them. What had happened was that, engulfed in his green, without having ever looked closely at his face, she had fallen in love with Jack; though, unfortunately for her, and for him as it would turn out, she was utterly unaware of this. She ran weeping towards the light and then there was Jack hanging on to her arm.

" 'The trees are alive,' was all she said to him.

"And when they made love Jack kept his eyes open so as not to ignore the hundreds of shades of green."

"That is a wonderful story," says Ann.

"Oh, no, it's not. It's a sad story and a grim story and it's not over yet. For, you see, she never returned to the forest or even to the rose garden, for Jack looked for her there. He waited for weeks and weeks on the edge of the very forest from which she had run weeping, and as he waited he kept absolutely still, never once attempting to be the wind. Finally, in despair, and as a last desperate gesture, he picked a leaf bouquet, a stem from every tree on the property: beech, ash, oak, pine, laurel, and so forth. He walked, for the first time, up the wide stone steps of the great house, under the gaze of all its windows, and knocked on its high front door. One of the servants answered and Jack asked that the bouquet he held be given to the Missus.

"Whether those leaves ever reached the tall lady or not we'll never know. But we do know that she never came out to Jack. Not that day, nor any of the days following. And in a month's time Jack left the rich man's land forever with his heart set against trees and his back turned to all his forests. And as he walked away, the woods behind him – the trees of the woods – lost their individual gestures and became just like those shaded thunderclouds he had drawn on his map paper.

"It's my thinking that he believed that the woman had been a tree, so tall and straight she was, and wearing green. That she had been a tree and that she had betrayed him.

"He would suffer, then, whenever he saw a tree.

"He came here to the moors because, as you can see, this land has few trees. The views from his windows, therefore, would not disturb him with memories of the tall green woman or of his abandoned, beckoning forests. He set himself up in the big house of Oldfield – for he had quite a lot of money from the rich men – and began to write a long book condemning the tree. 'It obscureth the view,' he wrote, 'It hideth slugs in its flesh, the rodent inhabiteth it, it blocketh out the sun, it maketh shadows on the grass,' and so forth: a chapter for each idea. And then one day, in the valley below the house, near the beck, he found the huge black stone.

"He had walked by it, already, hundreds of times, of course. It's just that, until that particular moment – maybe it was the way the light was – he had never really looked at it. But this time he did and he was right pleased with what he saw. He circled once in a clockwise direction, and then again in a counter-clockwise direction, and while he was doing this he scrutinized the rock's surface. It had come to his attention, all of a sudden like, how completely unlike a tree that rock was and how there was nothing at all frantic about its gesture: nothing that could propel sorrow to fling itself, weeping, into your arms, for instance, when you'd never even gone courting her. And there was little about it as well to make a man want to pretend he was the wind, for Jack knew looking at it that the wind would have no effect upon this rock at all. Yes, Jack as he had become then thought the old stone was beautiful, and he resolved to have it for the headstone of his grave.

"So he marched up the hill and into the village to find four short, stout, strong men – he'd gone right off tall, lean people had Jack – and then he marched with these men back down to the stone. Jack wanted the stone rolled up the hill to the little graveyard near the chapel at Oldfield. Not that he intended to die just then, but more that he felt that the big beautiful rock was in danger in the fertile valley where, Jack couldn't help but notice, small growing things that looked suspiciously like saplings flourished, now and then, until the sheep ate them. Jack certainly didn't want his beloved boulder growing roots or sprouting leaves or displaying any other signs of germination that might cause him to become anxious. During this time, you see, even a tall buttercup could cause Jack to become anxious. He were trying his best to remain, always, in a horizontal frame of mind.

"Well, the four short, stout, strong men used their eight stout, strong arms and their four stout, strong backs and they rolled the huge black stone up from the beck into the first pasture. But when they stopped to mop their brows the stone rolled right back down to the beck again. After going about this task three or four more times the four short, stout, strong men decided they would rather be lifting a tankard than a rock and they returned to the Grouse and Rabbit whence they had been fetched, leaving Jack alone with his boulder.

"In subsequent weeks he couldn't eat or sleep for thinking of the stone, all silent and brooding-like down by the water, and for his wanting to move it to higher ground. This in its own way were a relief to Jack in that it were a change from not eating or sleeping because he was thinking about the sorrowful woman. And a change too in that he was temporarily distracted from his preoccupation with creating venomous sentences concerning trees. Except that now Jack began a chapter in which he chastised the trees for being so unlike the rock. 'They do not keep still in the face of the wind,' he wrote. 'Sap riseth in them in certain seasons and courseth through their veins and sticketh on the hands of those who touch them. Their surface doth not remain smooth but rather is complicated and textured.' Anyway, after days and days of thinking about the rock he decided that he himself would roll it up the hill to the graveyard.

"From that decision onward his days were filled with activity. In the daylight hours he wrestled with the boulder, inching it upwards with the aid of a crowbar and then positioning it with wedges that he had chiselled into the correct shape from smaller rocks. He had no use for wood any more, Jack hadn't, for, as you know, it is simply the flesh of various trees, and were therefore, to Jack's mind, deceptive and unreliable. He had written in his book, 'The flesh of trees is untrustworthy as a material for building houses. It bursteth into flames at the touch of a match and small insects gnaw at its heart.' And, I believe, he added, as a footnote to that particular page, 'If a tree hath a heart, which is doubtful, it is one liable to change and eventually to decay. It is not constant like the heart of a rock.' In the evening he wrote such things in his book, and being so engaged in hours of light and in hours of darkness, there were no man in the riding who could match Jack for sustained industry.

"After about a year of this employment Jack had managed to push the boulder to the top of the hill – almost. He had maybe ten feet to go, when a strange thing happened. Right in the middle of the afternoon the sky turned a disturbing shade of green. It was the exact colour of the sorrowful woman's dress and also the shade of one of the larch trees that Jack, in the past, had shown great affection for, and he knew in his heart of hearts that there was some uncommon weather on the way. So he angrily wedged the boulder and reluctantly entered his house just as hailstones the size of large grapefruit began to pound the earth around him. They changed, in time, to rain, and there were this great green weeping sky that could not help but remind Jack of the woman, and that angered him even more than having to abandon his daily application to industry. He had hoped, you understand, to forget all about her in the midst of rigorous and sustained activities, but the colour and the moisture of the atmosphere had brought the idea of her so close again that it were like the feel of her breath near his shoulder.

"Now Jack did have some wood in the house at the time in the form of a wooden table, for he were not an uncivilized man and took his meals as we all do, and he began pounding this with his fist, so great was his wrath. And, of course, his candlesticks and cutlery jumped as he pounded and then, when he grew tired of his tantrum and ceased thumping, his candlesticks and cutlery continued to jump without his assistance. When he rushed to the window to look outside he saw all the hills of the moors heaving and swelling and rolling because this were the day of the Great Bog-Burst, which Reverend Brontë, over in Haworth, said was God's response to the sins of the parishioners. The mud from the burst poured down the next valley, coming as it did from Crow Hill, but the earth itself shook as far as Bingley so you can imagine what happened to our friend Jack's boulder."

John pauses here in order to allow the full impact of the bog-burst to settle in Ann's mind.

"The Brontë children were out on the moors that day," she says to him, "but fortunately they were taken to shelter. Otherwise *Wuthering Heights* might never have been written."

"Jack finished *his* book by suggesting that, and I quote, 'the green from southern forests doth reflect itself wantonly upon the roof of the sky causing great tempests and whirl-winds therein and bringing forth great eruptions out of the heart of the earth when it looketh thereon lustfully.' After he wrote these words he walked up to the Grouse and Rabbit to collect those same short, stout, strong men who at first refused to go with him thinking that he would make them push the rock again. But that wasn't what Jack had on his mind.

" 'See there,' he said to them as he stood at the top of his own hill at the door of his own house. 'There is where I'm to be buried.' And the men looked down and saw the rock, halfway down the valley, arrested by a small natural plateau of land just at the point where the little stream that rushes down to join the beck divides into two parts. 'A right nice burial plot,' Jack said to his four friends, 'and chosen especially for me by the boulder.'

"After this there weren't much left for Jack to do except die and this he did with expedience. The four strong, stout men convinced two more of their comrades at the Grouse and Rabbit to help dig the grave and to carry Jack's coffin down to it. They put up a headstone beside the rock and they built drystone walls around the little plot. Jack must have confessed his sad story late one night at the Grouse and Rabbit for on his tombstone you may read these words:

Here lies Jack Green
Kind as can be
Who died in mid-life
For love of a tree

"If you go down there, and you should soon – for the fresh air which can be got in the valley without suffering the wind on the moors – you will see that there are four laurel trees growing: one in each corner of the plot. Some say that they were planted, one apiece, by each of the four short, strong, stout men who had come to be quite fond of Jack as he had often dropped by the Grouse and Rabbit late in the evening after a regular fit of written tree deprecation. But my father always said that it were the wind that brought the laurel seeds to the spot from a tree in one of Jack's southern forests, a tree that had been watered over time by the woman's tears. Because, you see, all his forests and the trees in them and the sorrowful woman herself had loved Jack much, much more than he ever knew."

"Do real stories end like that?" Ann asks John.

"More often than you think," he replies.

"DID YOU know Latin?" asked Emily.

The ghosts had been amusing themselves in the fog by disappearing, and then coming gradually back into focus, making a guessing game of it. Thick mist: at ten feet everything was invisible, even phenomena that were normally visible.

"Have I dematerialized or am I swallowed in the fog?" they called to each other. Emily kept score and had become bored only when she was certain that she was winning. Then she wanted to talk.

"I didn't know it exactly, but I learned a little at school."

"And so, did you read the *Aeneid*?" Emily began to fade as she asked this.

"Come back." Arianna searched the vapours for her companion and eventually discovered traces of her near her right-hand side. "No," she said, "I never got further than some noun declensions. I wasn't much for books."

"*My* favourite part," said Emily, snapping into clear focus and startling Arianna a little, "is when Aeolus unchains the winds so that Juno can shipwreck the Trojans."

Arianna sighed, "You and weather. Who is Aeolus?"

"The king of Aeolis: land of storms."

"I might have guessed."

"Juno was Jove's wife – *and* his sister I might add. She harped away at Aeolus until he unleashed all these winds that he kept in a cave. The winds picked up ships and smashed them into rocks, they gathered up huge waves and dropped them onto the wooden decks, they blew scores of men right out of the rigging and into the deep. They howled and shrieked and caused tremendous havoc."

This last sentence was pronounced by Emily with great satisfaction.

"Good Lord! What happened to the balloonists?"

"There weren't any, but if there had been, your misadventure would have seemed like a fairy tale."

"I can't imagine Latin telling any of this. Puella, puellae . . . puellam," she added uncertainly. "*Now* where are you?"

"Back here. I've found some even denser fog. Venus, who was the mother of Aeneas, covered him in a cloud of mist so that he could enter Carthage unobserved, all the while observing what took place around him. Aeneas . . . the hero of the story."

"I only remember one story. Something about an angel with wax wings who flew near the sun."

"Icarus. He was Greek. He fell out of the sky like a stone. You would remember him. He wasn't an angel. His father made those wings for him. Afterwards he may have been an angel, but I doubt it. From what I can gather of his temperament it seems more likely that he would have become a ghost. It's good to be a ghost, don't you think?" Emily evaporated once again, as if to prove her point.

"Are there angels really? . . . And come to think of it, why aren't we?"

"I've only met one . . . an aggressive sort of beast. I think they all are, flapping away in that disturbing fashion. And those wings! Their wings are quite dirty really. Not white like you'd think but a sort of dullish yellow-grey. And often there's lice." Emily floated nearer to Arianna who, although she could not see her, was aware of her proximity. "I suspect that we aren't," she confided, still invisible, "because we never expected to be. *I* certainly never did."

"*I* never expected to be dead," sniffed Arianna. "Who was the angel?"

"My brother Branwell . . . and in such bad temper. It was before you. Several decades ago. I'll tell you about it if you like."

Arianna was silent. She knew Emily would tell her about it even if she didn't like.

" 'What do *you* want?' he asked me, very rudely, as if I'd called him down, interrupted him. He was all dishevelled . . . very untidy, probably drunk. 'You're always so demanding!' he said.

"This angered me not a little. '*Me* demanding!' I said. 'You were always the one who was demanding. Attention! Attention! I'm setting the bedclothes on fire now! That was you. Rescue me! Rescue me! I am drunk! I am a drunk genius. I deserve attention!'

" 'I was not like that,' he replied, 'I was retiring, sensitive. . . . Clean my wings!'

"This infuriated me. 'I will *not* clean your wings,' I said. 'Clean your own wings.'

" 'I can't,' he whimpered. 'I can't reach around the back where the itch is the worst. It torments me.' "

Emily's tone when imitating her brother was very sarcastic. She continued the story.

" 'Well,' I said, 'it was you who decided to become an angel.'

" 'I did not,' he whined. 'it wasn't my fault. It just happened.'

" 'There you go again, never taking any responsibility for anything. When are you going to grow up?'

" 'I can't grow any more,' he roared . . . really angry now. 'I'm dead.'

" 'Excuses, excuses,' I countered, 'you'll never change. You'll always be baby Bran, bedwetting and complaining, and furthermore I did not invite you here, regardless of what you might think.'

" 'Well, then what am I doing here?'

" 'Who knows? You've probably been thrown out. You're probably a fallen angel. What have you been up to?'

" 'Oh, nothing.'

"This was a typical answer. I decided to scold him concerning his apathy. 'Angels have chores,' I said, 'the good ones do them. But you probably haven't . . . '

" 'I've not been feeling well,' he said.

"I became impatient. 'You're *dead*, for heaven's sake,' I said, 'dead people always feel fine. Angels feel wonderful! Beatific! Ghosts, on the other hand, are capable of a range of emotions, revenge being one of the most prevalent – though personally I think it's a waste of eternity–but *angels*, angels are always supposed to be in good humour.'

" 'Well, *I'm* not!'

" 'So I see,' I said. Then he ruffled his feathers testily." At this point Emily shook her shoulders, demonstrating this angelic activity and Arianna laughed at her.

" 'You always knew it all,' he said. 'You were so bossy. Lording it over everybody. Your attitude was terrible. Imperious! Outrageous!'

" 'What an ingrate! Who helped you upstairs?' I demanded. 'Who told Papa you were in bed asleep when in fact you were still drinking at the Black Bull?'

"We argued on and on like this for some time, and the wind got into it of course, tossing words around as it does, and all the while this voice inside me kept saying, *I love him, I love him*. And I did, you know, he always touched some bright fuse in me. He ignited me like a torch and the world became clear in the eye of anger. I loved the way he left the house, a whistling boy, and then I loved the way he crashed drunkenly back into it. I cherished and protected the tormented side of him, the side that angered me, and I called it out of him too so that I could watch this side of myself reel clumsily through life meeting all the brutality head on. And there he was, a poor excuse for an angel, thrown out of heaven in exactly the same way he'd been thrown out of every pub he ever frequented. There he was, rending his celestial garments and holding forth about how he'd died for love. In the middle of this we both broke into laughter and I said to him, 'Branwell, I've really missed you. I'm so glad to see you.' "

"*Did* he die for love?" asked Arianna, immediately interested.

"He died for an idea of love, that unattainable married woman. But he really died of drink. I was the one who died of love."

"But Emily . . . you said . . . "

"Not that romantic kind of love. I died for love of him: that furious, catastrophic side of myself that was buried with him. I never went out the door of the house again after his funeral, didn't even come out here. They wanted me to see doctors but I knew I was dead already. I couldn't live without his complexities, which were really my complexities. So I just died!"

Arianna pondered this for a while. "Isn't it odd," she said, "that I didn't die for love. Isn't it ridiculous, when you think about it, that I had to die just at the moment when he started loving me again?"

"Not as ridiculous as you might think."

"What do you mean by that?" asked Arianna suspiciously.

Emily floated backwards in order to resume the game, her voice becoming softer as she slowly disappeared. Her words, when they reached Arianna, seemed to have no source.

It's not as odd as you think, the wind seemed to say.

A FEW EVENINGS later, John returns to the cottage and Ann, pleased to see him, brings the bottle of whisky from the kitchen to lace their tea and make the talk easier. She is burning a new form of coal: large, round, flat lumps.

"They look like hockey pucks," she says.

"What's this, these hockey pooks?"

"A Canadian game . . . with skates and sticks and ice."

"Ah, yes . . . " He has almost forgotten her foreignness. "Wilt tha have another story tonight?" he asks, using the Yorkshire, asserting the ground they stand on in the face of the pucks, in the face of her belonging somewhere else.

Ann pours the tea and adds a splash of liquor. This is a form of assent.

"The story is of Grief Mill, where I worked years ago as a young person – a child almost – and where my father worked before me. An odd sort of name for a mill, I suppose."

"Is it is a true story, then?"

"Why, Ann, they are all true stories that I tell." John opens his large hands towards her, as if by investigating his palms Ann should be able to read his honesty.

"But Jack Green, and all those things he felt and all the times he was alone in forests pretending to be the wind, how could you know that? You could never prove it."

"I know the truth of the idea of it and have no wish to prove it otherwise. And you, listening the way you did, knew the truth of the idea of it as well. And I know," he adds quietly, "that you will tell that story to someone else some day and that's how the truth gets passed on."

The wind groans in the chimney and forces a tattoo of sleet against the window's dark panes.

"I call this story 'Footpath to Fire.' "

"Did your father call it that?"

"No, he did not, for this story is my own. And you're the first I've told it to except for myself. I tell you because you are an *oftcumdun.*"

"Pardon?"

"One who comes from far away."

"So that's what the small Heathcliff was, and she . . . Emily . . . never even explained where he came from. And then later he was a revenant."

Now John looks confused.

"Revenant . . . :" Ann explains, "one who returns after a long absence or, like Catherine, for half of the book a ghost, a spirit, one who returns from the dead. But, enough of that, tell me the story."

"Two hundred years ago these hills were inhabited by hand-loom weavers. In the summers, when the rows of the windows were left open, the air filled with the sound of banging shuttles. And no one had clocks. Weavers rose at dawn and retired at dusk; in between they wove a highway of cloth and tended the sheep who provided the wool. Once a month they set forth on the old pack-horse track in order to take their wares to the Piece Hall in Halifax. All in all, it were happy time. Nobody had to murder anything in order to survive, the water in valley was pure and chose its own direction, followed its own inclinations like. Spirits lived there. The Pennine people were strong from long bouts of walking over moors, from breathing fresh air, and from good work that involved a transformation process that they themselves controlled: from lamb to spindle to loom.

"Then, men from the south came and put factories in the valley where cloth was made speedily on steam-powered looms and sent out into the world on steam-powered locomotives. And all the hand-loom weavers whose cottages had been absorbing the light of the hills for years had to come down from chambers – their upstairs rooms – close their oak doors, leave the high clear places, and descend into the dark souls of the cotton and woollen mills in the valley. At first it were just the men who'd go but then, as the pay was so little and all their independence gone, the other family members as well. Sometimes the women, but in particular the older children, the ones over eight years old.

"The lad I'm speaking of was one of these – began working in the mill at fourteen – following every morning the footpath down to Grief Mill that other children had made a hundred years before. Children that were now sleeping in the chapel graveyard. People these days have thoughts about this and they call it child abuse. But he were a happy lad, knowing nothing else but clogs on a footpath with his mates or his father, the haze of the sleepy afternoon schoolroom and the high roar of the machines all morning–except Sundays which were spent over yonder at Scar Top Sunday school, and evenings with his mother and father where they stayed on the little hilltop farm.

"Once they were inside a mill these people of the hills could speak no more; their voices being lost in the noise of the looms. And yet the conversations continued, for lipreading flourished. Think of it: silent gossip, voiceless invitations to religious meetings, the telling of folktales and current events, the words to hymns and popular songs all passing like minnows through that sea of noise.

"There were a peculiar soft look to the air around the workers in these mills, as the dust from the sizing filled every shaft of light from all the windows. And it fell down on everything in the room, this dust; on the floor, on the heads of the workers, and on the looms themselves – their steel framework. That were the lad's blackboard. He could write words of Greek there and rub them off, wait a few moments for the constant clay rain to cover the iron, and begin again. For he were learning the classics, but not in school. There in the mill where his mind was set free by the drone of the machines.

"There's something to be said, I suppose, for clouded vision and ears filled with wind. Working in one of those mills could be like standing on a seashore immersed in blinding spray, if you look at it from that point of view."

Or the highway in a snowstorm, thinks Ann, remembering.

"Now and then," continues John, "the owner of the mill, Thomas Grief the Third, would stroll up and down the long aisles between the weavers, inspecting not so much the cloth as the diligence of those making it. He would be an odd sight, would Grief: a tall, thin man, darkly dressed, and emerging from a shaft of dusty sunlight. He would be becoming clearer and clearer as he approached, until every detail of him were looming and breathing over the poor weaver–the way the teacher does in school. It were enough to make a lad lose his place and enough to distract a lad from learning the classics. But our lad–out on some windy sea with Odysseus–didn't even notice that his master were in the vicinity. Just kept on writing and erasing those words in Greek until he felt a hand on his shoulder.

"He jumped then and his heart beat harder than all the shuttles around him and he began to mouth desperate excuses and apologies into the noisy air. Thomas Grief, however, had never learned lip-reading and so he heard none of this. He picked the lad up like a kitten by the scruff of the neck and carried him, nearly choking, into his frosted glass office at the other end of the mill.

"The lad had never been in mill owner's office before and as he rubbed his neck he looked around and were right dazzled. The mahogany desk! The brass plaques! The polished porcelain knobs and handles on any number of drawers and cupboards! And most of all the paper, the great beautiful piles of paper which were situated to the left of a silver-topped glass inkwell. But even as he looked covetously at this, he was paying attention to the mill owner who was pacing angrily up and down on the carpet of coloured geometry problems that covered his floor. Mostly the lad were astonished by the man's height and by his long, long face, how his eyes and brows seemed to slide down the immense length of his face and then be pulled back up again by some kind of extraordinary inner effort. The trouble with this lad was that he would always be doing at least two things at once: working the loom and learning Greek; fearing Grief's retribution *and* examining eyebrows and carpets and facial tics. Perhaps it came from his father who would never stop moor edging though he worked, dawn till dusk, in the valley.

" 'How did you know those words?' the mill owner demanded, his active face pushed up against the boy's.

" 'Please, sir,' he said, 'I have a book.'

" 'Yes, I understand that must be so. But where did you acquire this book?' The volume, which lay beside the boy on the bench, had been confiscated by Grief at the same moment that the owner of the mill had lifted the boy into the air.

" 'It's my father's, sir, and he lets me have it.'

"Thomas Grief the Third stood with the book in his hand and, now and then, he opened it up and closed it again with a snap, without reading. 'Go back to your loom,' he said to the boy and as he said this his facial features flew into action and then reorganized themselves again. He did not give the lad his book.

"The next day the lad was miserable at his loom, for, as I've said, he was always wanting to be doing two things at once and, apart from the Bible, that were the only book his father had. He could remember quite a lot of it, however, having taught himself the letters and the words from the glossary at the back and so could run through some of it – the part with the Cyclops for instance – in his mind as he worked. But with the book not there nothing moved him to learn new Greek words and so by the end of the day the sizing lay, an undisturbed blanket a quarter of an inch

thick, on the metal frame of his loom. He were right dis-
pirited, cast down like, not by the loss of the story, for he
still had the first part of that – the part he'd been able to
decipher – in his memory, but by the loss of the beautiful
and frightening words that told the story, the words that
leapt out at him from the puzzle of the dead language.

"It were two or three weeks later when Thomas Grief the
Third once again appeared, coming into focus out of the
fog of sizing dust, and this time the lad saw him and bent
his head down to his task so that the mill owner would not
perceive that his eyes were filled with hatred for the man
who had stolen his book. Then all of a sudden he felt his
collar tighten in a familiar way as Grief pulled him to his
feet and dragged him, more gently this time it's true,
towards the office.

"There, a magnificent sight awaited the lad: seven books
piled high on Thomas Grief's desk, and his own among
them. 'These are for you,' said the mill owner, 'and during
tea I'll teach you if you like. But you mustn't read or write
while you work the loom, or there'll be an accident.' And
then his eyes and nose and mouth visited one another as
I've said before and flew apart again."

John pauses here and the wind rattles every door in the
cottage. It bangs its fists up and down the chimney. Ann
shifts uncomfortably in her chair.

"Is that all?" she asks. "Is that the end of this story?"

"I wish it were."

"But it isn't."

"No." Silence. More wind. "About this time there were
problems in the mill, though the lad knew little about
them, travelling around the world as he most often was in
his mind with Odysseus. Silent, mouthed words, however,
were moving across the floor, through the bright river of
threads, concerning the founding of a union which would
force the owners to pay fair wages and give the weavers a
better life. Much of this talk must have gone on during tea,
while Grief and the boy decoded Euripides or Homer.

Whatever the case, the lad were amazed to see his father enter the frosted glass office one day with several of his mates and a list of demands in his right hand.

"It's a funny thing about politics—how even if you don't go looking for them they will always come looking for you. The lad had heard his father and the men speaking of·the union in angry voices in the kitchen, but he hadn't believed that their talk would move beyond the realm of ideas. But now, when he and his father milked the cows, he could tell by the light of the one candle they used that the older man were angry. At night he went to sleep with the words 'Our demands have not been met!' bursting through walls of his room, interrupting his dreams of ancient Greece.

"You can't, perhaps, imagine what a fire in the valley looks like at night from above. No, it wouldn't be likely that you can imagine that . . . so I'll tell you. It looks, at first, festive – the way that sparks fly into the air – like the Queen's birthday until you see that it's all the wrong colours, dark oranges and reds. Then it looks like an inferno of Dante's, but man-made because, of course, this particular fire were burning architecture the square lines of which were especially obvious battling with the more unpredictable shape of the flames until, as you might expect, the fire won. The lad could see all this from his chamber window and the whole time he would be thinking how his books were gone. He could see in his mind's eye each of their pages slowly glowing beside the flaming mahogany and bubbling molten brass. He could imagine Thomas Grief watching his mill burn from the big house on the opposite hill. And he could imagine his own father's hand lighting the fire.

"No one ever asked how Grief Mill burned. The workers never got their union, at least not then, so the only result of the conflagration were that blackened ruin, now covered with vines, and a longer walk, a different path to the mill at Lumbfoot. The lad never saw Thomas Grief again, as he left the district soon after the fire. And so, at the age of fourteen, he gave up the study of Greek. His father never asked about the whereabouts of the first book, perhaps because he suspected the truth about it. Life at the little moor-edge farm continued as usual.

"Except that book were gone, and the others as well, so that the lad had to keep the memory of the stories and the wonderful language that told them in his mind or else, he knew, the books would be forever erased from his life.

"But memory has a way of playing with things – perhaps you've noticed that yourself – and as time went by the lad began telling himself stories that were not quite like the original. And since he often told himself the stories at night before he went to sleep, his dreams crept into them and, as time went by, some of his own memories. And because he lived here, on the moors, it were impossible – you'll like this – to keep the weather out of the stories. He had learned, with the help of Thomas Grief the Third, all the Greek names for the winds, amazed at the language that knew and expressed the differences that make up the turbulent ocean of air.

"Eventually, the stories were all his. A bit borrowed, true, from the Greek and a bit from the Bible, which were now his only reading material, a bit from his father, a bit from his mother. Very little from the afternoon classroom. More, much more from the silently mouthed rumours of the mill, his memories of Thomas Grief, and the persistent surrounding weather that nudged its way into his mental narrations whether he wanted it to or not.

"That were how he became the local story-teller and it made him right popular too – a good person to sit beside in the pub, entertaining like. But only he himself knew the agony of it, the loneliness: telling the stories, often ones of lies, betrayals, injustices, and broken hearts, over and over to himself in the dark until they came to be just right. And always the far chambers of his brain were holding on to whispers of a dead language that he had once learned but had now forgotten. Then there were the glimpsed images of a man's face; one that could disintegrate, then reassemble itself before your very eyes. That and one memory he could not erase: the fire in the valley reflecting from the windows of workers' cottages where he believed the ghosts of the hand-loom weavers must have puzzled over what it was that had suddenly turned their upstairs rooms orange."

John pours whisky into his cup and drinks it, neglecting to add the tea. Ann notices that his neck is flaring, red with emotion.

"You?" she asks.

"Myself," he confesses.

She creeps across the room and settles near his chair, placing her cheek against his knee so that he can easily touch her hair. Later, when they make love, she is a river of pleasure, a garden of fire; the unravelled story, the architecture of the upstairs room. The landscape belongs to John, and through his attentions to Ann, to her as well; the tributaries of his stories travelling over the moors and into the valleys.

They are in place.

"WHEN I SPOKE to you about building my house, Polly/Arianna, I did not tell you what else I built."

Arianna stopped watching the clouds, comparing them with the sheep that grazed nearby, and turned to her evanescent friend. "All right, Emily," she said patiently, "what else did you build?"

"This landscape and a lot of talk. Some people – not all pleasant people either. *And* I had to sew their clothes as well, *and* I had to set their tables."

"You could not possibly have built this landscape!" Arianna gazed down the groin of the valley: burgundies and ochres and greys. Fierce, breathing wind and everywhere black stone heaving out of the earth. White circles of snow on the heights, visibly shrinking. Lapwings, curlews, grouse – a profusion of springing rabbits, and all the various moor grasses astir.

"But I did, I did! I invented, I built it all!" Emily laughed and shot up, like an ascending Virgin Mary, straight towards the sky in order to survey her creations. Then she settled back down again. Arianna did the same and the two of them bounced like this for some time, twenty or thirty yards into the air – little girls joyfully skipping in a playground of ether.

"I did, you know," said Emily, eventually coming back to earth, lying down, relaxing on a couch of heather. "I knew it the day I finished the book. My dog Keeper and I set out on our daily walk and, suddenly, the landscape had altered. There it was, the landscape of my novel! I could never see it any other way again. It was mine, mine! I'd made it mine! And I'd changed it, forever. It is hard work too, building landscape. The rocks were particularly difficult, and that is what Mr. Capital H was made out of – different shapes of black stone. And he was obdurate, unyielding, fixed, unchanging, difficult to describe, and originating God knows where. Practically unkillable! A landscape can only be killed by dynamite or natural disaster – especially landscape formed by millstone grit. And even then the death is *very* slow. First it merely fragments.

"Mr. Capital H lost his soul when Catherine died. He was broken, fragmented. The stone centre of him, the black core was shattered and even so it took him thirty years to die."

"This Mr. Capital H sounds like a tyrant," remarked Arianna. "I don't think I should have liked him."

"O-o-o-h . . . ?" asked Emily sarcastically. "Really? Not interested in fierce men, nasty ones . . . is that it?"

"Well . . . I . . . "

Emily, having made her point, continued to explain her craft. "I had to build a farm and then this very pretentious manor house in the valley," she said. "I had to put tea tables and armchairs and chandeliers and all sorts of other things I'm not very interested in inside it too. God! . . . linen napkins and goblets. All these external objects in the manor house on the inside, in the valley, when most of the time I wanted to talk about the innerness of the landscape outside and above. You see what I mean? But I controlled myself and built it all very carefully, recording speeches, no matter how silly, and letting the landscape intrude only at significant moments, mostly through windows."

"I was always looking down on everything," said Arianna uncertainly. "It was always passing beneath me."

"I know everything about the stones beneath my feet," said Emily with pride, "and I talked about that. I know everything about kitchens, copper pots, and cinders and I talked about that too."

"It was always happening down there and I was two miles away. But, you know, occasionally something would reach me, some sound: a laugh, the bark of a dog, a cow bell, the whistle of a farm boy and once a phrase of music from a violin I couldn't see." Arianna was silent, thinking for a moment or two. "Perhaps if I could have followed one of those sounds to its source I might have . . . But it was no use. I was too far away and moving, always moving farther away. Except at night when he was so close . . . I didn't know whose hands, whose hair . . . mine or his. Too close and no love. And the rest of the time too far away, and love coming up to me in those sounds. In Devon a sob reached me from the centre of a forest. Someone who could have loved me was there weeping. And I, knowing this, was a mile away and moving on. I was always a mile away and moving on."

"Until you crashed into my geography."

"Yes . . . until then."

A KIND OF beautiful order steps with John into Ann's life: an order all the more clearly visible set as it is against the chaos of the surrounding moorland, which trembles daily under the touch of the wind.

In the mornings, Ann and John rise to the sound of glass milk bottles being set down on the cottage's stone doorstep, clinking together like Japanese chimes. As John dresses in his work clothes, Ann descends the stairs, an expert now, to stoke the fire, and then further down to the cellar to fetch a fresh scuttle of coal. In the kitchen she chooses plates and bowls whose flowers she has become fond of, leaving the little cracked cup of her illness on the windowsill: enshrined, a relic, a magic object. The morning cat, a creature who visits only once a day and always at this time, rubs against the window behind the cup, flattening his fur upon the glass. It is waiting for a saucer of the milk that Ann brings, along with a remarkable quantity of wind, in from the front door. John appears in the kitchen and fills the kettle for tea. He is, she realizes, the most scrubbed man on earth, his face aglow, his hair neatly combed and parted.

They talk at breakfast, quietly picking the lock of each other's pasts.

"Didst tha never have nowt but the city tha left behind?" John often, now that he is always with Ann, lapses into broad Yorkshire.

"Ah, no," she says, "I had the countryside – I've told you about the little church – in my childhood. But if I were to go there now I would find it all changed. They've built suburbs and shopping malls. They've bulldozed all the secret hidden places – all the little forts I made as a child near the creek."

"Creek?"

"The beck," she explains. "It's not like here. In Canada much of the past has been thrown away. No one cares. No one records it. It was very hard for me, losing the past like that. I honestly believed nothing would ever happen to me, because my past was gone. Only the lake stayed the same: at least it looked the same. It's poisoned."

"Who poisoned it? What has poisoned it?"

"Nuclear power plants, chemical companies, cement factories, sewage."

"Yes, I know about the poisoning of water by factories. Still, with them all closed here perhaps our water will clear itself."

"Perhaps."

After John leaves for his workshop or the farm, Ann sometimes walks over the moor and into Haworth, passing through the old crowded graveyard, past the church and the Black Bull Inn to the town's main street. Here she enters Tyson Mather's High Class Butcher Shop, Mrs. Eccles' Bakery and the greengrocer's – the location of tulips and figs. Occasionally she rides an old groaning bus deeper into the valley, and examines, through its sooty windows, the abandoned mills and the desperate, idle people. The mill where John most recently worked is now a gaping hole in the ground the size of a city block; not only closed but utterly demolished. Ann tries to imagine him, one of several workers, in a room full of noise and labour, but can bring him to mind only as an isolated figure in the carpentry shop that she now knows well, or in the barn out on Moor Edge Farm. Places that he controls, that are his own.

Her book about weather continues, Arthur's remembered face intruding now less often into this solitary activity. John, amused and fascinated by her work ("Tha writes a book about a book!" he has commented, amazed), has made two objects for her in his shop—objects that he claims will capture the wind. The first he presents to her one evening after work. For days it sits, a long thin box graced with a circle of pierced holes and several taut gut strings, on the windowsill in the light, demanding that Ann decipher it. It isn't until John takes it out into the garden, until she hears its voice, that she knows it is an Aeolian harp. It moans outside all night, weeps its way into Ann's dreams, until the wind, tired of its plaything, smashes it up against the garden wall. In the morning there is no more weird music, only the gasp of atmosphere and thin random shards of wood scattered among the tilting crocuses.

John replaces this with chimes made from old keys whose locks and doors no longer exist. "That were key to Scar Top Sunday school before t' new door." he explains or "these were for t' church in Haworth during the time of Reverend Grimshaw. They had six padlocks on all doors for fear of Luddites. And this . . . " he says to her, winking, "were key to Top Withins before it were abandoned. I've given tha' key to Wuthering Heights, I have."

"And where did you happen upon all these keys?"

"From my father. He kept a drawerful out at Moor Edge. It were pity, he always said, not to keep something of habitations vanished from the hills."

This source of music proves sturdier and more lyrical: laughter tossed by a turmoil of wind.

"Ah, but I regret the harp," John says. "I must have wanted it because of the Greek that I learned and forgot. But they have different winds there I suppose. Neither their words nor their harps are suitable to express this climate."

It is a Sunday in April, a combination of sun and showers. Black rocks, onyx-like, glisten in the sun or become sullen and removed under brief bouts of rain. In the village now each window, each small display case directed at the street, holds not only the customary Staffordshire lad and lassie sick with love, or doggies made by Royal Doulton, but also bright bouquets of daffodils in dazzling cut-glass vases. These flowers flourish in gardens as well, sometimes flying their yellow flags for a full week before being flattened by the wind. The green of the reclaimed pastures on the moor edge is beginning to deepen; March lambs are daring to leap and spring ten to fifteen yards away from scolding ewes. The windows of the upstairs room reflect solid white clouds hurrying through azure. The moors are alive with noisy, hidden, hurrying streams.

In the afternoon, after he returns from the chapel, John takes Ann out to the farm in order to fly a kite he has made. When they have moved away from the enclosed area into the open moor, he grasps one of the strips of crossed wood of which the kite is constructed and pulls it outwards into the shape of a bow. Then he ties a thin piece of sheep gut to each end of the curved shape, producing one taut string.

"What are you doing?"

"You'll see. Keep your eyes and ears open. Out here you learn either to fight or to play with the wind. Over the years I've chosen to play."

The kite in John's hands falters once or twice and is finally jerked aloft by forceful currents of air. It pulls and thrashes for a few moments like an angry fish on a line and then, resigning itself to its leash, it sails, as yellow as daffodils, proudly above. Ann watches and then she listens.

The kite is singing! The kite is singing to the hills in a strange and joyous voice.

John shouts with pleasure. "I was na' sure that kite would sing but that it does!"

Ann is laughing. Her shoes are filled with mud. Her head is filled with breeze and sunshine. Even the several sheep surrounding John and Ann lose, for a moment, their vacant look, snap out of their life-long trance long enough to look upwards, seeking the source of the sound.

"We could make more," says Ann, "we could make different colours and sizes and then we would have a regular orchestra."

"The wind section."

Sunday walkers approach singly and in pairs, pause to chat, to discuss the kite, tell their own tales of airborne miracles. Kites stolen by the wind and delivered, unscathed, to Loch Ness. A three year old kidnapped by a kite and transported to Hebden Bridge. A forty-year-old man, father of five, choked to death by a kite string. The kite that was reeled in with a tenacious hawk in tow. The bridge that was begun when a kite was flown over the Niagara Gorge.

"I'm from Canada," says Ann proudly.

"Aye," says the old man who is telling the tale, "it were begun on British side. But how dost get kite to sing?"

That night for the first time John speaks about his wife.

"There were a completeness about her death," he says, "that did not leave me torn. Left me empty, hollow, but not broken. Like a cup whose contents have been drunk, which is waiting to be filled again. She were a good lass who never knew, till she became ill, what it was not to be working; neither she nor her people, always getting up in the dark and going down to the mill. She knew that there was nowt for it when she became ill but that she were going to die."

"And there were no children?"

"No children. There were not yet any children. It were a pity; that, and her being so young."

"You loved her."

John passes a large hand over his forehead. "Yes . . . but I was undamaged by it – saddened, but still whole. With you it's different. Something has torn you, left you raw at edges."

Ann is silent. For a moment Arthur's body fills the space between the chairs that she and John occupy, blocks her

view of the other man. The condensed world of the highway and its rooms knocks at the cottage door. No breezes
bouncing melodious kites there. Inner weather: despair,
passion, some joy. Weather confined by the limits that gold
frames impose on paintings. Tintoretto's angry storms and
sudden celebratory showers of tumultuous stars. The man
whose name she has spoken only to herself, never to John.
The mystery of the man who wounds and then, seconds
later, is able to move the ships of drastic joy out of their
safe harbours into some dark, beautiful, inexplicable sea.
He is unstoppable. He cannot be cancelled by absence, by
distance. Transparent in this landscape he is nevertheless
around Ann all the time, an idea touching all her nerves.
Even here, even now, as she bathes in John's warmth.

Ann seeks John's eyes. He sits with his elbows resting on
his knees, his large hands clasped in front of him in an
attitude of supplication, perhaps of resignation. His eyes
are down. He will not look at her. Eventually he speaks.

"He has torn you and you still love him."

Ann does not answer. The wind becomes uneasy; its
palms testing the window glass, the doorframe for weaknesses, for access.

John looks up now, directly at her face. "And does he
. . . did he love you?"

"I don't know . . . no. I don't think so." Ann rises from
her chair, walks to the window, lifts a dying daffodil out of
her otherwise healthy bouquet. "I wonder why, if they are
all picked at the same time, one would fade before the
others." She shows John the flower. "It seems odd, doesn't
it?"

John takes the flower from her and drops it gently onto
the coals. Ann watches it convulse, bubble, blacken.

"And yes," she says, "I still love him."

It is surprising to them both when, all the same, they
awaken the next morning to embraces and sunlight. At

breakfast John tells the story of an old lady of the dales who, having resolved to commit suicide in the Wharfe River at the stroke of midnight on New Year's Eve some years back, was surprised to discover, at the end of her descent through the water, the Bolton Underwater Club clothed in scuba-diving gear, celebrating the New Year at the bottom of the strid—a small whirlpool formed by a bend in the river.

"They rescued her, of course," says John, "but her mind were never the same again."

"What about the Underwater Club, was it ever the same again?"

"Oh, aye, except they had developed a new appetite for thrills and adventure."

They laugh together, stroke the morning cat, pour steaming cups of tea. Their conversation of the previous night is, temporarily, laid aside.

IN THE YEAR 1805, a British naval commander became, not surprisingly, obsessed by the air currents upon which the movements of his ships depended. A rational man, he felt he could not rest until he had identified and described the wind's activities; until he had, in fact, labelled them. This must have involved years of observation, years of using his frigate as the subject of a long experiment, years of testing the soundness of the conclusions he gradually began to draw. Eventually he devised a system whereby the wind could be divided into thirteen categories, and since he was, by then, an admiral, these divisions became known to the world as Admiral Beaufort's Wind Scale.

Ann has come to the section in her scholarly writings where she feels she must apply Admiral Beaufort's Wind Scale to the weather of *Wuthering Heights*. She believes she has come to understand this obsessed admiral. She can see him in her mind's eye standing on the bridge of his ship at the turn of the nineteenth century, sniffing the wind, scrutinizing the ocean, writing his observations in a small notebook. "Calm, brisk, blustery, smooth, erratic," would be some of the words he might use as he quantifies the wind. Was his large admiral's hat ever carried off by the force he was describing? If so, would he then write "Wind strong enough to remove military apparel?"

The Beaufort scale, Ann discovers, has been adapted over the years, and applied to objects other than frigates; it has described the response of trees, chimney pots, insects, birds, children, architecture, clothing, and smoke to varying degrees of wind. Adjectives have been attached and discarded by succeeding generations: "intensely devastating, inconceivable, tremendous, overpowering," or "light, gentle, soothing, moderate, fresh, bracing." The nouns used in nineteenth-century descriptions of the levels of the scale have changed in the twentieth. Roof shale has been replaced by telephone wires, chimney pots by television antennae. Ann is particularly fond, however, of the Admiral's own elucidation of number 13, the hurricane-force wind as "that which no canvas could withstand." She wants to tell the forever absent Arthur about this, wants him to apply it to the canvases of Tintoretto. And she wants him to be pleased that she suggested this–pleased with her cleverness, her humour.

She also likes the way the admiral refers to a light breeze: its sea criteria. "Small wavelets, still short but more pronounced. Crests have a glassy appearance and do not break."

But most of all she loves the ancient seaman's descriptions of storm: land storm, sea storm. He gives ten points to this angry activity on his scale. He is clinging to the mast of his man-o'-war in ecstasy. "Very high winds with long over-hanging crests," he shouts in Ann's imagination. "Foam in great patches, blowing in dense white streaks along the direction of the wind! Surface taking on a white appearance! The sea! The sea! The sea is tumbling, heavy, shock-like!" The admiral is drenched, gasping. "Seldom experienced inland," he roars at her across the tumultuous ocean, across the yawning gap of time that separates them.

Oh, really. . . .? thinks Ann. *What about* King Lear? *What about* Wuthering Heights? *What about last month?*

There is only one scene in *Wuthering Heights* that Ann believes she can place at zero on the wind scale. She reads the few sentences describing it.

They sat together in a window whose lattice lay back against the wall, and displayed beyond the garden trees and the wild green park, the valley of Gimmerton, with a long line of mist winding nearly to its top . . . . Both the room and its

occupants, and the scene they gazed on, looked wondrously
peaceful.

Zero on the wind scale. Calm. "Sea like a mirror," the
admiral whispers, amazed, peering over the edge of the
mighty bark whose sails hang limp and lifeless behind him.
The cultivated garden of Thrushcross Grange holds its
breath, plays statue, becomes the perfect setting, the perfect
atmosphere for Catherine and her contented husband, for
their marriage.

But Ann, the reader, can predict the weather, can move
her mind around the park and investigate. She can see just
the suggestion of a nimbo-stratus cloud formation peeking
over the horizon. Unlike the couple in the book, who sit
as if posing for a portrait whose setting is Eden, Ann knows
that a change of barometric pressure is on the way.

Night of full moon, still night. Smoke rises vertically, mist
hangs. Black windows of the Grange reflect a quantity of
moons. No light glows inside, throws itself into this garden,
which is a still, silver sea, a mirror in which waits the gypsy.
Ann knows he waits there; his tense breath is the only
current in the surroundings, that and the air he disturbs
when he shifts with restrained impatience from one foot to
the other. Ann knows that, at this moment, the blades of
grass that felt the weight of his approaching foot are, hours
later, struggling to unbend themselves, struggling to reach
towards the moon. Ann understands that the curved mass
adjacent to the clean slice of black exterior wall is his intruding shoulder. Catherine and Linton inside, locked in the
unmoving trance of compatibility. Heathcliff outside, waiting to gain entrance.

Ann is certain that, as he waits, the wind scale is beginning, subtly, to alter. "A person from Gimmerton wishes
to see you, ma'am." Leaves rustle. A spider-web curves
outwards, like the belly of a sail. Catherine feels the light
air on her eyelids. "Someone mistress does not expect."

Twigs move. Dust is raised on the path leading to the house. "What, the gypsy – the ploughboy?" A leaf disconnects itself from a tree that has too long been its home, becomes airborne as Catherine walks onto the outside steps and sees the revenant, hears his speech – his eyes, his hair disturbed. Large branches move, winged seeds glide, plumed seeds are airborne. Her own sleeves rippling as her arms rise through the troubled air to meet him.

"Waves taking a more pronounced long form. Many white horses on the crests. Chance of some spray," says the admiral, in a strong, assured voice.

Number five, perhaps six on the Beaufort scale. And rising.

PART THREE

Revenants

Oh would that I were a reliable spirit careering around
Congenially employed and no longer by feebleness *bound*
Oh who would not leave the flesh to become a reliable spirit
Possibly travelling far and acquiring merit.

–STEVIE SMITH

I N L O V E A N D alone, Jeremy Jacobs, the Sindbad of
the Skies, was hovering over the white shores of Edge
Island. Above him loomed an enormous globe – a balloon
of scarlet silk, a breathtaking drop of blood poised over a
frigid, still landscape.

"White," he mused, as he touched a square inch of the
silk absently, with numb fingers, "always magnifies colour." And then he remembered *her* colour, pale though
she was, vibrant against the Arctic white of bedsheets. He
remembered the wet, plum-coloured mouth and yellow
hair – the long white limbs, beige inside the room's blank
interior.

He was not even sure, now, that he was travelling over
land, and that excited him. Just the idea of entering a
territory where land and sea camouflage each other, where
sameness and mimicry abound, where his form is the only
detail and his actions the only adventure, made him almost
wince with joy. Behind him crouched white mountains, in
front the hummocks of polar sea.

He had already sailed over the mountains of Spitzbergen,
over the sharp blades of the western range and the flat
platforms of the eastern, over Stor Fiord, past Whale's
Point, knowing the names from long nights spent with
polar maps. Tomorrow he would sail over North East Land,
leave the earth behind at Dove Bay, and aim for White
Island. But now, with the drag lines anchored on ice, the
red balloon remained stationary, and he had time to reflect,
to remember.

She was gone. And so was he. They were so marvellously gone from each other. Touch, talk, impossible. While he had floated over open water, he had sent cryptic messages to her by means of buoys. One had said, *My pale rose, I carry you here, a weightless light, near my heart.* Another: *Angel that you are now, I give you colour, have seen your splendid wings awaken . . . a borealis.* The hurling of the buoys over the edge of the basket had filled him with pleasure. He watched them somersault through air and then waited to see and hear them splash into the frigid water. Then he imagined their complicated journey to the country where she now lived; the fiords of *nothing*, the long estuaries of *never*, the country of *nowhere*. *Ah, maiden of feathers and snow*, he had written on the piece of paper attached to the third buoy, *because you are nowhere, you have entered the ocean of everything. I've seen your hair in the sun's rays and you crystallize around me. Small drifts of you fill the folds of my clothing.*

Then there was the moment when the dark fluid beneath him changed texture, became grey, opaque. The first evidence of polar ice. The ruffle on the bottom of the Arctic skirt. This was followed by painful, dazzling, unbroken white and the mountains of Spitzbergen, an enchanted glass castle on the horizon.

He was delighted, charmed by the snow-covered ice, even though it effectively put an end to his water messages. He loved to watch the wind play with the surface, creating small blizzards with available snow, without the help of clouds. The low sun wheeled across a sky so blue it was impossible to believe. Jeremy felt, in fact, that blue was absolutely the wrong name for the colour of that sky. It needed something clearer: a sound composed of long vowels and knife-sharp consonants. Something like *strike* or *take*.

From now on his messages to Arianna would, of necessity, be airborne. These, of course, would be the purest statements of all. She had been, he remembered, afraid of the water, an element that really had nothing to do with who she was/had been. With communication in mind, he had brought with him a cage of untrained white pigeons. Where these birds eventually landed mattered little as long as they flew away from him, because there was one thing certain about Arianna's whereabouts, and that was that she was away from him.

Now, anchored over Edge Island, he began to compose the airborne messages, ones that he knew had to be beautiful, exact, and pure. The paper, he decided, would not be folded, would rather trail from the ankle of each bird, banner-like across the sky. For this reason he tore several pieces of paper into long ribbons and then anchoring these with a milk-white paperweight on his small wicker table, he pulled out his pencil and began to write.

That night the aurora borealis did not appear. Instead there was a carpet of stars so thick, a meadow so crowded with bright flowers, that Jeremy stood at the outer edge of the wicker gondola, believing that, had he wanted to, he could have taken one or more on the journey with him. "Oh, Polly," he whispered as all sense of space – upper, lower, near, far–disappeared. "Oh, Polly . . . see how close the farthest distances are."

He was rapturously happy. He had never been so deeply in love. Alone, on a suspended wicker floor, he bowed and began to waltz, under the celestial grandeur, with an invisible partner.

It had been days and days since he had felt the cold.

The next morning, the wind, co-operating, blew lightly in a north-eastern direction. Jeremy cut his drag line and, with compass in hand, manipulated the white sail at the front of the balloon into the correct position. He looked through his mother-of-pearl field glasses towards the north for some minutes. Then, having established utter emptiness, he began to dispatch his white birds. In a vacant region it is unnecessary to complete any task in haste, and knowing this, he allowed an hour or two to pass after each release.

The small banner attached to the first bird said: *Oh, white maiden, frost's mistress, how I long for your icicle thighs.*

It was the moment when his hands opened and the bird's wings unfolded that he most wanted to freeze in his memory. He could stand outside himself now and see the exact image he was creating: his dark form in all the endless bright, his arms raised, the confusion of flight's inception bursting from his hands. The message lifting heavenward like a banderole of prayer emerging from the mouth of a painted saint.

I have seen you in ice floes, the second message read, *silver in your veins, the gentle snowdrifts that are your breasts.*

The third bird had shadows of grey here and there on its white feathers. Jeremy chose it for his darkest message.

You are night's negative, the blaze on the other side of the globe; I cannot see your dawn but believe none the less in its shine.

He floated over the mountains and glaciers of North East Land, noting Arctic foxes and their blue cousins who sometimes trailed behind them like shadows. Various birds visited the balloon: snow buntings, ivory gulls, Arctic terns. They seemed completely unafraid and would perch on the edge of the basket for hours. When he again left the land behind for a combination of solid ice and broken floes, he twice saw polar bears feasting on seals. Irregular swaths of blood on snow. Such purity. Such clearly documented, innocent murders were these fine red statements of survival.

Finally, in the middle of an afternoon (though by now he had stopped counting and so couldn't say which afternoon), just as the sun began its descent below the horizon, when all the ice and bergs and hummocks had turned orange, he saw a surprisingly regular dome-shape coming into focus in the distance. "White Island," he breathed, astonished that because of its unbroken cap of ice it was, in fact, blue. A single cloud of approximately the same shape hung over its summit. The left side of the island was covered with shadow.

"Home," shouted Jeremy, enjoying the sound of the word: a deep, bell sound in the emptiness all around him.

The balloon landed, scudding gently across a thin, icicle-shaped stone beach, the only exposed earth for hundreds of miles: an inexplicable dry lip on the edge of the island. Jeremy, standing on land for the first time in days, felt disoriented but content. He began, at once, to deflate the balloon. He had no intention of returning. "Home," he said, almost sang as he watched the globe change shape, tilt to the right, and finally become a huge puddle of scarlet silk. Then he climbed back inside the gondola to prepare his evening meal of champagne, *pâté de foie gras* and hard tack. He toasted the island, himself, the collapsed balloon, and his cherished absentee.

It was now quite dark. The wind, having completed the task of propelling Jeremy to his intended destination, was still. Jeremy toasted the wind, but with less exuberance, wine dampening the excitement of his brain. Soon he climbed inside his reindeer-hide sleeping sack. He was almost at once lost in dreams of his dear departed, his abandoned one.

The following day was green! Pale green sky, emerald-green sun, very low, like a patinated bronze disc rolling along the edge of the horizon. The mountain of ice behind Jeremy had turned an interesting shade of turquoise, and behind it stood a half moon of an olive colour.

On the strange, naked beach the grey stones were black-ish-green and scattered on top of them was the world's oddest collection of driftwood: water-smoothed huge branches in whose erratic shapes Jeremy believed he could see suggestions of dark warriors, the ruins of Bavarian castles, Bernini's sepulchral monuments, The Albert Memorial, The Trevi Fountain, all tangled together and darkly silhouetted against the approaching ice. He stood off shore for some time, savouring the formations, playing the same visual games with them that he had played as a child with passing clouds. Curiosity eventually moved him closer and he discovered, amazed, that the currents of the world's oceans had transported fragments of their nautical kills to these shores so that, mingled with the parts of the gigantic pines that had been ripped by turbulent spring waters from the banks of Siberian rivers, he found relics of demolished Norwegian sloops and Siberian river craft. These consisted of fishing floats, an elaborate desk, table legs, half of the face of a figurehead, a wooden bathtub, and something resembling a pulpit. All this wood, hundreds of miles above the spot where the last stunted tree struggled into existence.

As he ambled back towards the gondola, Jeremy noticed something just beyond the driftwood, which he took to be the skeleton of a small boat, but which, on further examination, proved to be a sledge. To the right of it there were two pieces of crumpled fabric – one plaid, one solid blue – and then, to his surprise, one boot; all of this strange, unreal in the greenish light. Jeremy began to examine the ground more carefully and found, to his great excitement, several leather notebooks, a bundle of letters, a tin box, a pair of field glasses, and a large case containing five cracked bottles of French champagne – all partly exposed but cemented to the ground by ice. On a neighbouring rock lay a perfectly beautiful compass glowing in the green light and pointing, relentlessly, towards the north.

Jeremy rushed back to the driftwood and gathered its smallest pieces for a fire, hungry for the words he would thaw out of the notebooks and letters. Arctic messages! The white truth! As he scurried over to the gondola to fetch matches, his foot slipped on the lip of the glacier and he fell towards the turquoise ice. It was then that he first saw the emerald-green skull, floating there, six inches down.

During the next few days, when he wasn't reading the journals and letters, he would stroll up and down the beach looking for and finding bones: thigh bones and scapulae, cages of ribs and one perfect spine curled, like a long still snake, on the rocks. But none of this would strike him hard in the chest the way the skull had. It was the recognition and then the denial of access that shocked him. It was the familiarity. How clear, how vulnerable the skull looked, encased forever in that cold, solid, unbreakable glass.

Jeremy knew that at this moment he was looking at himself.

"How tranquil everything is becoming," said Emily wistfully. "Spring was never one of my favourite seasons. These playful breezes annoy me. What has happened to the wind? We could go back to winter if you like."

"I *like* spring," said Arianna, "at least I like what I can remember of it from before him. Some of the girls from the factory would go out walking in the afternoon on Sundays, along the embankment or to the park. And when I was a little girl I *loved* spring. I remember birds from then, and daffodils. After him I couldn't seem to bring the seasons into focus . . . or anything else that happened regularly, predictably: days of the week, holidays, mealtimes. All that seemed to be gone, after him, because his unpredictability became my reality." Arianna looked straight ahead, right across the valley. She crossed her thin, translucent arms. "I suppose I should have liked spring when I was ballooning . . . it was the easiest time."

"I think my early interest in the Arctic must have had something to do with my dislike of spring, my love of winter. You see," Emily was incandescent with enthusiasm for her chosen season, "much more is happening in the winter. It is a more active state. None of this slow, practically imperceptible growth, this steady, dogged unfolding. The wind attacks everything around it, it makes instant contact, it changes the landscape in a great big hurry. A blizzard changes everything. It's as if it cares about the landscape so much it simply has to touch it recklessly, has to fling itself upon it. Inappropriately sometimes, yes, but always fearlessly. Passionately. None of this gentle, sentimental coaxing." Emily looked indignantly towards some cowslips growing nearby. "Aren't they a bit much, don't you think? They positively scream, See how sweet I am! I'm a flower! I'm a flower!"

Arianna examined the little blossoms thinking that, yes, they were sweet and they were flowers.

"You're just like my sister Charlotte," said Emily. "She would write something ridiculous about those flowers I'm sure. Anne would have, too." She paused and eyed Arianna closely. "As a matter of fact you *are* quite a lot like Charlotte. Proficient at pining, wanting to haunt, and all that." Emily laughed. "You should have seen him. Nothing resembling a perfect profile there."

"Was Charlotte in *love*?" asked Arianna, surprised. She had already heard quite a lot about the famous Charlotte, about the huge numbers of books that she had sold, about her desperate desire to please, socially. About her exhausting trips to London, and, in conjunction with these, about Emily's utter refusal to have anything to do with the place. *Literati*, she had sniffed. Hrumph!

Emily was not answering, but she had stopped laughing.

"Well, *was* she in love?"

Emily winced. "I don't really like to think about it."

"Oh . . . *please* tell me."

"It was . . ." Emily began, "pathetic. He was her teacher, she actually called him her master. This was in Belgium. I hated it there."

"*You* were in Belgium? It isn't possible. You could never have been anywhere but right here. I can't even imagine you in that parlour we haunted, or in that kitchen. I've been all over the sky, but I've never been to Belgium."

"We went to school there, Charlotte and I, for a while; she for a longer period than me. I came back as soon as possible, but Charlotte stayed on, as a teacher. It was awful. She wasn't very large to begin with and she just got smaller and smaller in all sorts of different ways. His name was Monsieur Heger."

"Did he seduce her? Did he love her?"

"Absolutely not. Oh, I think he admired her intelligence, but, good heavens, he was married and had a hundred children. Not that that matters, God knows. And there was something else; I think he was interested in his own power over her. She would have done anything to please him. He must have known that."

"He must have known that," said Arianna, trailing off into her own past.

"Finally, she came home defeated and then began the worst part of all."

"The worst part of all," echoed Arianna, slowly re-entering the subject.

"The waiting . . . the waiting for the letter. She had written to him, you see, and he hadn't replied, so she was always waiting. She only spoke about it once but I could *feel*, first the anticipation, and then this desperate waiting. It went on for years. After about six months I began to wait for the letter, too, even though I knew it would never, never come. Charlotte wrote to him again and again. I could tell by her face peering down at the paper that that's what she was doing. I began to imagine what might be in his letter if it did come. The unwritten paragraphs haunted me – not because I wanted it to arrive but just because it never did. In fact I wanted it not to arrive because I knew about Charlotte's capacity for suffering. The arrival of that letter could guarantee her ten more years of agony. She said that she wanted very little from him; a sort of intellectual correspondence, so she said. Of course, she was lying. What she really wanted from him was pain, deceit, secrecy, mystery, and darkness. And that was the announcement that the letter would contain regardless of what the words said. That was what he was withholding from her. Not simple friendship.

"You should have seen her wait . . . it became her employment . . . exhausting work. She waited all night long, awake, asleep. She waited for the kettle to boil in the morning but she was really waiting for a non-existent piece of paper to arrive. When she was waiting for Branwell to come home from the pub at night she was waiting for the letter to arrive. While she waited for Papa's long sermons to end she waited for the letter to begin. She waited for a cake to rise but she was really waiting for the letter to appear magically in the little silver tray that sat on the hall table."

"He never sent me any messages," said Arianna, "not even a postcard. I never saw the word *love* written by his hand."

"You were never apart . . . how could he? But" – a mysterious look entered Emily's eyes – "don't worry about that, he will send you messages now. He probably already has."

"Oh? is that because he's dead? Let's haunt him. Let's read the messages."

"No."

"Why is it that you are all in favour of haunting places, but people are somehow out of bounds?"

"Places are much more satisfactory."

"For you."

Emily ignored this last comment. "I thought I should go mad if Charlotte didn't stop waiting," she continued. "The arrival of the post was the most excruciating time of the day. Anything for me? she would ask lightly, and there often was something for her, she had girlfriends who wrote hundreds of long, tedious letters. She would sift eagerly through the envelopes and gradually a puzzled look would come over her face when she discovered no Belgian stamps – as if she were confused about the fact that, on the four hundredth and seventy-third consecutive day, there was still no word from him. I couldn't bear it. I, you see, had begun, not only to mentally write, but to visually construct this vagrant missive. I was certain it would be written on blue paper and that the ink would be black, the stamp cancelled in a fuzzy unreadable way. I began to wonder if *I* were in love with this Monsieur Heger whose presence I had been barely able to tolerate while I was in Belgium."

"But Emily, you said you were *never* in love."

"I wasn't . . . and I wasn't then either. I was deeply attracted, however, to this darkness, this deception that Charlotte wanted, though she probably didn't even know that she wanted it. I was attracted to the conflagration and the charred ruins that she unwittingly desired. I suppose I wanted them too.

"I remember one day when waiting and wanting hung all around the house like blue smoke. The post had come into and out of this blue mist almost unnoticed because, by now, the waiting had become an ordinary state, like breathing. The arrival of a letter into the lungs of the house at this stage would have been impossible, suffocating, no . . . more like choking or strangling. It simply could not happen and so, although we still waited all the time for the letter, we no longer looked for it. Yes, by then, the waiting had taken us over completely. It had invaded every corner of the house, this blue smoke, as if it were evidence, a reminder of a conflagration that had never happened. Then, quite suddenly, in the midst of kneading some dough in the kitchen, dough that looked blue because of the smoke I've been describing, I felt cold, apart, the outside edges of my soul registering an absence, and I knew I was waiting all alone."

"What had happened?" asked Arianna, appalled.

"Charlotte had stopped waiting. She'd started writing."

"Not another letter."

"A kind of letter, yes, I suppose it *was*, in a way, a kind of letter to him. But it didn't matter any more whether or not he received it. And it mattered even less that he would never respond. The book made her famous. There was lots of fire in it and some wonderful charred ruins."

"And what about you . . . did you stop waiting?"

"Not for a long, long time. I sat, awake, near my window at night and waited and waited. Not for a letter any more but for something else, unnameable. I wrote a lot of poetry and watched winter. I courted desire, alone, by the window. And once it all became mine: all the wanting and waiting and impossible conflagrations and terrifying vast charred ruins, I became quite happy. It was pride of ownership, I suspect."

Emily turned her gauzy back and floated down the valley. She pivoted once and called to Arianna in a hollow, confident voice, "Yes, I was, I was really quite content."

C O N S I D E R A M A N who is trying to write a letter he does not wish to write. Almost any other task will suffice for him at such a time: paying taxes, taking the car in for its twenty-thousand-mile check-up, cleaning out his desk drawers, walking a dog that has not seen a leash for two years, reading books of no interest, developing personal relationships with the intellectually limited students that fill his lecture halls.

But then consider a man who is trying *not* to write a letter that he honestly believes he does not wish to write. This is more difficult because he must spend at least some of his time convincing himself that he really has no wish to write it: a complicated activity that involves thinking about what he would say if he were to write the letter he really does not wish to write. And when he is not composing in this manner it is necessary for him to discover the whereabouts of the object of the composition. For if he does not have all those facts gathered together, postal codes and, probably, air mail rates and the proper stationery, he can never be entirely sure that it is lack of desire that prevents the writing of the letter and not something external, such as lack of the necessary information and/or equipment.

It is not difficult for Arthur Woodruff to obtain Ann's new address. He teaches, after all, at the same university from which she has taken her leave of absence. It takes him two or three weeks, however, to admit that she is no longer on the premises and another two or three weeks to inquire, casually, where she has gone. Once the fact of her journey has been digested, the possibility of the letter becomes more real and his aversion to writing it more pronounced. He really does not want to communicate with her in any way, feels nothing but utter gratitude for her absence. Nevertheless, he finds himself standing in the English Department subtly requesting her address at the end of a conversation involving at least five or six other, unrelated subjects.

After he has written the strange English postal directions in his small address book – in pencil, in case he might feel the urge to erase them – he feels more settled, relaxed. All is as it should be. He knows exactly where she is and therefore he can be more specific about where he does not wish any correspondence of his to be sent. Then he engages himself in a regular flurry of letter-writing. He writes to women he hasn't seen in ten years, to an Eagle Scout he admired as a boy, to his mother's Italian cousins in the Abruzzi, to his now-retired thesis adviser at the distant university, to little-known colleagues all over the world. He writes a few letters to the editors of the three city newspapers concerning pertinent social and environmental issues. He writes to his local member of parliament regarding a proposed change in the zoning by-law in his city neighbourhood. He writes to a Canadian artist whom he does not know, but whose show he has recently seen, to tell him that he thinks his realist paintings are brilliant and moving. He sends each of his three children and his wife affectionate, mildly humorous cards with teddy bears printed on them. Finally, he joins Amnesty International and writes polite, firm letters to various corrupt dictators all over South America.

After a week of this he returns with relief to Tintoretto. His paper on the *Ultima Cena* finished, he allows himself the pleasure of reading and writing about the two cycles of paintings in the Scuola San Rocco: his real loves, the objects of his true desires. Saints and devils and prophets and apostles. Christ in various stages of perpetual agony. Lightning, thunder, gesture, and the complicated folds of vibrant drapery.

And angels. From now until the end of term, he decides, he will spend his time counting and describing angels. He begins with those who figure in *The Brazen Serpent*, the first painting to be completed by Tintoretto in the upper hall of the Scuola. Arthur is delighted by the maelstrom of angels surrounding God the Father in the upper part of this painting. They are urging their deity, encouraging him to pay attention to what is taking place below him. And they themselves are either part of, or playing with one of the most dangerous clouds Tintoretto ever invented – a true thunderhead. This mass of wispy drapery, solid cloud, beating wings, and turmoil could not possibly be a comforting sight on any horizon. There are no fewer than twelve angels fighting for space inside this cumulous formation and Arthur is fond of every one of them, knows their physical characteristics as well as if they had all played on the same football team, shared the same locker rooms. As if he has been involved in skirmishes with them, has tumbled with them over rough earth, has held their muscular bodies close to his in the heat of leaping victory. "The angels in this painting," he writes, "are filled with energy, vitality. They burst down from above in a state of positive turmoil which echoes the more negative chaos that is taking place on the earth below."

There are thirteen baby angels in *The Assumption of the Virgin*, one of the eight paintings that occupy the ground floor of the Scuola, thirteen *putti* forming a nebula, the nucleus of which is the rising Virgin. How wonderfully strange they look . . . like some kind of unidentifiable insect with wings for ears and no thorax or abdomen at all. Their wings, Arthur concludes, would not beat or fan the air like those of their adult cousins; rather they would whir like the wings of hummingbirds. Because of this the whole painting seems to vibrate slightly, as though the Virgin is being helicoptered into space.

While Arthur looks at the small reproductions of the enormous paintings, and turns occasionally to write his thoughts about them on clean white sheets of paper, the Canadian spring is making its muddy statement outside his windows. Banks of snow are leaving behind winter refuse, gutters run, and a robin hops on newly emerged grass. Arthur, lost in crowds of angels, notices none of this, keeps time by his desk calendar, by the knowledge that it takes him five or six days to feel he has satisfied his curiosity about certain sets of angels. By the time he has finished with these and has begun to consider the personalities of the angels that God and Tintoretto have chosen to play starring roles, the ones that make important announcements or take CARE packages to the desert, it is the middle of April. He is no longer lecturing. There is a plane ticket to Italy on his desk.

He is surprised by a mild breeze creeping through a crack under his window while he is gazing into the soft face of the devil-angel in the *Temptation of Christ in the Desert*. There is this fragile moving air, and then the delicate pink that clothes the creature's wings. Almost absently, Arthur reaches for the airmail stationery that has been pushed by angels to the farthest corner of the desk.

On one thin sheet of onionskin he writes:

"I am going to Venice for one week . . . alone." He folds it, unsigned, into the miraculously addressed envelope.

He is certain, as he walks towards the corner, that he will never post the letter.

THE MORNING cat has caught a bird – an English robin deafened by wind and busy with worms in the little rocky garden.

The feline has begun the day early; leaving the stone barn that is his home and meandering slowly through the village, investigating garbage, sitting for a while, placidly in the low sun, sheltered by a drystone wall. He steps carefully around the edge of roadside puddles and walks fastidiously away from the ever-present animal excrement on the streets. He is aware of sleep breaking open to wakefulness in any number of the cottages whose foundations he skirts; still he struts slowly by, uninterested. He freezes once and stares down one of his brothers who is working the opposite side of the street. Both animals bristle briefly, hold the pose and, then, as if by mutual agreement, turn and walk arrogantly away; a contest of power that each of them believes he has won.

When he reaches Ann's cottage he is mildly annoyed to discover no one stirring, the soft cloud of deep morning dreams drifting as surely as an aroma through the outside walls. He leaps up to the ledge of the kitchen window, brushing his fur against the cool glass, looking into the dim, unlit interior. His tail flicks back and forth through an assault of wind. He turns and sees the two bottles of milk on the stoop, left by an even earlier creature: the milkman. The cat's breakfast is being kept from him by glass – glass and sleep.

Hearing self-confident, directed footsteps on the walk, the cat takes no time to look but jumps silently from the sill and hides behind the garbage pail that he knows, from previous morning excursions, to be tightly sealed. As the crunch of gravel grows quiet and quieter and finally fades, the cat walks coolly across the path where he watches with restrained curiosity as the wind picks up a blue envelope that has been left on the stoop and sends it flying towards the little garden where its journey is halted by the bare thin arms of a rose bush. It twitches there like something alive, something the cat might like to play with. His attention is divided, however, for at this exact moment he becomes aware of indoor activity, the creak of casual steps on stairs, and clamorous goings-on in the coal cellar. There will, he knows, be a saucer for him soon, but this struggle of wind, branch, and paper interests him. He begins to amble towards it; the centre part of his body sways slightly. It is then that he spots the preoccupied bird.

What comes bearing down on him after several splendid moments of utter engagement in the pastime of distributing equal doses of fear, hope, and pain to the bird, is a furious woman who is intent on giving him a broom for breakfast. He bounds over the garden wall and runs off onto the moor, domain of field mice. Ann stands, breathing deeply, looking stupidly at the spot on the top of the wall from which the cat has disappeared; the bristles on the bottom of her broom soaking moisture from garden earth, the bird turning heavily at her feet.

She brushes the hair from her eyes and looks down. John calls from the doorway. "Leave it," he says, "it's probably just stunned. It will fly away in a few moments."

She is not so sure of this, but pivots, nevertheless, in soft earth away from the tragedy, the sleeve of her sweater catching on a thorn in the rose bush as she starts to move away. As she unhooks the wool, the letter sails on the wind and is stopped a second time by the dark stone wall. Instantly, she knows what it is and by whose hand it was written. As she returns to the house she hides the envelope in her snagged sleeve.

The next morning the cat will return, as though no acts of violence have been committed, as though nothing whatsoever has changed.

The bird dies a slow and painful death.

"HE WAS YOUR shadow self. He was 'the former of your shadow self.' Part of you was drained by him, practically annihilated, and another part sprang into being, energized and whole. It's as though he gave you order and its chaotic opposite all at the same time. All of this he gave to you. But he needed something white and empty for himself. Do you understand?"

"No, Emily, I wanted pleasure and warmth from him. Surely, eventually, he wanted that too . . . he understood that, I think, when he began to love me again."

"Oh, Arianna, oh, Polly, don't you see? He had only discovered a new approach to whiteness and emptiness."

"But we don't know that, because I died before his new love for me could express itself over time. Such is the irony."

"Such is the actuality . . . the inevitability."

"I shouldn't have died."

"It was, for what you wanted . . . his love . . . inevitable." Emily looked around, all over the soft white moor. "This is storm's aftermath," she said, "storm's legacy. How smooth, eventless, comforting. Sometimes it's enough just to know this quietness, if it's a quietness born of tempest. Then it is like evidence; a letter full of small, unexaggerated words describing a disaster in the passive voice. A letter like a sigh, filled with resignation and reconciliation."

"Every jagged edge is gone," said Arianna. "I can see nothing of the rocks, or stiles, or even blades of grass. And there are no paths at all. Travellers would be lost in this."

"Travellers, yes. But not ghosts. Ghosts always know exactly where they are."

S H E C O M E S T O Venice unencumbered by the details of her journey there, by the interiors of trains and ferries, the expressions of ticket agents, the shaved necks of cab drivers in major cities, the changing railway stations. Unencumbered by the landscapes that stream past windows, the border police stamping her dark Canadian passport. All this she sloughs off as her mind returns like a trained bird to the idea of Arthur, his residence in a city where she knows, at last, she can find him. She is bringing light with her, and air. She is bringing clarity. She will remove the fear from him, remove the dark, heal him as she has been healed. And then he will place his inner self in her uncomplicated hands. She is lit from within by this concept. It is the electricity operating the trains that carry her there. It is the energy.

John, sensing the energy, the unstoppable forward momentum, silently packed a bag for her, and drove her to the station in his old grey van. On the platform he looked hard, for a moment, into her face, and seeing the idea glowing there, he said quietly, sadly, "It suits tha', this gypsying about." Her suitcase hung heavy, like a growth that had suddenly sprouted on the end of his left arm. And for just a moment as he stood before her, Ann saw his suffering. "I will come back . . . I'll be back," she said, not knowing whether or not she spoke the truth, pausing for several seconds in the midst of obsession to place her face against his.

Now, as she enters Venice on the Grand Canal vaporetto, she can barely hear the roar of the churning engines, barely see the night-lit water. The famous architecture parts like an inconsequential curtain, allows her to pass through, to get to Arthur. She remembers a ground-floor room on a highway, herself entering by a sliding glass door, fumbling with the heavy motel curtains in a panic to get to the other side. Here, palaces touch the top of her head, slide past her shoulders while she stands straight, ignoring them. She is propelling herself through the exotic night towards Arthur, while everything around her repeats itself in swaying inky water; this inappropriate distracting outer life, these buildings with other histories, people with other appointments to keep. She is not on a boat, she *is* a boat – clear sailing, number four on the wind scale, the admiral relaxed on deck enjoying the breeze, land sighted just minutes ago through his telescope.

In the small hotel room Ann does not sleep, still feels herself moving towards Arthur, the wind pushing her across a liquid surface. She *must* not rest, even after she finds him, must gather him up in the arms of this breeze and take him with her into clarity, into a new morning as spiritually nourishing as white bread and communion wine. One sweeping, graceful gesture will lift him up with her into this clear river of air.

She sails through the dark hours, past the unvisited islands of the rest of her life. She is breathing the air that fills her lungs and stretches her sails. She begins to construct the beautifully simple life she will give him, the order of appropriately filled daylight hours and nights rich with rest. She hears their two sleeping hearts drum uncomplicated messages into the air of some future room.

Outside the hotel, the city reeks with assignations. Plans are being made or carried out, strangers occupy café tables, dogs lick spilt ice cream in the corners of campos and the seams of calles, waiters bend and scurry. She knows none of this and cares even less, is conscious only of her voyage to Arthur and the form it is taking, this easy, joyful drift. She considers, as her eyes stare wide and dry into the dark, Emily Brontë's sleepless nights, her poems concerning "the visitant of air," "the wanderer." Who was he? Who was he? Who held the nineteenth-century, housebound girl transfixed, entranced? Who created the ghost, the weather in her?

The weather in Ann is calm all night long: untroubled, unchanging. The ship she has become is like a vast open sky sailing across the night looking for the perfect spot over which to settle, the perfect man. She can barely remember what Arthur looks like, how his face changed during the act of love, but can recall his hesitant hands, how rarely he used them. And his beautiful mouth, speaking.

When she walks out into the first light of dawn she is startled in the midst of her own transparency to find fog, and everything she disregarded the previous evening veiled, secretive. Across the Grand Canal one decaying palace is displaying all its chandeliers; boasting of an all-night dinner party. She is transformed by purpose. Turning a map in her hands she follows the maze of canals and calles that leads to the Scuola San Rocco, passing cats absorbed by garbage and the odd dog-walking dawn person. Occasionally, her own fixed concentration is interrupted by the staccato sound of early merchants flinging up the metal curtains that protect their shops.

It is a long way from the hotel to the Scuola San Rocco and there is much of which Ann is not aware as she walks. She is unaware that she has caught the attention of an elderly lady who watches her pass from an upper-storey window; that as she steps over a bridge a soccer ball lost elsewhere in the city floats beneath her, heading east, its destination the Adriatic; that in one dim, watery garage three empty, floating hearses nudge and scrape each other. She is unaware that the morning mist has invaded her hair, is causing it to curl in peculiar directions; that from the back of a dimly lit, as yet unopened café, a mopping *padrone* has eyed her lustfully and has whispered the word "*Americana*" under his breath. She is unaware that certain indi-

viduals who visit Venice often are pushing open hotel-room
shutters and saying to themselves, "Ah, . . . a misty day
. . . this is when it is best. . . . "

For Ann there cannot be any best or better, locked as she
is in the perpetual present of her own emotional landscape,
and the path through it to Arthur. It is as though she were
bringing with her all varieties of event and weather into a
city that has held itself alert and frozen until her entry and
her search.

Her inner voice is conversing with him. *I'm coming*, it
says, *I will find you. It will be pure now. A clean wind is moving
me.*

Something colder than her imagined wind blows across
the surface of a canal. She keeps walking.

Every morning for three weeks she repeats this journey, her
mind never once losing the focus of her intention: to find
him in the correct setting and then to place herself beside
him in its light. And still she registers no details of the
approach. Only her legs remember and guide her, with
confidence earned by repetition, up steps, across campos,
around corners.

Every day, inside the Scuola, she is handed a mirror by a
man whose name, she has learned, is Carlo. "For looking
at the ceiling," he explained, that first morning.

Now she knows how to operate the mirror; how, depending on where you stand and at what angle you tilt the frame,
the glass will allow you to concentrate on details or to hold
the whole ceiling in your hands. When she swings it back
and forth, like the flat top of an adjustable drafting table,
she is able to move angels, devils, storms, rapidly towards
her, or fling these same entities hastily away.

Carlo, who greets her cheerfully each day (*"Giorno Sig-
norina"*), stands discreetly in the corner of the vast upper

room, the buttons of his guard's uniform glowing on his round belly, while Ann engages in hours of this activity. Not knowing that her absorption is merely the cover for another form of absorption, he is amazed by her concentration.

"Maybe you are a scholar . . . ?" he asked some time after the first week.

"Oh, no . . . not at all," she replied.

After the second week he walked up to her and announced confidently, "Now I see you are a sister, a nun, who is studying the Old Testament prophets and wearing, as they do now, no habit. I am correct . . . yes?"

Ann surprised herself by laughing loud enough at this remark to make the empty room ring like a bell. Carlo retreated, puzzled, to his corner.

Now, at the end of the third week, Carlo is friendly enough to speak to her constantly of Signore Tintoretto. While she gazes into the height of the mirror he abruptly leaves this topic, makes a pronouncement that causes her to look directly into his dark eyes.

"You are looking for something else altogether, then. This is what I now know is true."

"Yes," answers Ann, unaware that her mirror, relinquishing its hold on the ceiling, has caught a sun ray and is sending fiery signals to each of the four walls.

"I am not a wise man," says Carlo thoughtfully, "but it seems to me that if you cannot find it here you should put the mirror aside and examine, for a while, the paintings on the walls of the ground floor hall. Perhaps, whatever it is, you will find it there."

Ann smiles at him, but tightens her grasp on the mirror. As he returns to his corner, sighing, she looks into her own obsessed eyes. She examines her face and head and hair and all the painted wings of angels that seem to extend from her curls. She walks around the room one last time, moving her face across miracles and tragedies, across brutalities and acts of unspeakable kindness. Then she hands the mirror to Carlo and prepares to leave the room.

She meets Arthur on the stairs.

"I have never seen so many angels," she eventually says to him, "they're all there . . . the Rockettes . . . all the ones you told me about."

Arthur stands, one foot poised on marble, silent.

"But now I'm finished up there . . . " Ann continues, "I've given the mirror back to Carlo. Do you know Carlo? He has a grandson in Toronto."

Still he does not speak.

"I've been looking at the miracles . . . for days and days now. They seem . . . I don't know . . . different, not what I thought they would be . . . darker. Somehow I never associated darkness with miracles, and you didn't say anything about the darkness. The miracles up there are like storms . . . the manna . . . you know, the manna, it really is like a bad hailstorm. How can this be?"

"I don't know, Ann," Arthur says quietly.

"And it's true about the lightning . . . absolutely everything is struck . . . you described that perfectly."

They haven't moved one inch on the stairs. Ann feels perspiration forming along her hairline. She does not look at him; looks at the patterns in the different colours of marble instead. She runs one hand along the cool stone wainscoting and leans her forehead against the damp wall.

"I came here for you," she whispers, and the clarity begins to disappear down the deep well of his silence. "I caught the train because of your letter. I knew I would find you here." The marble pattern against which she has rested her face is out of focus, foggy.

Arthur says, "I know," and nothing else. Ann can hear Carlo pacing back and forth on the upper-floor parquet, waiting out another afternoon, imprisoned by Signore Tintoretto. She wishes that he would walk over to the edge of the staircase, is certain that unless he does, she and Arthur will never be able to break their pose: a man arrested forever in the act of ascending a magnificent marble staircase, a woman with her face pressed against a marble wall.

There are centuries contained within this moment.

Then Arthur says, "Would you like to go now, Ann?"

On their way through the ground-floor hall they pass by Annunciations, Adorations, and Assumptions without pausing to admire. Arthur stops, however, for a moment in front of each of two painted female saints. "I never spoke to you about these," he says to Ann, "I knew you would have to see them." Both women hold books and are seated in tempestuous landscapes. "There is an Emily Brontë for you, two in fact. Solitary women of words."

He doesn't speak again until they reach his room.

ONCE SHE IS indisputably in his company, Ann is unperturbed by Arthur's quietness. She is clear, again – full of what she feels is love for him. She will break his silence. She is certain of this. The city clicks into life around her now that she is with him, delights her. "Look," she says to him, "look, look!," pointing out details, showing off her splendid eye as if she, not he, were the expert. She brings large bottles of cheap red Italian wine back to his room, day after day, hoping to open him, to release words. "We are here," she tells him in an orgy of speech to which he is barely responding, "we have a setting. Look out the window, see what we will have to remember."

"We already," he replies bitterly, "have more than enough to remember."

She beats back the pain statements such as this cause, drowns it in a sea of red wine as she talks and talks. She tells him of the letters that she wrote to him and didn't mail, how mentally she called to him and called to him, knowing, just knowing, that eventually he would reply.

"And you did," she says, smiling at his blank face, "didn't you?

"It isn't that I can't live without you," she says, "it's just that I love you so much I don't want to live without you. I should have known this in Toronto. I would go home after we met and it would be as if I hadn't gone home at all, as if we were still together, which is funny because at the same time I would feel so abandoned. Nevertheless, you *were* there with me, weren't you? You must have been because otherwise how could I have thought of you so constantly? And I never stopped, you know, even in Stanbury. Sometimes, there I thought I *had* stopped, but then you'd walk into a dream I was having, and it was just as if you'd touched my shoulder to remind me, as if you didn't want me to forget you. *Were* you trying to remind me?"

"No . . . Ann."

She pours herself more wine. "Well, then," she says, after a long swallow, "I must have been trying to remind myself, because of the truth of this. You see what I mean; the truth is unkillable. I tried, yes, I did try to kill it, but that was foolish, almost wicked of me. What I should have done was try to show it to you instead." She begins to pace up and down the hotel room's patterned rug. "I was afraid you'd reject me, but then I realized that didn't matter. What mattered was that I would never reject you. I remember every single shirt you ever wore when you were with me. When I got home, I mean back to my apartment, I would imagine those shirts hanging in my closet."

"Ann, you knew that wasn't . . . "

"Oh, no." She pulls aside the curtain and looks out to a canal bubbling under forceful rain. "No . . . that's not what I meant, not that. Just the shirts. I suppose I wanted a museum of you. Just those shirts . . . not any others. I didn't want any part of you that didn't concern me. But I wanted more of you to concern me. For instance, now the way you sleep concerns me . . . it didn't then. I didn't know that you cross your arms when you sleep and you look stern . . . like a genie. Yes . . . that's how you look, like Aladdin's genie; proud and slightly disdainful. As if you knew that any and all of the wishes that you might be about to grant were really trivial, inconsequential. As if there couldn't really be a wish worthy of the enormous power you have to make it come true."

Arthur smiles ruefully.

"But I know you're really not like that. You're not really disdainful. You *have* considered my wishes and you granted one of them . . . at least one of them. You wrote to me. Why did you write to me, Arthur?"

"I don't know."

"That's all right . . . that's fine . . . because I do know. And soon . . . I feel it, you'll know too. You already do know, you just haven't admitted it to me, to yourself."

"I'm not in love with you."

"I might have let that hurt me," says Ann, thoughtfully, "but my heart is so perfectly mended by us being here together that even that can't hurt me. You've let me sit close to you, sleep in the same bed . . . I've, I've seen your angels. You let me talk to you. And it's such a pleasure . . . such a relief, to be able to talk to you like this. And think of what we've seen here in this city. Absolutely everything we've seen together is a part of you that concerns me. All of it, all of it will go into that museum of you. Do you know how wonderful this is? All this walking we've done, all those paintings, every forkful of food we've eaten together, this wine – " Ann pours herself another glass. "The label of this wine will go into the museum. I don't mean I'll really save the label or anything like that, but I will never ever forget it."

Arthur closes his eyes and leans his head back against the tall, overstuffed chair in which he has been sitting. He rubs his forehead as if trying to massage away a headache. But he has no headache. He is exhausted, stupefied by Ann's talk. He has no answer for her. His notes on the Scuola San Rocco lie interrupted, abandoned on the table in this room. When he closes his eyes he sees the drapery of angels, but he has nothing to say about this. During the past three days he has moved from the bed into this river of talk and back to love-making again, over and over. He is surprised, when he opens his eyes, to see that the streetlights outside the window Ann stands near are illuminated. Time is beginning to evaporate, to dissolve, in a thick river of words.

"Sometimes I thought I had forgotten what you looked like," Ann is saying, "but then, quite suddenly, your face would flash into my mind, as clear as if you were standing right in front of me. I know it sounds mad but it was at those moments that I knew we would never be apart . . .

not really apart because I would never stop thinking about you." Ann kicks off her shoes and throws her legs over the arm of the chair into which she has suddenly collapsed. "I wasn't always happy about this. I admit. I wasn't always pleased that you had become the only thing I could think about. I wanted to stop; that's why I went away. I tried many, many things to get myself to stop."

"You should stop."

"But no, I don't think so now. I think I should be thinking of you. Look at the way we make love. Look at the way we walk together."

This time, when Arthur closes his eyes, he sees singed feathers; as if his angels were burning up, burning away. "I should work . . . " he whispers.

"Yes, yes, . . . I want you to work. I want to watch you work and then that will be a part of you that concerns me."

"It's late and I . . . "

"Don't you see, if you work it will be all right because I love your work. I love everything you say about Tintoretto . . . I love Tintoretto. Because of you I was able to stand in Emily Brontë's landscape and think about Tintoretto. His lightning was there! Think of that! It's like a miracle . . . he, Tintoretto, would have appreciated that, might even have painted it somehow. And you, you . . . did you ever think of Emily Brontë being transposed into the landscape of Venice?"

"No."

"Well, think about it now, think of how miraculous that is. Because of our . . . connection we can move forces as powerful as theirs from landscape to landscape. They were both, after all, deeply concerned with weather. Tintoretto would have loved the moors . . . all that wind and everything moving . . . the ideal setting for angels and miracles." For a moment as she says this, John's face leaps in her memory: his face and his warmth. The words *he has torn you* echo.

"You never really meant to hurt me, did you?" she asks.

"No."

"I know that now . . . and because I know it . . . you'll never hurt me again."

They crawl, shaky, exhausted, into bed at the beginning of a grey, weak dawn. Ann has begun to weep, her talk de-escalating into a choked whisper. "I'm not unhappy," she sobs, her voice becoming less and less audible. "There are all these miracles around us."

Outside, the rain has stopped. The canal has become an aluminum-grey replica of the sky, dotted here and there with floating objects that pass slowly under the nearest bridge. One of these is a dead bird which, during the night, has been taken on a complicated tour of the city. Positioned with its wings outstretched on the opaque, featureless surface, it appears to be coasting calmly through air on a benign wind. But this is neither flight nor freedom, and when the small boat with the wire basket cleans the canal in an hour or so the bird will enter a steel bin with all the other garbage.

"I'm not unhappy," Ann says to her pillow, "because of this wonderful chain of miracles."

Arthur has turned his face to the wall, has fallen down a well of sleep so deep not a single detail of his angels appears in his black dreams.

"EMILY, I AM getting very tired, and you don't seem as clear to me as you used to." Arianna looked earnestly at her friend. "Is it possible that we have talked ourselves silent?"

Sh-h-h . . . sh-h-h, whispered the wind.

They had discussed everything, each nuance of their lifetime of emotion, all the frivolous details of taste: favourite jams, best hymns, secret pleasures, most becoming colours, hair styles, fashions, methods of building fires, the making of watercolours, music, sewing machines, pony traps, embroidered cushions. Emily had spent several weeks describing a wooden tray she had painted with elaborate birds, and had later pitched into a fire. They had haunted every inch of this particular moor, making significant appearances near standing stones for the benefit of unsuspecting solitary travellers. This activity was allowed, now, by Emily, to prove that she was not narrow-minded about humanity, she merely preferred to inhabit unpopulated wastes. Branwell had fallen in once or twice, temporarily expelled for forms of behaviour he had no desire to explain. He had amused Arianna with descriptions of Emily's behaviour as a child, had quarrelled constantly with his sister, and was conveniently called back to his celestial abode just as he was beginning to sigh melodramatically and make sheep's eyes at the ghost of the balloonist.

"How awful he is!" Emily would announce after his re-ascension. "How awful he is! How wonderful!"

Now, nearly a century after Arianna's arrival, they leaned, rather anemically, against the broken walls of the farmhouse called Top Withins while Emily quietly cursed the Power Authority for turning her favourite glens into reservoirs.

"You knew they were there," Arianna argued, "they were there when I fell in. They've been here as long as I have, longer in fact. I told you. I glimpsed myself for the last time in one of them."

Emily paid no attention. "Imagine," she grumbled, "calling yourself the Power Authority, combining those two words into one name. It's worse than Mr. Capital H!"

It was then that Arianna complained of feeling weak. "We never leap up into the air like we used to," she said, "and we don't make time go backwards any more. We just don't seem to have the strength to control it. Why don't you make the reservoirs disappear, Emily? You'd feel a lot better. Let's go back to the day of your funeral, or even Charlotte's funeral. Everything was much more picturesque."

"I suppose we should," said Emily listlessly. Both ghosts made an effort to concentrate. The waters of Ponden Reservoir began to shrink. Workmen appeared, carefully lifting one stone at a time and carrying them to waiting wagons. These were pushed by draught horses who stepped gingerly backwards towards the Peniston quarry. And then, when the walls were almost dismantled, both ghosts collapsed. The reservoirs filled with water and behind their backs Top Withins fell into ruin.

"It looks," sighed Emily, "as if for some reason or other, we can no longer transcend time. We're attached to it again. What can this mean?"

"I think it means that you should tell me what happened to me. I think it means we are not going to be together too much longer. You should tell me, Emily, before it's too late."

"You fell out of a balloon."

"Why?"

"How should I know? What makes you so certain that I know?"

"You know everything."

"Why should I have to be the one to tell you?"

"You tell me everything."

"Maybe Branwell will be expelled again. He can tell you."

"I don't think he knows. Besides, the last time he was here he spoke only in Latin . . . and I couldn't understand him . . . or you. The two of you making classical jokes at my expense. Anyway, we haven't seen him for a long, long time."

Time . . . time, barked the wind.

Emily looked up toward heaven. "You don't suppose he's reformed?"

"Perhaps."

"If that's the case, then all is scattered and everything will just fall away." Emily eyed Arianna closely. "Do you still want to haunt Jeremy?"

"I'm not certain . . . " said Arianna slowly, "but, you know, I really don't think that I do. Now I just want to know."

The wind ripped three or four clouds in half and broken light scattered itself over the hills.

"That kind of light looks like falling angels," said Emily sadly. "It's odd, but there's very little about that kind of sunlight that resembles ghosts."

Arianna looked for comfort at several stone outcroppings, some close, some far away. These never changed regardless of the games the spirits had played with time. "Emily," she eventually said in a soft, hollow voice, "do ghosts ever just . . . stop?"

Emily did not reply, because as the wind gathered the sunlight up in its arms and sealed it again behind the clouds, both women became aware of the answer to the question.

ARTHUR TELLS her that she cannot come with him when he makes his daily journey to the Scuola. She has not stopped talking. Each sentence of his is transformed by her into several paragraphs.

"It's not that I have to be with you all the time everywhere," she says, "but I have to be with you all the time here. Anywhere else it's all right, my not being with you because, in a way, I really *am* with you all the time in my mind. But here, I want to see everything the way you see it. Even before I found you I saw some of the angels the way you would see them. I know I did because I would be looking and looking in the mirror at some of the angels, at the light of their faces and suddenly I would have this flash and I would know that this one or that one was a particular angel of yours because of the way it suddenly moved me. I must be with you while I am in this city. That's why I came here. That's why you wanted me to come here, why you wrote the letter."

He walks quickly through the streets to lose her voice in the crowds but she follows him doggedly. He is pale, drained, weak . . . filled alternately with fear and compassion. He desperately wants her to stop, her dark love, her talk. But she does not stop and he is mesmerized by her obsession, half believes that it carried across the ocean, forced him to write and mail that one unwise sentence. The beginning of the epic she is speaking now.

"If I could paint the way I feel about you," she says, "it would be all explosions of light and bright: pure lightning and wind . . . but clear. Summer sheet lightning and Arctic winds in a clear sky. Everything moving and pulsing and orbiting and just being! Shimmering! It's the wind, you know, that makes things shimmer; leaves, ponds . . . look, the canal is shimmering. The sun makes things shine, glare, but it needs wind to create a shimmer. When you touch me I swear I start to shimmer. I can't help it. I know you have the rest of your life. I know this. But think what you are to me. I can hardly sleep at all because I am so alive with you, so awake. And it doesn't matter that I don't sleep. It hasn't affected me at all because of the energy I feel in your presence."

Arthur looks at her drawn face and trembling hands and silently disagrees. He does not know what to do, vows to expel her, then inexplicably finds himself burying his face in her hair. Later, he is flung into a devastating sea of guilt and remorse. Please stop, Ann, he says silently, please, please leave me. If she would only stop talking he might be able to explain himself to her, to himself. Last night she fell asleep in the middle of a sentence and awakened two hours later, at dawn, picking the thread of words up exactly where she had unwillingly dropped it.

He has tried to move the ship of conversation into other ports. How, he asks, is her work going, her book? She tells him that the book, she now knows, is not really about weather as such, it is really about him, about her response to him, which, she says, is just like the emotional weather of *Wuthering Heights*. Without him, she explains, she never would have understood this the way she does now. And perhaps, she suggests, without her he would never have been able, really able, to understand Tintoretto.

A part of him wonders if this last statement might not be true. Then his daily self shouts out in panic, for God's sake don't listen! Make her stop!

On the steps of Scuola he pleads with her. "Please, Ann," he says, "I must look at the ceilings alone." To his surprise he feels his eyes filling with tears. "Please . . . I have to take some notes."

"I have wonderful ideas for your notes . . . you could do a whole section on scribes. What kind of notes were they taking, I wonder? Probably ones very similar to yours. There is something of the Old Testament prophet *and* something of the New Testament Evangelist in you, you know."

"*Please* Ann," he whispers chokingly, "let me go up there alone."

Ann is startled by this first suggestion of emotion in his voice. "Alone . . . ?" she echoes. They walk through the entrance together but on the ground floor she finally stops following, talking, and he ascends the staircase by himself.

She stands stunned, arrested in mid-sail, in front of the two paintings that Arthur pointed out the day she found him. The two female saints are remarkably calm in the centre of storm-torn landscapes, their bodies perched on the edges of shimmering streams. While palm fronds rake the air above them, their minds occupy the serene country of aftermath. Whatever it was they were meant to learn from experience has been taught, reflected upon, and allowed to drift away. Everything they are now, emotionally, is contained in the landscape in which they sit. The past is somewhere else, beyond the borders of the gold frame that holds them. Ann sees this and almost understands its possibilities. Then, she turns and the opposite wall reveals an aggressive angel hurling himself through a brick wall in order to bring impossible news to a startled Virgin Mary. A thunderstorm of *putti* and the Holy Ghost complete this invasion.

Suddenly Ann is very tired. She slumps onto a wooden bench where she sits for several hours staring at the two lone, contemplative women. Once in a while she closes her eyes and places the back of her head against the wall. Behind her an angel is frozen forever in the act of delivering a brutal message. In front of her two silent women occupy the eventless regions where no more stupendous announcements are necessary.

Walking back to the room Ann resumes her monologue. She is speaking about the wind, but now even Arthur knows that his name could just as well be substituted for every noun she articulates.

"Isn't it funny," she says, "how, because this city is all palaces and churches and museums and restaurants and hotels and shops and water and piazzas and bridges, how nothing bends in the wind here. Everything that can move at all does so awkwardly. It flaps," she points to a café awning, "or, when the wind gets strong enough, it crashes and smashes. If the wind got strong enough those tables would tumble around in it and those glasses would smash. There are no trees or grasses, you see, that's why nothing bends. The wind has to get really strong and then it would have to do damage before it would be felt at all."

For a second or two the memory of the glass dome on the side of the highway makes itself felt in her mind, but she shakes it away in favour of the present.

"You've taught me all about this," she says, "all about varying degrees. You must see how I am responding, and responding always differently, sometimes more than others but never with neutrality. But I suppose neutrality would be a lack of response, and that could never happen to me, not only while you are with me but while you are in the world. No, that's not quite true, I almost stopped responding while you were upstairs in the Scuola, maybe because of those two saints I was looking at. They seemed so, some-how . . . well . . . neutral. But the minute I saw you, when you came down the stairs, everything in me burst open again. If we had never been together I might have lived my whole life closed. And you, would you have lived your life closed if you had never been with me?"

"I don't know. Ann . . . I think not . . . how can I know?" Arthur is awash with longing for his daily life; the sound of the television in the next room, his wife's voice, a child stumbling through a piano exercise, car repairs, a Canadian newspaper, the untidy region of his academic office. "You can't live your whole life," he says, "with your nervous system exposed to the air."

"Yes, you *can*," she says, while he fumbles with the key at his hotel room door, "you can, you must. That is why we found each other, that is our purpose, to open each other. You've done that for me, and I know it's only a matter of time until I will do it for you."

"Please stop, Ann," Arthur's inner voice whispers, begs.

As they make love he has the impression that he is disappearing, each wave of pleasure peeling off another layer of his personality, his intellect, until he is raw, shuddering flesh, flayed alive, burnt, howling in agony as he comes. The word *stop* is all that is left of his vocabulary, while she repeats her tragic litany whimpering beneath him. "You see how it is?" she says over and over. "This, *this* is how it is."

He collapses into sleep and wakes again to find her staring into his face. "This time," she says, "while I watched you sleep, I was almost able to see your dreams."

"I wasn't dreaming," he says coldly. And then he flings himself away from the bed, away from her, stands naked in the fading afternoon light, and hisses, a cornered animal, "Don't you understand . . . I don't want you to see my dreams."

"I don't believe that because, otherwise . . . "

"No, no . . . believe it. I don't want that. Who do you think you are looking into me, scrutinizing me like this. God damn you!" he shouts, his voice rusty from days of inactivity, "looking into me like that. You fool! There's nothing there to look into!"

"Yes, yes, there is," Ann says, her heart cartwheeling in panic. "There's all this activity, this emotion . . . I've glimpsed it. I've seen your face, I've seen . . . "

"You've seen nothing." Arthur reaches for a full package of cigarettes and rips it open angrily. "I want you to stop! Whatever this web is that we're trapped in, you wove it!

God, Ann, why don't you look at me, just once, why don't you really look at me?"

"But I do, and I see everything alive and moving and vital."

"No, you *don't*! Or maybe you do. But you don't see me, Ann, you see yourself!"

She has begun to weep, has covered her eyes with her hands. "Without you I was vague, nothing. You awakened me and then I saw what you were and I fell in love with you."

"For God's sake, Ann, stop it! Look at me!" Abruptly he sinks into a chair and turns his back on her. Then, just as abruptly he rises and crosses the room. "Look at my hands, Ann," he says, thrusting them near the vicinity of her covered face. "We've been together all this time and you've never looked at my hands."

"You're not being brutally honest," she sobs, "you're just being brutal."

"Look . . . at . . . my . . . hands!"

"Oh . . . " she says, gazing at smooth, seamless skin. She has never seen flesh like this. Poreless, tight, stretched across bone and muscle, it appears completely unvisited by experience, instead of what it really is: the product of an experience from which it can never recover.

"Doesn't that tell you something?" Arthur asks. "It should tell you everything." Sitting on the edge of the bed he turns away from her. "I'm not what you think," Arthur's voice is practically inaudible, "and I never will be. I'm not desperate or passionate. We tumbled into each other, that's all. I'm fixed, Ann, stationary. Nothing like this should have ever happened to me. I'm just trying to live for the rest of my life."

"Your hands," she whispers, awe-struck, "is there pain?"

"No . . . not now. Now there's just nothing."

"Nothing?" Ann repeats. "How can there be nothing?"

Arthur does not immediately answer, carries his hands in front of him to the other side of the room. Then he speaks.

"I wanted to touch you, to love you in that way, but I can't just stop living the rest of my life. I'm terrified that my life will collapse around me and then I will feel nothing."

"But I feel everything."

"I know."

Ann looks at Arthur and sees his averted face, his spine curved like a scythe near a table filled with sad, neglected papers. She remembers the beast that prowled through her illness, how it was both male and female – the fused lovers – what she wanted to become, what she has been trying to draw Arthur into. It wasn't that she wanted *him* so much as that she wanted him to become her. That was how she was trying to tempt him. Like that other androgynous beast, the beautiful devil/angel in Tintoretto's wilderness, she held fragrant loaves in her outstretched hands, but they contained annihilation for him. She wanted him to feel only what she felt. A rush of moorland wind – the weather – and all the real details swept away.

"I am only an interpreter," he is saying. "I can't live this. I can't make the paintings. I can only interpret them."

"But I'm an interpreter too. I've always been apart . . . living my life through books. In that way we are alike." Ann would like to touch him again, to make this last tentative connection. "Neither one of us," she says, "has anything to do with real life."

But Arthur won't accept this either. "No," he says, "the difference is that you *want* to live the fiction or the life or whatever and I . . . I simply don't. You said it . . . you said you feel everything."

"Do you think I really meant that?"

"Oh . . . yes."

During the long night, while Arthur sleeps, Ann sits near the window at the little wooden table, one small light washing over all his scattered notes. As the hours advance, the air calms and clears and she, glancing at the unconscious man, is at last able to see his fragility and his imperfection. His age. The obsession is breaking, is falling away. She hears Arthur's breath, helpless, lost in the rhythms of sleep, while the night hours fill the space that has always existed between the man that he is and the woman that she is. The space that she has refused to acknowledge. The space that Arthur has had to cross each time they met.

Ann thinks of how Catherine described her adolescent dream in *Wuthering Heights*; how she knew that heaven was not her home. Ann can practically see this dream, in which angry angels toss a young girl out of the clouds and down onto the unreclaimed moor, as if her body were weather itself. Catherine asleep, her mind falling through air, the angels receding. And then the crash, the awakening. The real, the painful joy.

All through the night Ann falls, falls to earth, just as if certain angels had taken it upon themselves to toss her out of an inappropriate heaven. Everything she sees is draining downwards; the dim furniture, roses on the wallpaper, curtains, bedclothes. She can actually feel her own body gain texture, substance; the miracle of gravity guiding her towards solidity and weight. The city beneath her is rumoured to be sinking as well. She imagines it shifting and settling under her newly acquired weight. How the real earth holds, embraces, reclaims these built things; Tintoretto's painted tantrums or her own frail palace of romance. The man she built and now this breathing form. This life.

Every now and then Ann lifts her right arm up from the table and then lets it collapse with a satisfying thud onto the wooden surface, and, as she does this, she marvels at the construction of her own hand and the complicated grain on this one piece of ordinary furniture.

By dawn Ann has completed her descent, has fallen back into the world. She watches as the grey light turns to gold, fills with wind, parts the white curtains and dances towards her on a rug whose patterns she has never seen until this moment. She pictures herself an Elizabeth, a Magdalene, alone, surrounded by vital light and tumultuous weather – a still figure in a frantic landscape. She can keep it all: the idea of this man, this city, the ancient moor wind – even the currents of the highway with its clouds of fumes and thunderous noise, keep everything in the manner of painted saints, with patience, near trembling streams under glistening trees. The difficult love. The troubled awakening weather.

Before she leaves the room Ann goes to Arthur and reaches for his arm. "Sandy," he whispers, without opening his eyes.

"Who is Sandy? . . . your wife? . . . your little girl?" Ann tentatively approaches, now, the facts of his real life.

"My dog," he says, stirring. "You didn't even know I had a dog."

"No," says Ann, "I didn't even know you had a dog."

Without turning to look at her, he moves one hand to her wrist. "I told you I'm not in love with you," he says.

"Yes, you told me."

He is silent and still turned away from her. She places his hand on the pillow and lifts her own from his naked shoulder.

"PARRY LOVED the northern latitudes. He made certain that he spent a lot of time in them. No grand tourist he! He wanted to *live* in the countries he visited. There were two words in my father's book of Arctic anecdotes that described him perfectly. The sentence reads, 'Parry was the first explorer to winter deliberately in the high Arctic.' You see, he was a deliberate winterer. What a wonderful verb! To winter. That is what Parry liked to do most of all, he liked to winter. So first he lived in Halifax, Canada. But that wasn't wintery enough for him. So then he accompanied the whalers to Spitzbergen. Now there's a spot! After that he deliberately wintered in the high Arctic. I suspect he loved that! Oh . . . and he attempted to reach the North Pole by sledge over the pack ice from Spitzbergen. He was a winterer."

Emily was lecturing Arianna about the life of Sir Edward Parry. But she was not standing up and raising her clenched fist as she normally did when pontificating on this particular subject; rather she was quietly relating the information, as if teaching prayers to a child.

"Ross was different . . . a fool and a coward. He didn't enjoy wintering at all, I expect. He was a negationist. Nothing went anywhere as far as he was concerned. There was no Northwest Passage. There was no North Pole. There was no hope. There was no dream."

"I wish you'd tell me, Emily," Arianna insisted. "Why don't you just tell me?"

"So Parry said to Ross, 'Go your own way, then, and I'll be the Arctic explorer for both of us!' Oh, crime can make the heart grow old, sooner than years of wearing woe; can turn the warmest bosom cold, as winter wind or polar snow."

"Parry said that?"

"No . . . I said that."

"Please tell me. How did I die, Emily?"

"I wonder whether Parry is an angel or a ghost? Perhaps he began as one and ended up as the other. Did I tell you about his kingdom? The one I made for him when I was a child?"

Arianna was silent.

"I probably did, but I'll tell you again. It was white, well ordered, sparse, and, of course, cold. Ice palaces everywhere. And statues . . . clear blue, like glass. It is odd, but I seem to remember only my imagination now. I wonder, do I still have one? Perhaps I have become my imagination. I can see those statues perfectly, and the little snow paths around them, but I can't recall Anne's face. Poor Anne . . . what colour were her eyes?"

"You said they were blue. Emily . . . you do remember what happened to me, don't you?"

"Yes. And Charlotte's eyes? Did I mention them?"

"How do you know? Were you there? Were you out here watching?"

Emily was quiet for several seconds. Then she spoke. "I remember seeing your white balloon. And for some reason I remember haunting your hotel room. Why did I do that I wonder? That wasn't like me at all. Then I drifted around the village for a while the next morning, through the graveyard and into the house for a bit. Oh, yes . . . I was collecting views. You know what I mean. This was to be my last haunt, I meant to give it up completely. There's something cowardly about haunting, you know, trailing listlessly about, all unapproachable, and then vanishing at the least provocation. And besides, only certain gifted individuals can see you, even when you've materialized."

"Did anyone see you?"

"No . . . though I thought you did once . . . in the middle of the night. You spent a lot of time looking out the window. Wynken, Blynken, and Nod."

"Were you collecting views of me?"

"Good heavens, no . . . I hadn't you in mind at all . . . not at first, anyway. I just happened to see you and then I became a bit, well, curious I suppose. I was collecting views. I had this terror of forgetting them. Now it appears that I've forgotten everything . . . even the terror. At least I've forgotten what the terror felt like. But I'm glad I collected the views because I still remember them . . . a good thing, since it appears that we can no longer transcend time and everything has changed. The graveyard has trees full of rooks now. And the little lane that opens to the moor . . . trees line it as well. And then those reservoirs. The church burned, you know. Charlotte would have loved that! She became part of the Great Everything, I imagine, probably almost instantly. I haunted *him*, your Mr. Perfect Profile."

"Oh . . . did he see you?"

"Of course not . . . he was far too busy with his plans!"

"What plans?"

"*His* plans. Who else's? The only reason I paid any attention was because of the polar maps. I thought, foolishly, for a few moments, that we might be kindred spirits because of the maps. But his tundra and mine were placed in different regions. It was just by chance that I saw what he was thinking. The only reason that I was in the room at all was because of the view of the Black Bull that could be had from there. That and John Greenwood's stationery shop. I rather hoped that if I transcended time I could catch a glimpse of Branwell through the windows of the Black Bull, from the windows of the Olde White Lion. I had never been inside a public house and the fact that I was now a ghost did not alter my views of what was and what was not proper. Still, I was always curious about how he behaved in there. I did see him, too tipped back on his chair, holding forth on some subject before an audience of stupefied idiots . . . waving his arms around and toasting the air. Outrageous! Unthinkable! How wonderful he was! The stationery store I loved, because of paper, ink, pens . . . "

"Was I there?"

"In the Black Bull? I should hope not."

"In Jeremy's room . . . was I in his room?"

"No . . . you were in your room. He was alone . . . alone and making plans. Now I vaguely remember. I was standing by the window watching Branwell. You should have seen him, Branwell, that is. His mouth was open all the time. He was shouting and laughing and pouring tankards of ale down his throat. Once he lunged at a passing barmaid, he who was, at the time, supposed to be dying of love! What a farce that was! And behind me, in another time, Mr. Perfect Profile brooding boringly over polar maps. I was standing by the window experiencing all of the emotions that I always did when I looked at Branwell's bad behaviour: joy, sorrow, anger, hilarity, love, covetousness, envy. Then, suddenly, right behind my back, I felt the brooding stop, a kind of clarity was in the air so I turned to look at the brooder and I saw that his face was full of light . . . a look of real joy. And whether I wanted to or not, I could see his plans."

"He was planning to love me again," said Arianna, "wasn't he?"

"Yes," said Emily, uncertainly. "Yes . . . he was, but . . ."

"He was planning," Arianna continued, "to marry me. I know it now, that was what he was planning. It makes me so happy to know this, Emily, thank you for telling me."

"That was certainly *not* what he was planning. I didn't tell you that!"

Arianna floated to higher ground. Frost covered all the moorland and it softened the oranges and ochres and burgundies and greens. But, if you looked closer, you could see that each blade of grass, though gentler in colour, would be hard and frozen to the touch. The surrounding rocks, covered by this deceptive white cold, looked astonishingly like clouds.

"Emily," said Arianna, straightening her transparent spine, "you must tell me what happened to me."

Emily drifted up to her. "Arianna, Polly, I just can't."

"But I have to know!"

Emily felt very weak, her senses attached inexorably to the present, her memories fading, unclear. From where she sat she could see a banner of smoke issuing from the last cottage in Stanbury, and light glowing in one of its windows. There was a hearth there, near which, Emily knew, stories had been told, stories with the breath of the wind in them; told in a rich moorland voice. She could not say how she knew this, perhaps it was the look of the cottage itself. Yes, the little building had an absorbed, entranced look, as if all the while the spirits had been experiencing weather, the stone walls had been turning towards the inner voice of stories. And now those absorbed walls had an expectant look, as if there were one more story that they were waiting to hear. With a flash of her former ghostly intuition Emily realized why the cottage had caught her attention, which story was about to be told, and who would be listening.

"I *have* to know," Arianna/Polly repeated.

"Yes," said Emily, "I believe you do."

"Well, then, tell me."

Emily moved closer to her companion, her face open, sad, honest. "I can't remember," she whispered, "just fragments, and even they are going. It was something to do with a balloon. And just yesterday, even an hour ago, I would have known. I can't grasp it; I am suddenly so tired."

For the first time since she had been a ghost, Polly/Arianna felt despair. Her whole life, her existence, was being forgotten; even her death was disappearing. She crumpled into a heap at Emily's feet. "Why didn't you tell me before?" she sobbed.

"No, no . . ." Emily was gaining a little strength, reading her friend's thoughts, "you haven't disappeared at all. You are part of the texture of this landscape now. I know it. Look! That cottage is holding its breath because inside it you, your story, is on someone's mind."

Arianna looked down the seam of the valley to the warmth of one small rectangle of light. The wind nudged her non-existent back, tentatively pushing her towards the village.

Listen, listen, it breathed.

"Listen," said Emily. "Let's listen. Come with me."

AS THE GHOSTS accompany the wind down through the valley into a late spring day somewhere, some time, in the last half of the twentieth century, this is what they see.

They see that ruins of farmhouses vacated by saddened people in the nineteenth century are much the same as stones left by Vikings or monuments erected by Celts. They see that weather's main purpose is to melt rock and that that purpose is carried out with more tenderness than aggression. They see that storms are really acts of love and that the earth demands this passion, this tantrum of response to its simply being there. They see that every crack, every ripple, every undulation of surface, has been etched by wind requesting entry, by rain desperate for absorption; that weeds, heather, ling, the stunted trees are really currents of air reaching back to a heaven amazed by its own power. They understand that the birds, as they move, sail a sea, dive in an ocean of trembling emotion, the space of the first great union. They begin to read the language around them: a raindrop striking stone, a cloud coming apart at the edges, dust torn by wind from an ancient path in the midst of intense relationship. It is written on the land. It is speaking. The ghosts read; they listen.

Listen! Someone tells a story while bones bleach underground. The sky has changed a million times between the time of action and the time of documentation, will change again and again before the first sentence tumbles from the lips. Tell me. Listen. The dust the wind took clothes the glass of one warm window. The female faces of ghosts shine through to the interior. Tell me, Emily. Listen, Arianna. Here are some words; here is a voice: "The thing that irks me most is this shattered prison, after all." This is the language, the waiting, the desire: "I'm wearying to escape into that glorious world, and to be always there: not seeing it dimly through tears, and yearning for it through the walls of an aching heart . . . " These are the words the story leads to. This is where we are now. Read the weather. Listen to the storm. " . . . But really with it, and in it . . . I shall be incomparably beyond and above you all."

Listen to the story, Arianna.

Ann enters the room and John takes her hand. She feels the width, the generosity of his callused palm, can read by touch the story of his labours: the planer in his workshop and long days spent at looms; and hovering above the hard determined history of his hand, a mind free to gather the bright threads of his landscape, his community. The sweep of it. A long bolt of cloth, a track over the moorland, a linked chain of words. This is the jewellery he gives her.

John takes her hand and leads her to the fire. "I knew you would come back for the story of the sky."

"How did you know?"

"I just knew."

Outside, the ghosts flicker near the glass. They dissolve into each other and separate again. The wind passes through Emily's mouth, hissing the word *listen*.

Ann looks into the orange heat of the fire, remembering what she saw there when she was ill, and what she saw there later. Arianna sees the interior, the large man, the details of the room. *Who is at home here?* she wonders.

"I waited for you here," John says. "I didn't go back to the farm, except in the afternoons, to work."

Ann recognizes evidence of herself everywhere; her manuscript on the table, her pen, a huge exclamation mark across the last page, her waterproof jacket hanging from a nail on the wall, boots caked with mud from the moor lying on a mat near the door, the singing kite near them, quiet, motionless. Her quilted hen. Her Staffordshire friends. She is calm, waiting for the story.

John does not let go of her hand and so she moves with him to the kitchen, where he performs small tasks, awkwardly, with one free hand, collecting glasses and the bottle, cold currant buns, and then setting the kettle for the tea. Eventually he releases her and she sits carefully in the accustomed chair, attentive, wanting the structure of the story to build itself in the room.

John brings steaming mugs of tea in from the kitchen, places them beside the bottle and the glasses on the fireside bench. Hungry for the first time in weeks, Ann has already eaten two currant buns. She watches John stir a lump of sugar into the hot cinnamon-coloured liquid and then add two drops of lemon to clarify it, the fruit a semi-circle of light in his huge hand. "And your young man," he asks softly, shyly, "what of him?"

Ann colours slightly. "He's gone back to Canada." She pauses. "He's not so young, John." When John remains silent, she adds, "He'll be home by now."

"And you?"

"I will have to go back as well, but not for him."

"Soon?"

"Not too soon." Their eyes meet. They smile. The ghosts outside sway impatiently.

John relaxes in the chair, moving one massive shoulder into an upholstered corner. "The story I will tell you now is about a man who was known all over England as the 'Sindbad of the Skies.' He were a man who knew quite a lot about distance, quite a lot about the wind. He knew how to float away from things, but not how to travel nearer. As I said, he floated all over England but he came down to earth here in Stanbury, eighty years ago – or, at least, he realized that he'd come down to earth at that time. He'd actually been on ground for several years." John picks up the glass, moves a tablespoon of whisky around in his mouth, then swallows. "It were because of a woman."

"What woman?"

"That you will discover in the story . . . providing there are no more questions."

As John speaks, Arianna listens with such intensity that, behind the glass, her normally vaporous form becomes almost solid. Details of her physiognomy that Emily had never noticed before spring into view: eyelashes, a mole on her left cheek, the tendons in her neck.

"It were a life, for him, filled with one long farewell and the incessant fluttering of female handkerchiefs. He were a balloonist, moving from country fair to country fair, lifted into the sky away from village after village. The world were a map to him, something folded and carried in his back pocket. All was distance and he loved that. As far as he was concerned, nothing but the sky had any size whatsoever, everything else, you see, just fell away at his feet, just tumbled away into distance, and when the distance were great enough, into invisibility. It were perfect for him, this vocation, because he hated to be intimate, even with objects, and he knew he could travel the sky forever and never become intimate with it, it being so vast – infinite really, and the clouds, when they were there, being so large and mostly unapproachable and, to his delight, utterly lacking in substance, the few times that he did approach them."

Arianna/Polly turns to Emily, speechless, amazed, and she sees that her ghostly companion's lips are moving, are mimicking the shapes taken by the large man's mouth.

"Who is telling the story, Emily?"

"*Listen, Arianna.*"

"What a happy life he had, so far away from everything, so infinitely above and beyond. Birds bothered him occasionally – they were so detailed – but otherwise all was clear and empty. And quiet. In fact, when he travelled the sky, his senses were rarely assaulted by anything. He heard nothing but wind. He saw nothing but sky, when he looked up, and that map of the earth when he looked down. He tasted nothing but ether. He smelled nothing at all. But, most important, he was touched by nothing but air."

Nothing but air, repeated the wind out where the phantoms were. "Nothing but air," whispered Emily to Arianna, who stood, as if struck, her ghost's heart open to the story.

"But then he met her."

Arianna quivered at these words, became electricity, became light, her spirit ringing like a bell.

"She were light and white and pale yellow like clouds at evening. Her eyes were blue and infinite and he saw the sky in them. She were young and unformed and lacking in content. She seemed so beautifully vacant to him, so empty, so like the air that he loved her immediately. And so he, who had touched nothing but air, touched her, because she was so wonderfully like the air as to be entirely mistaken for it. He took her away with him and she must have loved him too, because she went without protest, walked with him out of her life into a sort of dream and groundlessness. And here I speak figuratively and only out of my own intuition, for, of course, I don't know. But it would seem to me that a love affair with the 'Sindbad of the Skies' would have to be all dreams and shadows, illusory and ungrounded. Loving a man who loved distance would be, in a manner of speaking, like embracing absence.

"They went on like this for some time, away and apart from the world, embracing the absence and each other. And he still sailed the skies for the love of distance and for the money it put in his pocket. He would lock her away, it were said, when he went to a fair, not because he were worried or jealous, but because he wanted her unchanged, as empty of experience as he had found her. He wanted her to accumulate no more memories concerning the details, the trivia of the world than she had already had, for he considered all the world's details to be trivia. In fact, he considered all details to be somehow unclean and wanted them all washed away by an ocean of emptiness, an ocean of air.

"Still, what he didn't know and what were his undoing, were that if you leave a mind alone long enough in a vacant region it will invent details. What he didn't know was that all the details of arranging to escape from details had occupied his own mind sufficiently that it sought no other employment. But with her it were different. As he had insisted that her outer life, with him and without him, be a blank, her inner life had flourished, inventing who knows what kind of landscape and architecture, friends and enemies, circuses and theatricals, possessions and trinkets, toys and games, for, as I've said, she were only a child. And when he returned one night she told him all her fancies and he were angered and all his love for her were broken.

"But he couldn't leave her, because she had come to love *him* in a difficult, in a stubborn sort of way, and he was held by her tenacity. That, and the fact that he had loved her and felt that, if he could only find the lost key to that vacuous region, if he could return her, somehow, to that state of beautiful beloved vacancy, he might be able to love her again. And so she went out into the world with him and up into the skies as well, for a while, for the people at the fairs adored her light foot and her prettiness. Sindbad could not bear, however, to be witness to all the details of her floating around in what was formerly nothing but air, and so eventually he decided to remain on the ground, taking care of details where he believed details ought to be. He was by then a sad and bitter man, full of self-loathing and longing for the Arctic; that being the only region on earth vast enough, empty enough, white enough, and cold enough to please him.

"They called her Arianna M. Ether, though her name were really Polly Smith. The 'M' stood for milkweed, for Arianna had to leap out of the balloon during each performance and drift lightly and gracefully down to earth by means of a parachute, which she did successfully time after time. It is significant, I suppose, to remember that while the most important part of Sindbad's performance had been the drifting away, the achievement of distance and emptiness, the most important part of Arianna's performance were her return to earth, to intimacy and detail. And so now there were poor Sindbad, the lover of nothing but air, harnessed to the details of the earth, watching his woman return from the regions of ether over and over. It weren't long before his broken love turned to hate.

"Now, before you being to think badly of our Sindbad, let me explain to you that he were not a hard man, not an unfeeling man – not a man, for instance, who had never loved at all. Remember, he had loved 'nothing but air' and he had loved a woman who he thought resembled 'nothing but air' . . . which is a lot more love than some men put into an entire lifetime, or women either, for that matter. Sindbad was always looking and not finding. Until he came here, to Haworth, to Stanbury."

Here . . . sighed the wind. "Here . . . hear," breathed Emily.

"You should have seen the galas in those days. *I* should have seen the galas in those days. Some of us worked in the quarries then, carving out stones for the reservoirs that were being built all over the moors, but most of us, my grandfather and all my great-uncles and many of my great-aunts, worked in the valley mills as usual. And all appreciated a good fair, a good gala. There were the men who played in the comic bands, the men who pulled white doves out of black hats, the men who made speeches, the men who performed juggling acts and cartwheels. And all of these practising and preparing for the day that Sindbad and his lady entered Haworth. It were a dark and brooding day, like himself. The next day were light and clear, like herself. And, for some reason, this dark and brooding man had become light and clear as well. Why? You may well ask. It

was because of love. Some time during the night, Sindbad
had discovered how to recapture love.

"It came to him all of a sudden like. At one point during
the evening the girl had been in his room, but then she had
gone – they never shared the same room when they were
travelling, something to do with propriety, I expect. The
important part were that she had departed from his presence when he was engaged in some other activity – reading,
or looking at maps – and so he had not seen her leave. Her
absence, then, had registered itself upon him less the way
a fact might and more like a state of mind. Concentrating
on something else he had felt her absence before he knew
the fact of it, and it felt wondrous, complete, miraculous
. . . the very room seemed to shine with her absence, the
walls of his heart were ready to burst with her absence before
Sindbad could say what all this shining and bursting were
for. By simply stepping out of his room when he were not
looking, she, Polly/Arianna M. Ether, had brought the
space back, the emptiness, the vacuum, and before Sindbad
had completed one thought concerning this, he were back
in love again. But with one terrible difference: he knew he
could love her only if she were utterly absent from him.
And then he knew what he had to do."

"What did he have to do?" asks Ann.

"What did he have to do?" asks Arianna.

Have, have, howls the wind.

"My father would end the story here by telling us what
Sindbad had to do and then telling us what he did afterwards, and then he would tell us about the dangers of illicit
love and we would read in the Bible about Jesus casting out
the seven devils. As I got older, though, I wanted to tell
the story differently. It seemed to me that the most interesting part of the story was the mind of Sindbad and so I
decided to stay inside that mind and tell the rest of the
story that way. Do you object to this at all, Ann?"

"No," she says.

"No!" shouts Arianna, who has acquired so much substance that she is clothed, down to the last brass button, in her aeronautical costume. Her call is mistaken by the couple inside for a strong wind sliding around the outside corners of the cottage.

"Sindbad stood on the edge of Haworth's West Lane field and watched all the complicated details of this woman float away from him, up into the uncomplicated emptiness of a clear blue sky. All around him there were the clamour of the world; the brass bands, the jugglers, and the clowns, and above him this woman moving farther and farther away. Then, as she neared Stanbury he saw her leap from the balloon into absence. His heart leaped with love, I might add, while she leaped into absence. He knew, you see, that she were leaping into absence–for he himself had prepared the parachute that morning so there were no chance that she could leap into anything else. And then he wept with all the colliers and mill hands that surrounded him; the difference being that they were weeping with sorrow at a young life cut short, and he were weeping with joy at reactivated love.

"Later, he went to the Arctic in a balloon and was never seen again. It were as though he had embraced a vacuum so complete that it erased every trace of him. Which would have been what he wanted in the end: white love, the absence, emptiness, and eradication.

"While he were up there, perhaps he found the remains of icemen such as himself, Arctic madmen who chose that particular kind of slow suicide. At least that's the way I see it. Perhaps he found their frozen journals full of awkward entries or maybe a packet of impossible love letters to a girl they left behind. Yes, I like this last part, so that is the way I am going to end the story, breaking into the white landscape just at the point when our Sindbad is reading impossible love letters."

John pours himself a large glass of whisky, then empties half of it into Ann's teacup. The ghosts pressed up against the pane become thinner, flatter. They watch the large man lean earnestly forward in his chair, speaking the last words of the story directly to the woman facing him.

"SINDBAD READ the diaries for three days in the ever-darkening twilight: each dawn dimmer, each day shorter. He read about days of gruelling travel over ice floes, about wonderful feasts on icebergs, about hunting bears. He read about the erection of ice houses and the frying of seal blubber. He read about the exchange of confidences under Arctic moons and about the odd, desperate confession. He read about illness and recovery; about the singing of the Swedish national anthem in the morning. He read about the sighting of the very island on whose shore he himself had landed, about a pet Arctic fox that you, Ann, would have loved to hold, about the malfunction of a primus stove. The last words written under the final date in each of the three journals that he found were: 'I climbed as far as I could and looked around in all directions.' These were oddly comforting in that Sindbad knew that all they would see in any direction was nothingness.

"On the fourth day he began to read the packet of letters. 'My poor darling,' the first began, 'what can you be thinking now that I have not returned?' Sindbad, reading this in the midst of emptiness, felt an odd tickling sensation in his throat and he knew that, for the second time in his life, he were going to weep. And then he did weep. Tears froze on his moustache, his eyelashes, his beard, and as he wept longer and harder, some dropped to the ground where they began to form the kind of small, conical castles children sometimes make with wet sand on the beach. He wept all through the long nights and the increasingly short days ahead, intermittently reading once again the seven letters which he came to all but memorize. 'If I could only,' so

many of the paragraphs began. 'If I had only.' Phrases from
the letters hung in Sindbad's mind, you see, even when he
were not reading: 'the colour of that dress,' 'As you listened
to the orchestra,' 'The first time we,' 'Your little cat,' 'Your
hair shining,' 'The last ride together.' And words, words
like 'known,' 'cruel,' 'madness,' 'open,' 'touch,' 'wait.'

"On the seventh day Sindbad could weep no more. He
had wept enough for ten men and could no longer keep
his senses tuned to the orgy of reading and sobbing he'd
been engaging in. Salty icicles composed of frozen tears
hung from every inch of him. They made a sound like sleigh
bells or wind chimes when he moved. And now he were
moving – moving everything he owned off the island and
far out onto the ice. The day was purple, the sun dark and
only half visible on the horizon as he eliminated every trace
of himself: balloon silk and wicker, tin cans and turds,
empty champagne bottles and drag lines – far, far out onto
ice so that when he stood on island for the last time he
could see a small dark mountain of objects silhouetted
against the mauve sky. He scattered the letters and journals
about on the rocks so that they would not appear to have
been disturbed. Then he walked away out onto the ice,
which he must have known very well would melt once the
few, brief weeks of summer arrived. He would think of all
the strange objects that currents of sea brought to White
Island when all the white nothingness around melted for a
month and he would know that all these details would have
to be brought from far, far away. And he would be content,
covered in a shroud of frozen tears fabricated by himself
alone, to wait for the thaw."

Arianna watches the words *wait for* move on John's lips and
then she watches the word *thaw* emerge from Emily's
mouth. The ghosts look long into one another's eyes. They
clasp hands, embrace the energy of the completed story,

touch reconciliation, become air, become wind, enter rock and ether, enter breeze and heather. Now they are shadows behind the glass, now they are clouds blown across the moon.

They are engaged in the great gasp of leave-taking, the long, relieved sigh of arrival. *Open the window, Nelly, I'm freezing.* On the other side of the window the ghosts are experiencing brilliance and fragmentation. Emily dissolves. Arianna evaporates.

When ghosts become landscape, weather alters, the wind shifts, and heaven changes. The shadows of great flocks of migrating birds tremble against the clouds, the seeds of wonderful storms are born and the winds are self-assured. A sixteenth-century painter holds lightning in his hands; a mill worker invents stories for the sky. Someone enters an ice-blink, someone enters air. She who loved weather becomes the weather, caressing the rock, the brown sturdy hills.

At the end of one dark village, someone illuminates an upstairs room.

Acknowledgements

Two books in particular have informed and inspired parts of this novel: Glyn Hughes' *Millstone Grit* in which I learned about lip reading in clamorous mills, and writing in sizing dust, and other beautiful details too numerous to mention; and Peggy Hewitt's *These Lonely Mountains*, from which I learned the facts about a certain lady balloonist whose tomb I had come across in a graveyard near Haworth. Thanks, also, to Peggy Hewitt for living in and writing about a certain old gentleman's house in Oldfield, and for the hospitality she and her husband lavished upon me and my family, when we visited one evening in May. And, of course, deep gratitude goes to Eric and Kathleen Cole for their many kindnesses to me, my husband, and my daughter, and for the cottage in which I dreamt the greater part of this novel.

Thanks to the Canada Council and the Ontario Arts Council for providing me with the time I needed to complete this novel.

I would also like to thank Diane Keating and Anne Pippin Burnett for their enthusiasm, their comments, and their encouragement; and, once again, special thanks to Ellen Seligman for her commitment and support.

Certain sections of this novel have appeared in *Exile* in a slightly different form. One chapter has been broadcast on CBC Radio's "Speaking Volumes" and "Aircraft."

Jane Urquhart
Wellesley, Ontario

ABOUT THE AUTHOR

JANE URQUHART grew up in Ontario, where she now lives with her husband and daughter. Her first novel, *The Whirlpool*, was published to wide acclaim in 1990, and received the Prix du Meilleur Livre Etranger in 1991. In addition to her two novels, Ms. Urquhart has written a collection of short stories, *Storm Glass.*

CHANGING HEAVEN

was set in Galliard, a typeface designed by Matthew Carter
and introduced in 1978 by the Mergenthaler Linotype
Company. Based on the types created by Robert Granjon
in the sixteenth century, Galliard is the first of its genre to
be designed exclusively for phototypesetting. A type of
solid weight, it possesses an authentic sparkle that is lacking in most current Garamonds. The italic is particularly
felicitous and reaches back to the feeling of the
chancery style, from which Claude
Garamond's italic departed.

Printed and bound by Haddon
Craftsmen, Scranton, Pennsylvania